THE ISLAND

Abnormal/Variant, Book Two

M. Rose Flores

A NineStar Press Publication

Published by NineStar Press
P.O. Box 91792,
Albuquerque, New Mexico, 87199 USA.
www.ninestarpress.com

The Island

Printed in the USA
First Edition
May, 2020

Print ISBN: 978-1-64890-006-8

Also available in eBook, ISBN: 978-1-64890-005-1

Warning: This book contains depictions of violence and some gore, vomiting, discussions of intrusive thoughts and self-harm, child and infant death, and biphobia.

Two years after the end of the world, Cate and Marco have finally found a place for their people to start over. Sustainable and safe from zombies, the island is everything they hoped it would be. It seems the worst may finally be over; they can stop surviving and begin to live again. But the arrival of two new people sets in motion a chain of events that throw the island into unrest, and Cate must fight for her love, her people, and her sense of self. Can the inhabitants of Alcatraz Island find a way to come together when everything around them is falling apart?

Almost two years before their arrival on the island, just after the event that ripped their family apart, Marco began an aimless journey. With his foster family gone—some dead, some vanished—once again, Marco was on his own and sure it was for the best; other people only slowed you down, ended up as liabilities, or worse. Alone was good. It was what he was used to. But on his journey south, he collected other wanderers and began to consider the idea of a cooperative group or, maybe, a found family. There was, after all, safety in numbers.

Finally, together on the island, everyone assumes they are safe. But assumptions in a world run by zombies can be dangerous. Deadly. There is something going on in the city, terrifying and unnatural. Something that will change everything they think they know about zombies. And it's coming to the island.

The Island is not a stand-alone. It's advised that book one, *The End*, be read first.

To Stephen, the best friend I have ever known; the heart of my chosen family.

One: Home

Those are not people. The way they move, the fact that when we wave, they don't wave back, and the way they are all shambling toward us down the paths to either side. It all collectively spells zombie.

"Hello," calls Calvin.

No answer. Damn it.

None of us has the energy to fight any more. We spent the whole night fighting to get to the island. We watched our people get maimed and die; Calvin's Nana Mae sacrificed herself to save him, my sister Mel, and their new babies. Five other people died too, though I didn't know any of them well. They were all Marco's people. Now we're all one another's people. What a way to make a family.

Toby is looking pale. His younger brother Jax, though much smaller than Toby, is doing his best to keep him upright. The place where Toby's hand used to be, before it was clawed by an Abnormal zombie and then cut off by me to prevent infection, is wrapped in a bandage from what I'm guessing is a very limited supply. I think everything is probably limited. There wasn't much time to pack or prepare after Mel's labor screams drew in the horde last night. It's not her fault. Birthing twins with nothing stronger than ibuprofen must be agony. But we had to leave in a hurry. We made it all the way to Alcatraz, barely. And now, apparently, we have to fight again.

I'm too exhausted to cry. We are broken, for the second time since this all started. It's cold and drizzling. There's a thick fog rolling in. At least it isn't dark anymore.

"What do we do?" asks Sylvia, holding her kids close to her body.

"Same thing we've been doing," answers Marco.

When he doesn't offer anything else, Calvin steps in. "We should get the injured and the kids somewhere safe, right?"

Marco nods.

"They're still far enough we can probably slip by them on that road—" Calvin points to the right. "—and come back out once you're all safe inside. Shouldn't take long to clear the island; there don't seem to be many here."

"It's a big island," says Marco. "There will be a lot more up there than you think."

"Can't say I'll be much use," says Captain Jacob, stepping forward through the group. He's cradling his arm. I can guess what comes next: He edges his sleeve up, wincing, to reveal a definite bite near his elbow. The veins around it are black, all the way up and down his arm, peeking over the collar of his shirt.

"Captain," breathes Amy, our doctor, "why didn't you say something?"

"Call me Jacob; I told you. I knew it wouldn't do any good. Happened so fast. Had to get us here either way."

Amy examines the wound, touches his arm where the veins disappear under his sleeve. "There's no way this hasn't reached a main vessel by now," she says, feeling his face for fever and shaking her head. "I'm so sorry, Jacob."

"I appreciate it, Amy. But there's no need. I'll have to show someone how to drive the ferry. Murray?"

"Of course, Jacob."

"It has been an honor to know all of you," Jacob says. "Marco, you take care of these people. You got us this far. Soon you'll all be safe."

"I'm sorry, Jacob," says Marco, who looks on the verge of tears.

"Don't be. I did my part. I can live with the result. Or, I guess I can't." He chuckles at his own dark joke, but it turns into a coughing fit that makes his whole body tremble. "Come on, now, Murray. We haven't got all day."

Murray follows Jacob, catching him as he stumbles getting back on the boat. Jacob looks back and lifts a hand in goodbye to all of us. He doesn't have long. Another family member lost, claimed by the infection.

"We should go," says Ana, ever the stoic. "They're getting closer."

We move up the wider path as quickly as we can, although every one of us is exhausted and several of us are in some way incapacitated, so we're not as fast as we need to be. The path switches back and forth as it ascends.

"Stay together," Calvin whispers as the first few zombies notice us.

We do as we did last night, shuffling the less capable into the middle of our huddle as we move. However, now, so many more of us can't fight than can. When the zombies get to us, we are less efficient than we have ever been. It takes me two hits to take down one zombie, even though I sharpened my axe the other day, and I have to put my boot on its head to get the axe back. I haven't had to do that in ages. Calvin gets one on the first try, but it takes him a second to pull his knife free. Somehow, we escape. But just up the path, more swarm toward us. Not many, but there are always more.

"I think we should run for it," says Ana.

"Marco, what do you think?" asks Calvin.

Marco deliberates for a beat before he answers. "Yeah."

Calvin takes the lead, and we run to the top of the path, which opens into a sort of courtyard surrounded by buildings. Up here, with nothing to follow, they have congregated. Gaping mouths and grabbing claws close in as they lurch toward us.

"What do we do?!" cries Adrienne, the oldest little kid.

One of Mel's newborns starts to wail in her arms.

"That way!" shouts Marco. "It leads to the cell house. Go!"

The path, which runs alongside a building marked Administration, is narrow enough that we have to go single file. Mercifully, it also means Calvin can easily fight off the two zombies in his way. One, Calvin throws over the railing. It doesn't die, but it's not right there anymore. The second, Calvin simply stabs.

Behind him, Marco is giving directions. "Turn here, this way!"

More zombies. Tons more. We run, faster, but not by much, and the fog is making it impossible to see more than five yards ahead. The dogs, running behind us, don't seem to be in danger. The zombies don't go for them when there are people around. I take out as many as I can, but it's not near enough, and what little energy I had left is sucked away. My knees wobble, and I fall.

"Cate!" Mel's voice sounds like she's sobbing.

The group stops. In the middle of a bunch of zombies. Because I couldn't keep my damn legs under me for a few hundred feet. Calvin rushes toward me as a zombie closes in. It's leaning over me, claws and teeth tearing at my jacket, my hair, my skin. I shield my face with my arms because I don't know what else to do. There is another one on me now, and I'm stuck. At least I won't come back. At least I don't have to put Mel through that.

I feel the weight of one zombie yanked off me, and as I peek through a crack between my arms, I see Calvin destroying it. But the one he didn't get sinks its teeth into my wrist. I cry out. It's an unreal kind of feeling, being bitten by something that intends to eat you. The terror and shock, the disbelief. But on top of everything, soaking through it, is the pain itself. The amount of pressure a human jaw can exert is unreal, and when it's applied to all the little bones and nerves in your wrist, it is excruciating.

"Cate!" shouts Marco as Joaquin shoots the thing, effectively ending it. But the shot has drawn in more.

"Let's go," I say through gritted teeth, putting as much pressure on the wound as I can with my other hand.

"Up those stairs and through the door," Marco says. "We're almost safe."

We're losing momentum again, and both Toby and Mel are very pale. I'm sure I don't look so hot either. My wrist is bleeding a lot. And I have no hand to fight with.

"There might be more in the cell house," warns Marco.

"Figures," says Ana.

"We can't go in, then!" Mel protests.

"Can't go back," says Joaquin. "They're building up out here. We have to go in!"

We file in as Calvin, Joaquin, and Ana try to keep them back. But before they can shut the door, the horde busts in.

"Run!" shouts Calvin.

"Run to the end, find a cell, everyone!" calls Marco. "The cells don't close on their own, somebody has to stay out here to close them. Hurry!"

He sprints to the very end of the long row of cells, up a staircase, and stops by a big white box on the wall.

"Marco, you'll die!" I shout, as Amy's wife, Tanya, ushers me down the row.

"He's the only one who knows how to do this," Tanya snaps, shoving me into a cell and stumbling in behind me.

The door slams shut. A million zombies claw through the bars at us, their trapped prey. Everyone is screaming. Both dogs are barking. All at once, the cell closes in on me. Four people and two big dogs seem like a lot more when the place they're crammed into isn't even five by ten. I want to escape, to breathe something other than putrid flesh and excrement and old sweat. The smells, the closeness of Tanya and Jax and Toby, it's dizzying. I sit on the cement-filled toilet. Chaz cowers behind me, still barking. In front of us, hands reach in, gray faces chew and snarl. Milky-white eyes stare through us. I put my head in my hands.

"Is everyone okay? Tanya?" Amy calls for her wife.

We are all trapped.

"I'm here," calls Tanya. "Cate's with me. We've got Jax and Toby in here. Dogs too."

At least the doors closed in time.

The doors! He closed them!

"Marco!" I scream.

"Cal?" Mel's voice is choked and shaky. Her babies wail.

"I'm here!" Calvin shouts. "Amy, Joaquin, and Ana—We're all safe. You okay? Babies? Kids?"

"I'm okay!" Mel says. "David, babies, and kids are here. Where's Sylvia?"

There's no answer. Only zombie groans and the sound of nails and teeth scraping the bars of the cell doors.

"Sylvia?"

"Where the hell is she?" asks Tanya.

Chaz and Duchess bark and snarl at the intruders still scrambling to get to us.

"Marco!" I shout once more. This time, it's my voice that shakes. My gut tells me he just sacrificed himself to save us. He would. I know that. But I can't make myself believe he's really gone. We just got here! He's my only friend in the world, and I need him. I get up and walk as close to the bars as I can, to hear him better when he answers. "Marco?"

No reply. *Come on. Say something.*

"I'm okay."

A small fraction of the knot in my stomach unwinds. "Where are you?"

"Second level. I shut the stairwell door behind me."

I want to tell him he's a fool for doing what he did. But he saved us, and he's all right. I accept the win in this avalanche of losses.

"Tanya," calls Amy. "You're with Cate?"

"Yeah."

"You have to help her."

Tanya whirls around. "Right. Cate, give me your axe. Roll up your sleeve; I have to see where the infection has spread to. Hurry up, or you'll lose your whole arm."

I lean back, out of her reach. "Tanya, it's okay."

"Damn it, Cate, we've lost enough today!" Tears fill her eyes. "I'll have none of that martyr bullshit. Give me your axe."

"No! It's..." I glance at Toby. Shit. This wasn't how I wanted anyone to find out. I'm not even sure I *do* want anyone to find out. But here we are, so I take a deep breath and say it. "I'm...immune."

"You're kidding," says Jax. It's barely audible over the din.

Toby watches me but doesn't say anything. I can't imagine what he's thinking since I was the one who cut off his hand not even five hours ago.

"You're immune?" Tanya repeats, narrowing her eyes. "How do you know?"

"I've been bitten before. Right after all of this started. And last week, before we left the apartments, an Abnormal scratched me."

I roll up my sleeve to show them. The scabs have finally gone. The black veins all around the new pink scars are hard to miss though. Below the scratches, the new wound still bleeds.

"My God," says Tanya. "Well, we have to stop the bleeding anyway." She takes a handkerchief out of her pocket and wraps it around my wrist. The pressure feels good, but it pulses underneath. My own heart, pumping the ineffective virus through my body.

Without warning, Toby stands up and stabs three or four zombies as they press against the bars of our cell. They drop but are instantly replaced by more. He stabs a few more, grunting and yelling every time. After a second, he sits on the one cot that has no mattress and puts his head in his hand.

"Tanya?" calls Amy. "What's happening in there?"

"We're all okay," Tanya says, still looking at me as though I'm not quite human. "Cate is fine. Apparently, she can't be turned."

"Can't be what?" asks Ana.

"I can't be turned. I'm immune to the infection." I say it so quietly I'm not sure anyone hears me.

"Well, lucky her," says Ana from the farthest cell.

I never intended to share this information with everybody, or anybody who didn't already know. Especially since I wasn't sure how I felt about it myself. I'm still not sure. When Marco compared it to a superpower before, I felt more optimistic about it. How could it be a bad thing, right? But now, when I'm staring Toby in the face, it feels unfair. How did we know he wasn't immune? He could be. Any of us could be. But then again, who would want to wait around and find out?

"What do we do about the zombie situation?" asks Tanya after the silence drags on way too long.

"We're stuck for now," calls Calvin. "Does everyone at least have some water?"

"We do," answers Jax.

"So do we," says Mel.

There's no answer from Marco.

"So, we wait it out," says Calvin. "Hope they get distracted, or we just keep killing them as they get close enough. Eventually, there won't be any more. Unless anyone else has a better idea?"

No one does.

There's grunting and the sounds of bodies dropping as the others start taking down the zombies they can reach. I force myself up and start to do the same with my uninjured hand. Tanya joins me. Jax follows. Toby stays where he is.

The dogs keep barking. Two of the kids are crying and asking for their mother in Mel's cell. Sylvia must be dead, but how do you tell two children who lost their father a few hours ago that their mother is probably gone too? And how did she get separated from the group? Mel tries to comfort them at first, but eventually, she deteriorates into sobs herself. She asks Calvin when it will be over, if it will be over, and between killing zombies, he says he hopes so, not to worry, and he loves her.

The fog had lifted for a while, allowing some blue sky to peek through the barred windows. But it comes back even thicker, and it starts to rain again. Big, noisy droplets this time. It's loud enough to compete with the sounds of death and heartbreak inside the cell house.

When the zombies have been cleared out, Marco opens the cell doors and returns to the first level, and Calvin strides over and slams the door to the outside shut. I turn back to the carnage we inflicted, and my stomach roils. I don't know if it's the blood loss, the number of dead bodies piled up around us, or the smell. I guess it's probably all of the above.

In the cell we just left, Jax and Toby sit with their heads together. Jax reaches out to touch Toby's bandaged arm, but Toby pulls away. When I see the expression on his face, the guilt makes my insides twist.

"Hey, guys," says Joaquin, walking into the cell. "Toby, can I pray for you?"

Toby nods, so Joaquin kneels, puts a hand on Toby and the other on Jax, and starts to recite a prayer.

In the next cell, Mel feeds one of her babies on the cot while Marco wipes the dirt and gore off Francis's little face. Ever since Marco found him in the dumpster, it seems Francis trusts no one but him. No one can blame him. Being five years old and orphaned would make anyone cynical.

"Here, let me help you," says Ana, kneeling in front of Adrienne, who wraps her little arms around Ana's neck and weeps. Sylvia is still nowhere to be found. Nick and Adrienne are likely orphans now too. The same as Francis. And Marco. And me.

David just sits there, staring at the wall. His face might appear blank at first glance, but there's unimaginable pain there. His wife Eunice didn't make it more than five feet onto the dock last night before the zombies got her. And David saw all of it. How does someone recover from losing their wife that way? If it's anything like losing my mom was for me, he won't recover. I don't think any of us will.

"Hey, my love," Calvin says to Mel. He picks up one of his babies and kisses the top of their head. He's leaning all his weight on his left leg. The prosthetic attached to his knee must be killing him.

"Did you get them all?" Mel asks.

"For now."

She takes off her glasses and bows her head. More tears slip down her face.

"So what now?" I ask.

Calvin waits, watches Marco for a second. Marco finishes cleaning Francis's face and moves on to Nick's. He says nothing.

"We'll sleep in whatever part of the building smells the least like death," Calvin suggests, "and take shifts through the night. Tomorrow, we can clear this block. Make it habitable. What do you think, Marco? Marco?"

Without looking up, Marco shrugs. "Sounds good."

He must be exhausted. He's not acting at all like himself.

"When you're done here, we'll suss it out, cool?"

"Don't worry about it; you go ahead."

Calvin regards Marco, narrowing his eyes. "All right. Cate? Shall we?"

"Why me?" I whine. I was this close to finding a place to lie down. Stink or no stink.

"Because the buddy system works."

"But can't Joaquin go?"

Calvin glances back at Joaquin, who is still on his knees next to Toby. "Joaquin is busy. So is Ana. That leaves you and me, kid. Let's move out."

I grumble into a standing position and trudge out of the cell. Calvin hands the baby he's holding off to Tanya, who sits down next to Mel and starts to sing the baby a song.

We end up having to search for no more than a few minutes. There's a library off to one end of the building, and it is totally corpse-free. It's also book-free. The smell isn't as bad, but there's nothing but a few wooden benches and some shelves.

"It will *not* be a comfortable night," I say.

"That's okay," says Calvin. "Probably safer to sleep light tonight."

I utter a one-syllable reply. "Mmh." At this point, I don't care how or where I sleep, as long as I do.

"You doing okay, kid?" asks Calvin, turning away from the bare-bones library to face me. "Hell of a night we've had."

"I'm..." I feel the familiar prickle around my eyes, the rush of heat to my face. I press my knuckles into the inner corners of my eyes, not gently. I don't know why, but I'm angry with myself for this sudden onset of feelings.

"Hey." Calvin steps toward me and puts a hand on my shoulder.

"This sucks," I choke out. Tears falling freely. "So many people died last night. And all the time. All the fucking time, Cal!"

Calvin scoops me into a hug. It's uncommon coming from him but welcome in my moment of utter, embarrassing weakness. "Hey, shh. I know it sucks. I know. But you want to know what?" He pulls back and smiles gently, inviting me to ask.

I wipe my eyes, more softly this time. "What?"

"We made it. Cate, we're here. Hard part's over."

The last couple of tears find their way down my face, but I smile. Calvin is right.

"So," he says, "go tell them what we found?"

Once everybody is cleaned up as much as they can be and wounds are tended, we all shuffle into the library and find a spot along the wall to lie down. Everyone except Jacob and Murray, who are still out on the boat. I'm glad Jacob isn't alone in his final moments. I hope Murray is okay. In the morning, we will check on them and find a place to bury Jacob or maybe both of them. It's still light outside; when I check my watch and it says 4:30, I wonder for a moment if the battery died. But of course it didn't, I remind myself. The watch is kinetic. It moves with me and stores the energy. It can't die.

Before I fall asleep, I think about the last day I saw my mom and stepdad alive, my seventeenth birthday, two years ago. The way my mom got all excited about giving me the watch even though we were experiencing the actual apocalypse. The way she told everyone to look for birthday candles when we went out searching for food. It's getting easier to remember the good stuff. I can't shut out the moment she died, but I can paper over it with random nice things most of the time. It's a temporary fix. I know the worst memories will sneak up on me eventually, but it's easier to fall asleep with a patchwork of happy thoughts than with the hole in my heart spewing the darkest stuff.

We spend the next day clearing out the cell block and the entirety of the next ten days making the island habitable. Sylvia isn't anywhere, inside or out, alive or dead. Not even a body. It's both a relief and not at the same time. At least no one had to find something horrible—a mostly-eaten Sylvia or worse, a mostly-eaten zombie. But the fact that we can't find her points pretty directly to the conclusion that she is not coming back. On the third day, Nick and Adrienne stop asking about her.

After the initial clearing, the zombies don't seem to be an issue at all. The ones we found on the island must have already been here when they died because we don't see any more after they're gone. They're still floating, bloated and gray, in the San Francisco Bay, and if anyone gets too close or makes too much noise it riles them up. But they're so immobile we don't bother killing them unless they're Abnormal zombies, and with their human eyes, those are easy to spot.

The seabirds that nest all over the island are an excellent source of food. I never thought I'd have scrambled eggs again, and the metal cups from the gift shop make excellent single-serving pots in which to cook the eggs. We do not eat the seagulls. No reason to risk it when nobody is quite sure of their role in the outbreak, and there are so many other kinds of birds to eat anyway. Mel says she is sure she can get some vegetables to grow, so we haul this creepy wax figure from one of the buildings out to the garden to use as a scarecrow.

We also find out from the informational plaques and brochures all over the island explaining that not only does the island run on solar power, but there is also a decent system in place for collecting rainwater in several giant cisterns outside the rec yard.

"And by simply boiling it," David tells us, "we can make the water potable, useable for everything from drinking to washing up."

Eventually, he warns us, when summer comes, or if it doesn't rain enough, we will have to find another source of fresh water. But we have time.

I'd have thought Marco would be a wealth of information about Alcatraz, and maybe he is, but he spends a lot of his time exploring the island by himself and cleaning the interior of the cell house. To his credit, it's spotless, and on one of his exploratory laps, he does find a small rowboat. It's too small for more than two or three people, but still worth keeping. Murray insists we use the ferry for as long as it's practical, and while it will be easier for heavy hauls when we go to the city for supplies, I suspect part of his reasoning is the ferry's connection to Jacob. The big giant boat and its salty old captain were the reason we all got here safely. Most of us.

We set up a patrol similar to what we had in the apartments in San Francisco with at least one adult awake and alert at all times. We all partake, even Mel after a few weeks. But when Calvin and Ana start leading group training in the mornings, Marco doesn't show up. After a few days, it seems as though he's finding reasons not to. After a week, he stops coming up with excuses. More than once, I see him hanging out in the Warden's House, this big overgrown structure that wasn't kept up the way the others were. He's usually drawing or sometimes just sitting, staring off into the distance. I want to join him, but it's clear he would rather be alone.

The days, having fallen into a routine, start to blend together. The grass and weeds begin to grow over Jacob's grave; the autumn weather gets colder and wetter. It doesn't sink in that this is a permanent arrangement, that we have arrived at our destination, until little green sprouts start poking up from the dirt in the newly tilled garden—the vegetable seeds Calvin's Nana Mae collected for this reason, and Mel somehow managed to keep after Mae died. Something about knowing we have our own food growing makes it feel real. We've made a home on this island. We're here to stay.

Two: Abnormal

"I'm telling you, the closest we have to a gardening book is *The Secret Garden*," says Marco, pointing to the meager half shelf of books on the far wall of the library.

"This is why we need a system," says David, shaking his head. "A list, at least. I'm going to start up a media catalogue."

"What media?" asks Marco. "We have the books from the gift shop, these six here, and the audio tour headsets."

"I believe you just answered your own question, Marco. Anyway, I'm sure we'll keep finding books on our runs into the city. Won't we, Cate?" David turns to me, hands clasped, asking for reassurance.

I make a noncommittal noise as I plop down on the bench nearest the shelf and scan the spines of the books just in case. Marco is right, though, there's nothing in the way of gardening books. "I miss Google."

"I told you," says Marco.

"Well you would know, wouldn't you." I'm more aggressive than I mean to be. And then, for no good reason, I continue, "You're in here enough."

Marco stares at me, chewing his lip.

David clears his throat. "Perhaps it's a simple issue of contamination?"

I turn to him. "Meaning?"

"Well, you brought these pea vines over after they were already established, bearing fruit and everything. They may have been sick from the beginning."

"Guys?" says Marco.

"Then why aren't the others sick too?" I ask. "Why is it only the one?"

"I don't know. Plants aren't my area."

"*Cate*," says Marco.

"Oh!" says David.

Marco and David are both staring toward the doorway. I turn around.

The thing silently peering around the corner at us, with black veins spidering up the right side of its face, is not human. It was, once, and its eyes still are. Unlike most zombies, which have pale eyes, this thing has dark-brown eyes.

"Variant!" says Marco.

As soon as he does, the Abnormal zombie lunges. I stab at it, but I miss by a lot, and it passes me. This thing is fast.

"Shit! Cate!" Marco grips his knife and trips over a bench, slicing his cargo pants and probably his leg.

I rush it from behind, but it must hear me because it whips around and stares me down as I skid to a halt. It creeps toward me, the look on its face eerily aware, calculating. I try to stab it, but it blocks my hand. I drop the knife as the thing continues to stalk me. It doesn't attack but watches me the way a person might. Or maybe it's just the eyes making it seem less soulless. Instead of the white eyes of a regular zombie, they're the human-looking eyes all Abnormal zombies have. It opens its mouth just as David picks up my knife and drives it into the base of the Abnormal's head. It drops, thankfully, the same way normal zombies do.

"Thank you," I say to David. "God, what was that? Was it watching us?"

"It certainly seemed to be," says David, handing my knife to me. "It's the first Variant I've seen since...well, since the ones on the docks, the night we came here."

"It was watching though," I repeat, and I want to crawl out of my own skin.

"I agree; it's cause for concern."

"Bet it was trying to decide who to eat first," Marco says from the floor.

It's a hell of a word to use, *decide*, but he's right. Abnormal zombies do decide, they do think. That's why they're far more dangerous than normal zombies, and why I'm grateful we don't ever see them on the island. So how the hell did that one get all the way up and into the library without being seen? Do Abnormals sneak now too? There's no way we missed one for this long, is there?

I hold my hand out to Marco and give him a look as he uses the overturned bench to stand instead. "You're getting soft. Why won't you train with us in the mornings?"

Marco winces as he puts his full weight on the injured leg. "Lay off, Cate. It's no big deal."

"No? Jesus, Marco. We've been here barely more than a month, and you've already run through most of the first aid kit solo. Need help?" I offer a shoulder.

Marco scoffs. "Please. I've had way worse than this. And I think you should be a little less worried about me and a lot more worried about the fact that a goddamned Variant somehow got to the island and walked all the way up the path and into the library."

I don't correct his terminology the way I normally would. It's a running joke between us, the Abnormal/Variant thing, but I am not even in the vicinity of a joking mood. "I can be worried about more than one thing. You just tripped over yourself dealing with a single zombie. When we were getting out of the city, even from day one, you kicked massive zombie ass. Maybe you should put your ego in one of those giant pockets and try training once in a while."

He glares at me, takes a couple of ridiculous wobbly little steps, and leans on my shoulder. "I'll train soon, okay?" he mumbles.

"You've said that before."

"Can we talk about this later, Cate?"

"Can you stop hogging all the med supplies, Marco?"

"Children, please," calls David from behind us. "We're all okay; isn't that what counts?"

"As long as Marco didn't slice an artery or something," I grumble.

"If I'd sliced an artery, I'd be dead. Calm down."

"I'll calm down when you show up at training. You know, you used to be stronger than me. Now, I bet I could take you down in ninety seconds flat."

"Well, with a wound like this, it wouldn't be much of a victory, would it?"

"And whose fault is the wound?"

We spend the whole walk from the library to the cell block bickering. Somewhere along the way, David ditches us, muttering about finding someone to help him move the body. I don't blame him. I'm annoying myself by the time we get there, but I can't help it. Or I don't want to. It's so much easier to snap and jab than to address what I'm actually feeling.

Marco is my best friend. Seeing him give up and retreat into himself leaves me with a whole lot of cloudy, spiky emotions I don't want to examine too closely. Even if he wasn't my foster cousin, even if he wasn't one of the only two family members I have left, even if I didn't owe him my life—a few times over—we just understand each other. But I don't understand this.

Calvin, carrying one of the twins, steps out of an empty cell to walk with us. "What happened this time?" he asks as we limp through.

"Variant," answers Marco.

"Are you serious?" Calvin glances at his baby. "Here?"

"It wasn't a big deal," I say. "We took it down easy. Marco stabbed himself running away from it."

Marco glares at me. "I did not run away, and I did not stab myself."

Calvin glances at Marco's bloodstained pants. "Looks like you did something. Amy, you home?"

"I'm here," calls Amy's tinkling voice. Her fluffy German Shepherd, Duchess, circles us while I help Marco onto the table that sits outside the cell we use as a med station. The table had a bunch of pictures of old Alcatraz inmates laid out across it before, but now it's Amy's patient table. Duchess whines and wags her tail.

"Marco, what's up?" Amy asks, gliding out of her cell and pulling a headband over her short black hair.

"Just a scratch," Marco says before I can get another dig in.

"Pants off, or cut?"

"Cut."

Amy slices up Marco's pant leg, all the way to the waist, and opens the flaps to examine the damage.

"You'll need to make another run to the city sooner than anticipated, Calvin," she says as she cleans Marco's leg. When it keeps bleeding, she unwraps a piece of new gauze and places it over the cut. "Hold this here, please, Marco."

She never sounds bothered; her tone is always that cool, easy doctor tone, but something about the way she doesn't make eye contact with Marco makes me think she's getting fed up too. Maybe I'm projecting.

"How soon?" asks Calvin.

"Very."

"Tomorrow, then?"

"I think so, yes." Amy stands and stretches her arms over her head. "Okay, Marco, you're done."

Calvin runs a hand through his thick curly hair, flexing his jaw. I can tell he's annoyed, but unlike me, he has the good sense to keep it to himself. "All right, tomorrow it is. What's on the list? First aid..."

"Food?" I ask.

"Cans are heavy, and we're doing fine with what we have," Marco interjects.

"Not true," says Amy. "We need all the food we can get."

"Okay. So, first aid, food, maybe batteries."

"Diapers, always," says Calvin, bouncing his baby gently on his hip.

"Pants?"

Marco shoots me another glare.

"With this kind of list, we'll need to head deeper into the city," says Calvin. "Mel isn't going to be happy about it though. She hates when we go."

"I hate it too," I say. "Murray almost died last time."

"That's a bit dramatic, but it *was* a close call…"

Marco pets Duchess with both hands, deliberately keeping his gaze low. His cheeks are flushed. Intermingled with my less identifiable feelings, I recognize a pit of guilt in my stomach. Sometimes it seems like all he wants is to be comforted. I don't comfort him though. All of my other, more complicated feelings stop me.

Calvin follows me out when I leave the cell house.

"An Abnormal?" he asks again.

"Yeah, in the library."

"How the hell did it get in there?"

"You're asking me? I was about to ask if you'd seen it on its way up."

"If I'd seen it, Cate, do you think I would have let it just waltz up on in?"

He has a point. "Well, were you outside? Near the path? Any chance it could have slipped by you?"

"I was in the rec yard, but Melody was gardening with the kids until right before I saw you. She can see the path from there, and she wouldn't have missed a whole zombie, I'm sure."

"So how did it get on the island, and into the library, without anyone noticing?"

"Fair question. We'll do more perimeter checks for now. I'll have Toby and Jax check the barriers and doors. Make sure nothing's loose, maybe find out where it got in."

"Good. Okay. You gonna go tell Mel about the upcoming adventure?"

"Nah." Calvin shakes his head. "I'll wait until dinner. She's resting now."

"She rests a lot these days, doesn't she?"

"Well, having twins will take it out of you."

Mel isn't too upset when Calvin breaks the news that night at dinner. She does chop the heads off the fish rather spitefully at first, but she softens and melts into Calvin's arms, whispering "please be careful" and "your babies need you" as though he wouldn't be careful if she didn't remind him ten times. It's sweet, I guess, but it's also kind of unbearable to be around. It's as if they forget anyone else exists. One of these days, they'll forget for real, and one of them will get bitten or something. That's how it works, right? Nobody gets a happily ever after. Not anymore.

And this is why I'm alone.

Well, this and the fact that my girlfriend probably got eaten by zombies.

Three: Potential

Something is poking my back. It's too jabby to be the dog's nose.

"Cate. Cate?"

Go away, go away, go away. I curl up and pull the covers tighter.

"Cate." Poke. "Boat's leaving in five."

Boat? I sit up and scowl. Boat!

"What the hell, Joaquin. Why didn't you get me sooner?"

"I've been trying. You're a real heavy sleeper."

I adjust my blanket over my waist. My dress is across the cell. I'm wearing nothing but a tank top and underwear. It's still weird, having people randomly come into my room. My cell. Well, not people. This one person. But not in a bad way.

"Calvin already on the dock?"

Joaquin nods. "Melody too. We've been there a minute."

"So you're saying it's really time to go." I stretch my arm out to see if I can reach the dress from where I'm sitting. Nope.

"Yes, Cate, it's really time." His tone is deadpan, but when I turn around, he's smiling.

"I don't even have time to wash up, damn it."

"So what? You're beautiful."

"Shut up," I mutter through my teeth as my face starts to burn around the edges. "You mind?" I gesture to the blanket covering my bare legs.

Joaquin smirks. "Not a bit."

I throw my shitty pillow at him, and he scurries out of my cell. I get up and grab my dress, but even the small bit of exposed skin is freezing, so I opt for the pair of jeans Calvin found our first time back in San Francisco.

Outside my cell, Joaquin is leaning on the opposite wall. I pull my jacket on as I pass him. I feel his eyes on me, but I stare at the floor, fearing my own traitor face and its propensity for blushing at the worst times.

"Hey, Cate?" he calls after me as I jog down the cell block. "Missing something?"

I feel for my weapons before the thought even forms in my brain. I jog back, grab them out of his outstretched hand, and we both fly outside.

It's chilly in the gray predawn, the mist is so thick I can feel it on my tongue and in my nose when I breathe. I tie on the green handkerchief I've been using as a headband. At first, I resented that Tanya had taken about a foot off my hair when she cut it, but she knew what she was doing. It's low maintenance and cute in its own unruly way. Andrew would have made some corny joke about it growing on me just then. The bad dad joke and subsequent realization I'll never hear one again make my stomach hurt. I push the grief back down where it belongs. They're gone, and that's that.

By the dock, Calvin and Mel are making out, and David is waiting patiently, though awkwardly, to hand Calvin the list. I take it on my way by.

"Thanks, David. We'll be back soon." I refrain from shoving the list into my pocket even though I know it will stay there for most of the excursion. It somehow feels mean after he went to the trouble of writing it. He nods, tells me to be safe, and shuffles back toward the prison.

Ana and Murray pass him on their way down the path together. Ana is laughing at whatever Murray is saying, and he looks pleased with himself.

"So, I'll see you this afternoon then," says Ana, her smile fading slowly.

Murray grins, arching an eyebrow. "Indeed, you will."

The pink in Ana's cheeks deepens as she tucks a strand of her white-blonde hair behind her ear. Her fingertips linger on the elastic of her eye patch in the same spot. I've noticed she only does it when she's nervous, which seems to be exclusively when she and Murray are together. "And you'll help me with the cisterns?"

"You can count on me."

Ana bobs her head once and leaves us.

"Don't do anything reckless," Mel murmurs to Calvin behind me. "Come back to us, okay?"

"Let's go, Loverboy," says Murray, slapping Calvin on the back as he stomps down the dock. The seagulls perching on the ferry protest and flap away as he boards. All but one. Murray swings his giant hand at the holdout, and I swear it snaps at him before flying off.

Mel and Calvin manage to pull their faces apart as Joaquin and I step onto the boat. Calvin jogs onboard behind us.

Murray starts the engine. "Gonna have to find a more sustainable vessel soon, lady and gents," he shouts over the loud rumbling. "More rowboats, maybe. This gas-guzzlin' wreck is about spent."

The zombies floating around the boat as we pull away don't worry me at all. If we're lucky, a few will get sucked into the propeller or engine or whatever makes this thing go. Some of them seem to be looking at us, others not so much. Same as always. The only ones who can see, as far as we know, are the Abnormals, and these all seem to be normal. I try to check the eyes of each one. It's not easy with the combined motion of the boat and the water.

"Got the list?" asks Calvin, making me jump.

"Got it. Same as we discussed, and David added 'books, please,' circled twice."

"He wrote please?" asks Joaquin, smirking.

"Can't blame him." Calvin watches the water ripple as we cut through it. "We all must've been thinking the same thing the first time we saw the state of the library."

"What a bullshit library?" I ask.

Calvin nods. "I expected there to be some room for improvement, but my God."

"The bookstore was stocked though."

"With a bunch of Alcatraz literature and postcards."

"And some clothes."

"There was a bible in one of the offices," says Joaquin.

"I guess it makes sense that he always asks," I say.

The city materializes out of the thick morning fog, at the same time both pretty and ominous. I can't see any individual zombies yet, just a lot of movement, but we all know they're there. When we're within twenty yards of Pier 33, the few undead walking through the area take notice. This engine is so loud, we can't help but announce our presence. Murray is right. We need another mode of transport.

"One hour," says Murray as we disembark.

Joaquin scoffs. "We won't need thirty minutes." He does look a little uneasy, though, as the zombies close in.

Shick-shick!

Thub.

The sound the blade makes sinking into a waterlogged zombie is somehow worse than the sound it makes killing a regular land-dwelling zombie. Do they dwell? Is that word reserved for the living?

Squish.

They're definitely way uglier when they're all gray and soggy.

Bang!

"Damn it, Joaquin!"

Calvin and I team up on the remaining two. When we're done, he wipes and sheathes those awesome Bowie knives of his and says, "Okay, to the checkpoint."

"You and your guns," I tease Joaquin as we take off running.

"What's that supposed to mean?"

"There are quieter ways to kill a zombie, you know."

"Just because I choose to shoot them doesn't mean I can't use my knife."

"Prove it," I say even though I know it's true. But that's part of the reason his preference for shooting is so irksome. Since I first met him—when he and the rest of Ana's men killed our would-be captors outside Santa Rosa—I've noticed he uses long-range weapons more than anything, even when we're fighting close-up. It gets the job done, and so far without further incident, but on top of being noisy as hell, it seems so unnecessarily macho or reckless or...something.

We have to stop twice on the way to the checkpoint, once for an Abnormal that drops off a fire escape right into our path (but runs away before anyone can kill it), and once for a regular half-rotten zombie that happens to stumble around the wrong corner. Which hardly counts as a stop since Calvin gets it on his way by.

The checkpoint, a VW Beetle propped up on its rear bumper and painted to resemble planet Earth, sits in the middle of an intersection about three blocks inland.

"Okay. Murray and I will get first aid and diapers and such," Calvin says. "There's a pharmacy we didn't have time to check last time, east of here. We'll be in there. Joaquin, Cate—food, water, batteries, and books. Try the apartment building we've been working. Remember, stay north, stay safe, and keep your eyes open."

"Like we'd go in with them shut?"

Joaquin snorts. "Smart ass."

Calvin narrows his eyes, trying to hide his amusement. "Hope your knife is as quick as your wit, kid."

"So meet back here at—" I check my watch. "—eight fifteen?"

"Right," Murray says, glancing around us. "Looks as though we're about to have company. Shall we?"

We all scatter, Calvin and Murray heading east, Joaquin and I jogging north toward our target, the fancy apartment building we're about halfway through raiding.

The door is already propped open with a rag. Joaquin's idea. The building's interior smells of dust and different kinds of rot. There's not a lot of light thanks to the weird, labyrinthian layout of the first floor. It's uncomfortably ritzy, with giant murals made of little mirrors and furniture I'm pretty sure all used to be white. In a couple of the chairs and on the floor, bodies are collapsed in the complete stillness of the long dead. Their skin sags like half-deflated balloons. They've been there since we first found the place, some chewed to bits and some that must have turned early and starved.

Joaquin and I spent our whole first run on this floor alone and came away with plenty to show for it. We've already cleared up to floor four, so we race through the lobby, to the stairs, and up, playfully bumping each other out of the way as we ascend. When I reach the fourth-floor landing first, I lift my chin in triumph before I crack the door open and peek through.

"Shit." I let the door close more quickly than I mean to. The *click!* sounds loud in the silent stairwell.

"How many?" asks Joaquin.

"Seven or eight, at least."

He moves to pull out his gun.

I put my hand on his to stop him. "Thought you were going to show me your knife skills?" I let my fingers linger for a second. His skin is so warm. Maybe mine is cold.

"Okay, fine." He slides his long skinny blade out of the duct tape sheath the kids made and reaches around and behind me with his free hand, leaning so his face is an inch from mine. "Watch and learn."

The zombies notice us as soon as we open the door and all eight or so charge at once. I say "charge," but it's more of a stumble in our direction. All of them are normal, which is always a relief. Joaquin stabs one right in the eye, but the next one goes for his face with its gross hands, and Joaquin fumbles backward. I take care of that one, knifing it in the back of the neck. I eyeball him as it drops from between us. For a second, Joaquin looks afraid. He seems so self-assured, except in moments such as this. When he's talking about zombies, he's a badass. In training, same thing. But when he's dealing with them, face-to-face, he's hesitant.

Even though all of us, including Joaquin, go through Calvin's four-step formation every single day in training, I'm the only one using it now. I don't get it—it's so automatic for me I hardly think about it. I duck out of the grasp of the zombie in front of me, roll to the side, come back into a crouch, and swing my leg around, taking the rotten bastard out at the knees. As soon as it's on the ground, I finish it.

After all eight are down, I notice Joaquin only killed three of them, which isn't so much annoying as worrisome. I can handle myself, but it would be nice to know the guy I'm fighting next to has my back too.

We pick a door and start our search. We stay together, not because we're afraid to split up, but because we can get through each apartment much faster this way. It's amazing how many people didn't lock their doors when the world ended. They must have thought they were safe up here in their big, shiny apartments.

We have the same arrangement every time: while I head into the bedroom and bathroom, Joaquin checks the living room and kitchen. I turn down the hallway and I'm greeted by the familiar sounds of kitchen utensils clattering as Joaquin digs through the drawers and cupboards. We learned not to open the fridge after the first time.

The layout and setup of each place is pretty predictable. For example, nobody in this building keeps much in the half bathroom attached to the living room, but if we're lucky, there'll be an extra toothbrush or travel tube of toothpaste or something in a drawer. Today, I am lucky: I come away with two toothbrushes, three rolls of toilet paper, and two mini toothpastes. I wander down the hall toward the master bedroom and attached bathroom. Joaquin sings while he searches the living room. I've never heard the song, but the way he's singing it makes me smile. He's really into it. I linger in the hallway for a second, out of sight, listening. When the singing stops, I hurry into the master bedroom/bathroom.

The big rooms always have more stuff, but whoever lived here was disappointingly thorough when they evacuated. I double-check the drawers and cabinets and shower to be sure there's nothing more of value. There isn't.

I back out of the bathroom, do one last scan, and go to the closet. I've already found some of what I'm meant to be searching for, but more won't ever go to waste.

"Perfect," I whisper as I pull two pairs of folded jeans off a shelf. The closets in this building are unreal. They're enormous, organized with tons of little cubby shelves built into the walls and long bars packed with beautiful, probably expensive, clothing. I run my fingers along the multicolored things and have a weird, long-dormant urge to feel pretty. Joaquin is still moving around in the other room, which means I have a minute. I check the time, just to be sure, then pull a red sequined dress off its cushioned silky hanger, take off my jacket, and hold the dress up against myself, over my practical but ugly new jeans. Swishing it back and forth, I watch the fabric move and sparkle in the dim light. I turn in a circle and retreat into my head, allowing myself to imagine a prom night I will never have, with music and finger foods; the way the lights would have bounced off the sequins on this dress.

There's movement in the bedroom behind me.

"Wow."

As soon as we make eye contact in the mirror, my spine tingles. I let the dress fall to the floor and pick up my jacket, careful to avoid eye contact. Joaquin watches as I walk out of the closet. He's leaning on the door frame, but it's as wide as two regular doors, so I walk by, chancing a second of eye contact as I do. He's looking at me, but not my face. He catches my gaze and smiles.

I smile back, surprised at my boldness even as my facial muscles move.

"Get anything good?" I ask, glancing back at the floor.

Joaquin follows me at a comfortable distance. I swear I can feel his eyes on me.

"Some vitamins. Expired. A few cans. Some spices. You?"

"Not much. More toothpaste. Stuff for the babies. Pants for Marco. Ready?" I turn and glance over my shoulder as we get to the doorway.

He pats his gun, and when he sees my expression change, he says, "Kidding, jeez," and pulls out his knife.

I turn away quickly. Why am I smiling again?

I don't even think he was kidding.

There are no zombies in the hall. Not that there should be, not after we've already cleared them once. Stairs aren't their forte. Usually.

We leave the building in silence anyway, because there's no reason to call attention to ourselves in case there are any lurkers. Joaquin walks right next to me; his hand is so close to mine that when it swings by, I can feel the air shift around it. A few steps later, his knuckle brushes mine. Neither of us says anything. I don't really know what to say. I feel *something* when I'm around him. A lot of things. Interested, in a way. He's cool so far, rarely obnoxious, and we get along well during these trips into the city. I feel easy around him, for the most part. Just a little awkward—the good kind. He's so cute it's intimidating; the shiny black hair, the smooth tan skin, the eyes so dark they seem endless. When I catch him checking me out, I feel desirable, which doesn't happen very often. I mean, there are only three of us on the island—people our age, that is—and one is Marco, who has never expressed attraction to anyone I can remember. So, in a way, the idea of Joaquin and me becoming a thing seems, if not inevitable, definitely an option. There's potential there. However, underneath all of that new, growing stuff—or maybe over the top of it like a plastic bag, sealing it away and suffocating it—is guilt. I have someone.

Had. I don't anymore. Sam has been gone for two years.

Maybe I should try to let go of the guilt finally. I haven't felt it long, because I haven't had a real crush on Joaquin until today, or at least, today is the first time I've allowed myself to entertain the idea. But would it be so bad? Does he even feel the same way? I glance up, and he's staring at me again. Or, still. I smile. So does he.

So, maybe.

At the checkpoint, Calvin and Murray are chatting. Their duffels sit overstuffed at their feet.

"I'm telling you, man, she likes you," Calvin is saying.

"Everybody likes me. What's not to like?" says Murray, resting a hand on his belly. "Ana is different. She's a special lady."

"Dude," calls Joaquin as we approach. "Are you ever going to go for it, or are you planning to harbor this crush forever like a wuss?"

I smack Joaquin's arm. "He's being respectful."

"You call it respectful," says Joaquin. "I call it single and sad."

Murray adjusts his beanie. Beneath his red beard, his cheeks glow with embarrassment. "Don't see the ladies linin' up at your door."

I look up, down, anywhere but at Joaquin. Is my face as flushed as it feels?

"You two sure took your time," says Calvin. "If you'd have cut it any closer, you would be living on the mainland for a few weeks,"

"You wouldn't leave me," I retort.

"No, you're right. Your sister would kill me if I did."

"Him though?" Murray shrugs.

"You wouldn't miss me?" Joaquin asks, opening his arms as if to hug Murray. "Come on."

Murray ducks out from under the impending embrace even though I'm pretty sure Joaquin would not actually hug him.

Joaquin drops his arms and punches Murray on the arm instead. "You two were just gossiping like a pair of old ladies anyway; there wasn't exactly a pressing need to leave."

"We were waiting for you to grace us with your presence."

"Did you run into any trouble in the pharmacy?" I ask.

Calvin shakes his head. "Nope, just a few half-rotten ones. Regular. Easy. You?"

"Nothing we couldn't handle," Joaquin says.

I reach out to unzip Calvin's duffel. "What did you find?"

"Let's show and tell on the boat," Calvin says, hefting the massive bag over his shoulder. "I guarantee Melody is already pacing the dock."

When we get to the boat, only two zombies block our way. Calvin and I each take one while Joaquin and Murray untie the boat. Once we're all aboard, Murray starts the engine. It coughs. Rumbles. Sputters.

The three Abnormals that gather on the street weren't there a second ago. They could catch us no problem if they're the swimming kind. It seems each Abnormal has a different and limited skill set.

"Okay, Murray," Joaquin calls. "Let's go!"

The engine goes *ruh-ruh-ruh*.

"Bloody hell!" Murray shouts.

The Abnormals all turn to face us at once.

The boat roars to life.

They charge.

"Hang on," calls Murray. "She needs to warm up or she'll die again."

Calvin drops his bag on the deck and takes out a knife.

Two of the zombies run right to the edge but stop at the last second. The third vaults off the dock toward us. Joaquin pulls out his gun and shoots the thing in the eye. It goes limp mid-jump and splashes into the water while the other two watch. I'm sure they're just attracted to the movement, though, not that they understand or consider the one Joaquin shot to be a fallen comrade or anything.

The boat takes off.

We stare at one another. I start to laugh.

"Hell of a shot, Joaquin," shouts Murray.

Joaquin grins at me as he holsters his gun. The blush returns to my face with a vengeance.

We rumble across the water, and the city disappears into the mist behind us. Once we're way out, I crouch and unzip Calvin's bag. I whistle as I riffle through it.

"You did well."

"I did, didn't I? Know what that means?"

"Means you're getting some tonight." Joaquin winks.

"No, you chucklehead. It means we won't have to go back for a while."

"Unless Marco injures himself ten more times this week," I say.

"Well let's bubble wrap him already, at least until he decides to train with us again."

"He's not gonna train with us," Joaquin says. "He's soft now, and if he tries to get into our routine, it'll be obvious how far behind he is. He doesn't want to embarrass himself."

"Better embarrassed than dead," I say, opening my bag. The first thing on top is jeans.

Calvin smiles at me as he pulls them aside. "You're a good egg, kid. Are these gonna fit him?"

"Got that covered." I pull open a side pocket to reveal a few leather belts. "We found books too. Mostly fiction, but we brought them anyway."

Calvin picks up a book of fairy tales. "Good find."

"My mom used to read these to me," I say, taking the book back and cradling it for a minute. "I thought it might be nice for the kids."

"There were a lot of cans of food," Joaquin says, patting his bulging bag.

Calvin pulls out something small and soft from the bottom of my bag. Two onesies, one yellow with a duckling on it, and one green with a turtle. "Cate..." His face goes all squishy.

"It's just a few things I found. They're going to need bigger stuff pretty soon. Think Mel will like them?"

"She'll love them. Probably gonna cry over it."

"Yeah, her moods have sure been something since she had the babies. She cried when Nick killed a spider by accident. Will she go back to normal soon, you think?"

"When my sister Angelica had her baby," Joaquin says, "she was all over the place for a while. Michael was eating solid food before she was totally herself again."

I turn around and face Joaquin. "You have a sister?"

He spits over the side of the boat. "Had."

"I'm sorry." Of course I should have realized he had family before, and that, obviously, they were no longer around.

He moves his mouth like he's chewing but says nothing as he stares out at the water, fiddling with something around his neck I never noticed before. A small gold cross.

I can't believe I've never asked about how he came to be a part of Marco's—our—group. Not that any of us love to talk about before. Why would we?

A loud rumbling sound startles all three of us. It's not the boat; it's different. Grating and higher in pitch. And getting louder.

"Cate." Calvin nudges me and points up.

"It's a plane," I say so quietly I can't even hear myself.

Joaquin traces a line in the sky with his finger. "It's heading toward the island."

Four: Alone

1 year, 10 months ago

The noise was incredible surrounded by that many zombies.

Where the hell was Bill? I had seen him, right there. I turned to Cate, but she and Melody were running. They turned back as if they could feel me watching.

"Go! The truck! I'll find you!" I shouted. I didn't know if they heard me.

The horde was closing in. I put my hands up to protect my face, but I knew I wouldn't get away that way, so I dropped to my knees and crawled as fast as I could to the other side of the throng, through the grabbing hands and pulling fingers. I emerged from between many, many legs, stood, and booked it. It didn't matter which direction I was going; I ran without looking or caring.

About a hundred feet away from the church, I stopped running, out of breath and lightheaded. My lungs felt like they had cigarette burns in them. In a way, I guess they sort of did. Wheezing, I bent down and checked my legs, felt around my back and shoulders. Not one scratch? How had I gotten away unscathed? I put my hands on my knees. No matter how hard I tried, I couldn't get a deep enough breath.

So many zombies! So! Many! There was no way in hell Bill got out alive, was there? I took pathetic little shallow gulps of air until my heartbeat came down to a manageable level, considering the situation— the one in which I was totally fucked. I straightened up, trying to blink away the little black spots all over my field of view. I was okay, for the moment.

Bill was probably being ripped to shreds as I sat there quivering. How far had the sisters made it? Probably not far at all. Why the fuck had nobody listened to me when I told them no goddamned guns?

Focus, Marco.

I clenched my fists and tried to take stock of what was going on around me. Okay, how long had it been? Ten minutes, tops? Cate and Melody were probably already at the truck waiting for me. If they'd made it. But Bill wouldn't be. I hadn't had a chance to tell him about it. Where would he have gone? He would have stuck close to the church, at least at first. The only place he might find his family, or the remaining three members.

Except they weren't there, none of them. Tess was dead, and Bill knew it. In fact, unless someone had put her down, Bill's wife was still in there, wandering around undead and mangled. I swallowed against the urge to vomit. Cate and Melody had run straight to the truck after Bill's son Gary had split with half their stuff. Nobody was left in the area except Bill and me. If Bill was still in the area. I turned back and started a loose lap around the church, just in case. No Bill, alive or otherwise.

I thought of going straight to the truck. Maybe Bill had seen the sisters running and joined them. Gary too, that asshole. They were probably all sitting there waiting for me. Would they wait for me? Maybe they'd cut and run as soon as they found the thing. If it started.

A flash of something black caught my eye. Hadn't Bill been wearing a black shirt? I ran toward it, keeping my knife ready. I was stopped seconds later by several brand-new parishioner zombies, people who had been ineffective fighters in life and were now lethal in unlife. None of them wore black.

I stabbed one old lady zombie, the first to reach me, in the temple. It reminded me of the first one I killed, forever ago, in Cate's back yard. My knife came loose after a good, hard tug. Fluids spurted out behind it, blood that had not quite coagulated narrowly missing my face. Unfortunately, as the knife came out, Granny zombie toppled, and we both went down as the others stumbled closer. A sharp pain cut through my leg. My gut clenched. I looked down, positive one of them had gotten me. But it was a rock. Just a rock.

Focus.

I made fists again and stood. I could survive this. Only five left. My taekwondo instructor had been right, though: sparring was completely different from having to defend yourself in real life. Especially alone, and surrounded, and terrified.

With a squelching sound, the zombie to my right dropped. Where it had been stood a man I recognized from the church. I couldn't remember his name. His shirt was black. Together, we got rid of the others a lot more easily.

"You good?" asked the man.

I nodded. "Thanks for that."

"Welcome. Come with me. There are a group of us over this way."

"Is Bill with you?"

"Bill? Don't know. But you're safer with people; come on."

He was probably right, so I followed him to a small house one block north, the opposite direction from where the truck was parked, hoping Bill and Gary might be there. We could still make it to the truck. The sisters would still be waiting, and we would all get out alive. Things could still work out.

When I found neither Bill nor Gary there, I wondered if I should stay with these people or leave and keep trying to find them. What if Bill was somewhere nearby and he found his way to me? Wasn't it more likely to happen if I stayed put?

No. Everyone who was going to escape already had, and the rest had to be dead already.

"You're Frank and Lucy's family, is that right?" asked a woman with a silver braid and a kind smile.

I wasn't sure what to say. I wasn't anyone's family; I was a foster kid. Tess and Bill had been the most recent in a string of foster families, and Lucy was Tess's sister. I'd only met Frank and Lucy recently, and now Lucy, Frank, and Tess were all dead inside the church. Undead, probably, in Tess and Lucy's cases. Nobody put them down.

"Yeah," I said, instead of explaining all that.

"I'm sorry about what happened to them," said the woman, touching my shoulder.

I thanked her because it seemed to be the thing to do and slid out from under her hand.

One of the kids from the group photo Cate had taken a few hours before—one of the few kids I'd seen in the church—sat alone on the couch, pulling at a string in his jeans.

"Hi," I said, sitting on the far side of the couch.

"Hi," he said without looking at me. He swung his legs back and forth. "My dad's dead."

A lot of people are dead, kid, was what I almost said. But what kind of person says that to a little kid? I said sorry instead.

"My sister might be alive though. That's what my mom said."

"She got lost?"

"I was supposed to hold her hand." His face scrunched and his lips trembled. Tears started to roll down his pale, blood-spattered cheeks. "I tried." He bowed his little head and started sobbing.

"It's not your fault," I said, echoing the voices of a hundred social workers, cops, and teachers. I didn't know; maybe it was his fault. But you don't say that to little kids either. "Do you want a hug?"

The little boy nodded. As soon as I scooted closer, he leaned on me, lightly. I put my arm around him. He sobbed some more, cried quietly for a while, sniffed a few times. Finally, his breathing evened out.

In some of the homes I got placed in, I wasn't alone. A few times, I was placed with little ones. They usually acted pretty stoic in the daytime, but at night, a lot of them cried. Since we often shared rooms, I would sit up and talk with them until they could fall asleep. Sometimes, I would wake up to find them curled up next to me, sleeping soundly. Human contact is such a powerful thing, especially when you don't experience it as often or in the same way as other people do.

"Are we still going to the safe place?" he asked after a minute.

"I am."

"What's your name again?"

"Marco."

He stuck his hand out and squeezed mine the way someone must have taught him to. "Hi Marco. I'm Ryan. Mom!"

A woman with long brown hair turned around.

"Marco says we can still go to the safe place."

The woman glared at me. "Well, he doesn't know what he's talking about. We're safer here."

"We're as safe here as we were in the church," I said, not quite making eye contact with Ryan's mom. "Except there are these big giant windows here, so actually we're less safe."

"We're a lot safer with four walls than we are out on the road. Did you not see what happened out there *because* of your ridiculous Alcatraz idea? My husband is dead, and my daughter probably is too!"

Next to me, Ryan tensed up. I patted him on the back and tried to give him a *don't worry* look before standing up and walking toward his mom and the people she was talking to. The blood on my leg, having adhered my jeans to the skin, pulled as I moved and felt like it might open up again. I tugged at the fabric, discreetly, trying to get it loose.

"I know it seems like a long shot," I said. "But it's doable. It's a chance to survive long-term."

"What do you think this is?" asked a guy who I figured was a few years older than me. "We already have long-term safety here."

"This is what you call safe?" These people were maddeningly naive if they thought this flat little house with windows all over the place and not even a damn fence was anything close to safe. "These things are relentless. They will bust in here without hesitating, and that will be it. If you care about your son at all," I said to Ryan's mom, "you'll get him out of here."

"Don't you dare talk to me about my family. As far as I'm concerned, you and your people got my family killed!"

"It was no one's fault," said the pastor. (John, I thought his name was.) "Marco, we appreciate your determination. I understand how this Alcatraz plan might seem like the best option to you. But we have homes here, people who may still be out there alive. We won't abandon them."

"If they're out there, pastor, they've either escaped already, or they're dead. Either way, they don't know to come looking for you here, do they?"

His jaw tensed and relaxed a few times. "We have faith."

Was he kidding with that passive garbage? "Faith? How about a plan? For all we know, some of the others who were going to go are still planning to. We could find more of our people on the road, we could—"

"Is that a scratch?" asked the woman with the silver braid, pointing at my leg. No kind smile anymore, just wide, accusatory eyes.

"It's a cut, I cut myself."

"How do we know you're not lying?" asked a man with a moustache.

"Look what happened to Frank," said the woman.

Things were getting tense, fast. In my periphery, I saw someone step closer to me.

"If Marco says he cut himself," said the pastor, "why wouldn't we believe him?" He put a heavy hand on my shoulder. "He's Frank and Lucy's family, and as long as he's here with us, he's our family too. How did you cut yourself, Marco?"

"I got knocked down and fell on a rock."

"How do you know you fell on a rock?" asked moustache.

"Because I was there?"

"I don't believe him," said Ryan's mom. She scuttled across the room to grab her kid.

"Me neither," said moustache.

Suddenly. there was a gun in my face. I froze. I thought—knew—he was going to kill me. I wondered if Bill was searching for me somewhere nearby. Would he hear the gunshot? The mustached man's finger twitched. I took a deep breath. Would it be my last? Over a fucking cut on my leg?

"Lower it, Ed," said the pastor.

The guy put the gun down surprisingly fast. His face was red. "You saw what happened at the church. He's going to do what the rest did and kill us all. He has to go."

My thoughts exactly, Ed. Except for the part about me turning. A mixture of residual fear and rage squirmed around inside me.

John seemed genuinely disappointed. "Where's your charitable spirit? At the very least, we should keep him here to fix up his leg and make sure he doesn't go the way of the others."

"I'm good," I cut in.

"No, John is right," said Ryan's mom. "If we let him go, he'll just be another monster for us to reckon with later. We keep him here; we can watch him. If he turns,

Ed can shoot him. If he's telling the truth, then he can go in a few hours."

"My people will be gone in a few hours," I protested, knowing that more than likely, they already were. But it sounded more compelling than "please let me go."

"You told John that everyone out there was gone or dead," said Ryan's mom, crossing her arms. "So, which is it? Are you lying to get away or lying to get us to come with you? And if you're lying about that, then who knows how you really got your wound?"

"Regardless," interjected John before I could tell her to go fuck herself. "Marco, I think you'll be better off staying here for now, as much for your sake as ours. We have first aid. We'll clean your leg, you sit with us a while, and if in three hours, you still want to go, then we won't stop you. Deal?"

"Do I have a choice?"

"I'm not saying you have to stay here. No one can make you."

"Except Ed and his gun, right?"

"It's for everyone's sake," said John. "Come, sit over here, we'll clean up that scratch."

His word choice made my skin prickle. Scratch. No matter how even-tempered he was acting, John saw me as a threat too. Another potential monster. He wasn't trying to protect me, not at all. He was trying to protect his flock; of course he was. And if that meant killing a teenager, I bet he'd be one hundred percent down. I sat where he told me to, glancing around as discreetly as I could with all those eyes on me, to see how many guns were present.

Lots, was the answer. Cate and Melody were probably gone, and Bill had either found them, found a spot to hide, or found a horrible end. Alcatraz would still be there in a few hours, and whatever John said, I could tell I didn't have a choice.

It was an unbearably long three hours. I didn't have a watch either, so I had to rely on the few people who did, all of whom watched me as if I might jump up and tear out their throats. Even Ryan was keeping his distance. Nobody spoke to me unless I spoke first, and then, it was short sentences or single words. At the end of three hours, or so they told me, when I showed zero sign of sickness (shocker), John took a bottle of water and a granola bar from their sizeable pile of stuff and handed them to me.

"Okay, then. Good luck, Marco."

"Yeah, thanks." Thanks for making me miss any small chance of finding anyone I knew. Thanks for trying to kill me.

I walked to the door, keeping my composure until I got outside. As John was about to close the door, I turned to him. "You should board up your windows."

He nodded. "We will."

The door shut before I hit the second step. As soon as it latched, I started running, letting all of the fear and absurdity of the last three hours go free.

"Fuck!" I shouted to the empty street. What the hell had I expected, going with some random dude? I should have known better than to trust people. At least zombies only operated on one setting. At least you knew what to expect from them. But people? People were scary.

Back at the church, the zombies had mostly dispersed, leaving only a few stragglers. I snuck past, not trying to engage. Definitely not wanting to see Tess or Lucy as undead monsters.

I found myself wishing it was the night before, and I was on a walk with Cate. If I closed my eyes and concentrated, I could hear her voice. It made me happy and really sad that she and Melody were probably hours away. If I was going to get to Alcatraz, I was going to do it alone. No Cate or Melody, no Bill, not even Gary. No big deal though. It would be easier if I didn't have anyone else to worry about.

I stopped running so abruptly I stumbled. Why was I running? Would I run all the way to Alcatraz? Was Alcatraz even a possibility anymore? Having a group was the only way it was going to work, and I was fresh out of people.

But...

What if Cate and Melody hadn't left yet?

The sky was still light...ish. It was a ridiculous long shot, but what if they were still there, sitting in the bed of the truck the way Cate and I had done, waiting? They wouldn't wait for me alone, probably, but as far as they knew, I was with their uncle. They'd wait for Bill, wouldn't they?

I ran for the truck. I was about a block and a half away when I saw it sitting there, all bulbous and rickety. When I got a little closer, I could make out the faint outline of exhaust pouring out of the tailpipe.

"Cate!"

That was what I had meant to say, but as I took a deep breath to yell, the cold air burned my throat, and I was incapacitated in a coughing fit.

Two zombies, attracted to the noise I was making, came at me from behind and knocked me down. I fought them off fine, but the few seconds it took to get back up were too many, and the truck began to pull away.

"Cate! No!" I finally managed to shout, but there was no way they could see me or hear me. The truck was so loud I could hear it from where I stood, and so could any zombies within fifty yards. I sprinted, my feet pounding the cement, the freezing air shredding my throat and lungs. I shouted again, coughed again. Waving my arms, I kept running and calling to them, but the truck's taillights got smaller and smaller until they were distant pinpoints, then nothing at all.

I stopped and watched the spot where the lights had been. If I had just come straight to the truck, if I hadn't wasted time with those people. But it didn't matter, because I had, and as a result, I'd missed Cate and Melody by seconds and sealed my fucking fate. I would never make it to Alcatraz alone; who was I kidding?

I took a few steps in the direction the truck had gone. Finding them again would be absurdly unlikely. I had no direction, no supplies, no map, and no people.

A zombie came at me, another damn parishioner. I swung a left hook at its face. It wouldn't slow it down, but I needed to hit something. It came back, and I hit it again. Again, again, again. The skin of my knuckles split against the insides of my gloves. When it grabbed for my hair, I leaned out of reach, landed a solid back kick to its chest, and stood on its neck when it went down. As the zombie gazed through me, continuing to claw at my leg, I axed its face and wiped the blade on its sweatshirt.

I stepped over it, took a few more stumbling steps. My head pounded from the effort. The sky got darker. Hopelessness crept in, and I stopped walking. For the first time in a long time, I let myself cry.

Five: Changes

Calvin jumps off the boat as soon as it's docked. Joaquin, Murray, and I are right behind him.

"What do we do?" I ask as we jog up the path. Smoke rises from where the plane must have crash-landed.

"We need to get everyone inside."

The little plane sits at the very edge of the open area below the lighthouse. Our people are creeping toward it, surrounding it. Mel steps closer as a person gets out, then another. All of a sudden, she runs and smashes into one of them. I shout her name. What the hell is she doing?

By the time I get to them, Marco is with her. And I recognize the first passenger. He's thinner than before, making his broad shoulders appear even more so. His beard is longer, and his tattoos are faded. But it's definitely him.

"Uncle Bill!" I run at him, same as Mel did, into the group hug already in progress. Mel is sobbing, of course, and now so am I.

"Hey, kiddo." Bill's voice sounds shaky too. He hugs us all tighter for a second before letting us go. "Gary?" His gaze darts back and forth between Mel, Marco, and me.

Nobody answers at first.

He seems to understand. "When?"

"Right before we got to San Francisco," Mel answers.

Bill doesn't seem surprised by the news of his son's death, but he does shrink under the weight of it. He takes off his glasses and massages the bridge of his nose. He stands that way for a long time, with his eyes squeezed shut and his mouth in a grimace. Mel and I lay our hands on his arm and his back, and eventually, he puts his glasses back on.

"How did it—" He swallows. "How did it happen?"

I shake my head. "It was fast."

Thankfully, he doesn't pursue it.

"We're glad you're here," Mel says gently.

"Me too." says Uncle Bill. He's smiling, but it's steeped in pain.

"So, pilot's license?" asks Marco, glancing at the plane. It's in one piece, but it's sort of smashed into the barrier, giving it the appearance of a minor crash rather than a landing. A foot or two more, and it would have overshot and tumbled straight into the water.

"Gimme a break, man," says Bill, wiping the last few tears away from his cheeks with his knuckles. "I did okay; I got us here."

"Us?" I ask. I'd momentarily forgotten there were two people on the plane.

"Yeah, us. Come on out!" Bill calls toward the plane.

The other passenger is standing back, peeking around the side of the aircraft. When I look right at her, she gives a small wave and steps out of the plane's shadow. Her hair isn't blue anymore. It's brown with silvery-blonde ends. Her face is the same though—every freckle. She steps toward me, one tentative step, then another.

When she's close enough to touch, I place a hand on her face. I open my mouth twice before any sound comes out. It's suddenly so dry. My heartbeat is in my throat. I get one word out. "Sam?"

"Hi," she says, smiling.

I move closer to her, closer, closer, staring at her. I linger on my favorite parts of her face: her twinkly eyes and thick lashes, the little gap in her front teeth, the constellation of freckles across her nose and cheeks. I never thought I would see this face again except for the pictures in my phone.

Before I can ask, Sam kisses me. Her lips, which used to be smothered in sticky, fruity lip gloss most of the time, are chapped and warm. The kiss only lasts a second before I have to pull away to examine her face. I've had dreams that start this way and end with Sam as a zombie. I bite the inside of my cheek to wake myself. But I am awake, and she is here.

"Hi," I whisper.

She takes my hands in hers, smiling though her eyes are glistening with tears.

"Somebody's gonna have to tell me what we're all clearly missing," Calvin says.

"This is, uh, Bill, our uncle," answers Mel, although she's watching Sam and me. "He and my aunt Tess adopted Marco just before everything happened."

"Fostered," Marco corrects her.

"Shush, you." Bill gestures toward the plane. "If flying about a thousand miles with nothing but hope and a very expired pilot's license isn't grounds for adoption, I don't know what is. You're my family, Marco. Cool?"

Marco smiles real and wide for the first time in forever. "Cool," he agrees.

Bill opens up his arms. "Come on, hug it out."

"And this is?" asks Joaquin, looking Sam up and down in a weirdly appraising way.

The specific kind of heat that usually comes with being caught doing something I shouldn't rushes to my cheeks. This time, though, nobody's catching me. Nobody, except maybe Joaquin, knows what was on my mind not even an hour ago. I don't realize the question was directed at me until Sam squeezes my hand and Bill lets go of Marco and speaks up.

"This is Samantha, Cate's...girlfriend?"

Sam and I both nod. I glance between Sam and Joaquin a couple of times. Sam doesn't notice. Joaquin does.

"Seems our family grew by a few people," says Bill, glancing around.

Everyone introduces themselves, except for Amy, Tanya, and the kids, who are all inside. Bill greets them all with the same genuine enthusiasm. Sam shakes some hands, smiles, nods a few times. She's making an effort, but her expression is strained, tired, anxious. She's overwhelmed, and I can't blame her: I know I would be.

Mel pulls Calvin close so he's standing directly in front of Bill. "And this is Calvin. He's the father of our babies."

Calvin extends a hand. "Good to meet you, sir."

Bill takes it, and tips his head a little. "Calvin, are you the hugging type?"

"I certainly can be."

Calvin seems surprised by the strength of Bill's hug. He has several inches and a few solid pounds on Bill.

"Welcome to the family, man," Bill says. "Thank you for whatever you did to keep the girls safe. I owe you."

"No," says Calvin. "Melody is the best thing that has ever happened to me. And Cate's not bad." He winks at me.

Bill startles, shakes his head, and turns to Mel. "I'm sorry, Melody, did you say the father of your babies? As in, plural?"

"Twins," Mel clarifies, tilting up her chin. "A girl, Maebelle, after Calvin's Nana, and a boy, Andrew, after—"

"After your dad, of course." Bill keeps smiling, but the sadness in his eyes deepens. Speaking from experience, I know the feeling will never truly fade.

Mel nods. "They were born right before we got here."

"Like, right before," Marco chimes in.

"Where are they?"

"Tanya and her wife, Amy, took them inside when you landed," answers Mel. "You made a pretty dramatic entrance."

"I didn't know if I'd ever see another child," says Bill, shaking his head in disbelief. "And you have two."

"We have five, including the babies," Marco tells him.

"How did you two find each other?" I mean to ask Sam, but Bill answers first.

"I went a little off the rails after Tess... After we got separated at the church. I got surrounded pretty quick, managed to get out from underneath them. Almost didn't. One ripped my shirt; I thought I would...but I didn't.

"I couldn't see any of you, I figured you must have gotten out. I grabbed a bike and rode. I rode for hours and ended up at the last place I saw her smiling. Your house. I guess I just needed to be near her however I could be. I found Samantha there, sleeping in Cate's room. She said she knew Cate, that her mom had been infected, and Cate's house was the only place she could think of to go."

"Your mom?" I turn to Sam again. She looks at the ground. "I'm sorry," I murmur, hugging her tight.

"It was just a scratch," says Sam. "We tried remedies, rituals. She even tried real meds for once. But, you know. When she, uh, woke up, she tried to get me. I ran to your house because your text said you'd be there. You weren't. I almost died, Cate."

"I'm sorry," I repeat.

Sam shrugs. "Bill showed up days later. He told me where you might have ended up if you were alive."

"She was half dead when I found her, poor thing. When I told her about Alcatraz, she jumped on the idea, and off we went."

"And you just got here?" asks Marco.

"We found the plane, like, two weeks ago," says Sam.

"Where were you until then?" Mel asks Bill.

"Some beach town in Oregon, mostly."

"We found this cute little hotel. One of the rooms was unlocked. It was full of supplies. No people though. One dead body in the bathroom. Bill took care of it."

"And you spent, what, the winter there?"

"We were there for..." Sam glances up, contemplating. "About a year and a half."

"Are you serious?" I gape at Sam. "How, why?"

Bill makes a chuffing sound. "One thing after another. First, too cold to move on. Then I got sick. Nothing life-threatening, but we didn't have basic vitamins and stuff, so it took me a while to be travel-ready again. Then, a big old gaggle of zombies came through chasing a deer. They hung around for weeks after they'd eaten the thing. That set us back on food, just having to sit there and wait 'em out. While we were gathering supplies after they finally moved on, some jackoff stole our bikes and what little food we had left. Well, we had to have bikes, didn't we? So finding them took time. We had to go two towns over before we found rideable ones. We camped out in houses, which by then were all but empty of food or water. It was rough going for a few months."

"Have you ever eaten squirrel?" asks Sam, curling her lip.

"Worse than that," Calvin says.

Bill nods. "So, it was a year and a half in the hotel. A couple of months finding and fixing bikes, living off practically nothing. Then, finally, we started to ride south. We flew out of a town right near the California border."

They walk ahead; Sam and I hang way back and let our steps fall into sync. We are still holding hands. I don't know if I can let go.

"I would have got caught by a few of them on the way out of town. Zombies. But Bill saved me. He did that a lot, protected me from them." Sam pronounces the word "zombies" as if she's not used to saying it yet, even though zombies have been a thing for about two years now. I wonder what she called them before? It seems like everybody called them sick people, but they aren't people, not at all.

"I'm glad you found each other."

"You look so different," she says.

"I am different."

"I guess we all are." Sam runs her fingers over the scar on my temple. For a quick instant, I'm back in the woods where I got the wound, an awful sick feeling twisting my guts, that bastard Alex's boot on my face. The closest I've ever been to death, and some of the most terrifying hours of my life. I stiffen, but Sam doesn't notice. She's staring at the cell house, her mouth hanging open. "You live in there?"

I breathe in and out, bringing myself back to the now. "We all do. It's safe. There's privacy, and, well, that's about all it has going for it."

"Safe is good. I've never been here before. I didn't expect these signs and stuff all over."

"It's a national park, or something. There used to be tours and rangers. There's even a gift shop."

"Seriously?"

I open the door to the cell house and hold it for her to walk through first. "We cleared out all of the useful stuff early on. We don't go there much anymore, but I think Mel and Calvin sneak over there sometimes."

"Why?"

I raise my eyebrows at her.

Sam's eyes widen, and she cracks a smile. "Ah. So, which cell will be mine?"

I lead her up the stairs to the second tier. "Whichever one you want. We live on tiers two and three. You can go anywhere but the bottom row. We don't sleep down there. Safety."

Sam peers up and down the row. I watch her eyes stop on every cell for a moment each.

"It's like a home in here," she says. "Can I have a curtain too?"

"You can have mine. Mostly, they're for nighttime coverage, but I don't close mine often since Chaz sleeps in there with me, and he likes to check on the babies."

"Chaz?"

At the sound of his name, the old white lab waddles out of my cell sleepily. Sam cries out and crouches to pet him when he sits in front of us.

"Mel and I found him in Oregon the first winter. She says we share custody, but we both know he's mine."

"Does that mean he's mine too?" asks Sam.

"What do you think, Chaz? Are you Sam's dog too?" I make a face like I'm listening to his answer. "He says he'll think about it."

After Sam puts her one little backpack on the bare bed of her chosen cell, we go to mine to take down my curtain, and back to hers to hang it. Chaz walks between us, occasionally touching Sam's hand or mine with his nose, and in my mind, it's like he's accepting her into the family.

"So I'll get a blanket eventually, won't I?" she asks as we leave the cell. The dog follows us carefully down the stairs and toward the door that leads outside.

"Yeah, of course. I'm sure we have an extra somewhere. Remind me to talk to David at dinner. He's in charge of inventory. His choice. He didn't even wait for anyone else to volunteer."

"He's the older guy, right?"

"Um, yeah."

The way Sam uses his age as his only descriptor reminds me that David is, indeed, the oldest person we have on the island. I don't know quite how old, but he has mentioned a granddaughter. Bill, in his late forties, isn't too far behind. After months with the same people, you don't think about that stuff.

But for a small second, I consider it—what little time he might have left, even here, safe on the island. Especially after he lost his wife Eunice on the docks. And for that matter, what little time any of us might have. Because no matter how safe we think we are, the collapse of society two years ago showed us there's no real guarantee. But good things happen, too, don't they? Sam and Bill made it here, after all.

"Cate?" Sam is watching me. How long have I been standing still?

"Yeah, that's him. He keeps the island running as smoothly as it does. Which isn't to say we don't have issues."

"Like what?"

"Little things. Our pea plants are dying, and no one can figure out why. And yesterday, a zombie got into the cell house."

"A zombie is a little thing?"

"One zombie is a very little thing when it's up against people who are trained to take it down."

Sam regards everyone else, most of them crowded around the babies, and Bill at the other end of the row. "Who's trained?"

"All of us. We train together in the mornings. Right out here."

I open the door, and we venture out into the rec yard, a large, walled-in area of grass and cement outside the cell house.

"All?"

"Yeah. Well, most of us. Mel comes in now and then, but she spends a lot of time with the kids. There are other people who don't train religiously."

Sam scrunches up her nose. "I would way rather hang out with cute kids all day than fight zombies and risk getting infected."

"Tell me that after months of nothing but cute kids. Mel has vomit in her hair at least once a week, and she hasn't slept a whole night since we got here. I'd rather fight."

Sam and I keep to ourselves for the rest of the morning. After the rec yard, I show her the garden where we are starting to grow our food. The kids, who are learning to tend the crops, greet Sam the same way they greeted me when I first met them. Adrienne is a social butterfly, asking Sam all about herself and her two-toned hair. Upon hearing about the blue it used to be, she announces that she, too, wants to give color a try.

"But orange, because that's the best color."

Nick, who still hardly talks, is sweet and shy, making himself busy with one of the plants while not-so-secretly watching us over his shoulder. Francis says hello, but as he did with me, he makes it clear he's not interested in being friends with Sam.

"Don't take it personally," I tell her as we leave them to their gardening. "Marco found Francis in a dumpster in the city. He only likes Marco and the other kids. He's finally starting to trust Mel."

On the way back up, we see Calvin, Murray, and Bill standing around the plane, scratching their heads. By the time we reach the top of the agave trail, they're climbing up behind us, having apparently decided to leave the plane where it is.

As we finish touring the island, Sam seems a whole lot more comfortable. She smiles and waves at Jax and Toby as we pass them. At mealtime, we make our way to the patch of grass where we all meet to eat. As we walk by Mel, she hands us each a cup of canned vegetables. To each of the dogs she gives a generous handful of kibble from a box we keep nearby.

"Is food scarce?" Sam asks, eyeing the meager helpings.

"No, but it's not abundant either," I answer, leading her toward the outer edge of the group.

"This is great. Bill and I ate whatever we could find. Some days, it was a big fat nothing."

"That was a lot of days," Bill calls from across the group. He's got a very content-looking baby Maebelle resting on his lap and his cup suspended under his chin. As soon as he stops talking, he starts dumping the food into his mouth.

"Been there," says Calvin as he scoots next to Mel with baby Andrew in one arm and a plate in the other hand. He settles Andrew on his belly in the grass. "I think that was when Cate asked about whether a person can survive on urine for hydration."

I groan through my mouthful of food. "Dude, I'm eating."

"You asked."

"Last year!"

Marco sits next to us, on Sam's other side. "Well, can you?"

"Not for long," says Calvin.

"What about other peoples' pee?"

Sam groans.

"Please don't answer him," I say to Calvin.

"Well, I mean if you can—"

"Stop."

"If you can drink your own, then—"

"Cal!" I squeal.

Calvin chuckles and rubs smalls circles on baby Andrew's back. "Oooh, I think we ruffled Auntie Cate," he coos. "What do you think?"

"How's the leg?" I ask, trying my very best not to sound judgmental.

"It's fine. Another day or two, it'll be like it never happened."

"Any chance I'll see you at training soon?"

"You see me all day, Cate. Don't you get sick of me?"

"Sick of you injuring yourself."

"How did he injure himself?" asks Sam, leaning forward into my field of view.

I say "Abnormal" at the exact same time Marco says "Variant." He makes a face.

"You are both ridiculous," says Tanya, sitting a few feet away from us with Amy.

"Seriously," says Toby, "who cares what they're called?"

Jax snorts. "They're scary as shit either way."

"Okay, wait." Sam says. "You're talking about what, now? Because Bill said you call them zombies, and at first it was like *whoa*, you know? But I get it—zombies. So what are Abnormals or Variants or whatever?"

"They're zombies, but worse."

"Worse?"

I search her face. "You've never seen any weird zombies? No? Bill?"

Bill looks as confused as Sam.

"Seriously?" Marco says. "How could you not have seen them? They're all over."

Bill shakes his head. "We spent most of our time cooped up in that hotel, remember?"

"I mean, we only saw one in all of Oregon, didn't we?" Mel asks no one in particular. "They were way more concentrated the farther south we got. If they flew in from southern Oregon, it makes sense that they never encountered one."

"Then they're damn lucky," mumbles Tanya.

"So what are we missing?" Bill asks. "What's a Variant?"

"They're sort of...super zombies," Marco explains. "They run and climb and stuff. Cate and I saw one who could talk. A little one, on a rooftop in the city. I told you about her, Ana."

Who. Her. I don't think he meant to say it, but the slip makes me wonder: does Marco think of the zombie kid as a kid more than a zombie? He called it "she" that day on the roof, too, even though he knew it was a zombie before I did.

"The zombie got away, correct?" asks Ana.

"Correct."

Sam shivers. "Well that's unsettling." She scooches closer and leans on me. I put my arm around her and pet her bicep.

Bill, having finished his food, sets his cup down and cradles baby Mae close to his chest. "I'll say."

"Any idea why they're like that?" Sam asks, perking her head up.

"Nope," says Marco. "Best guess, the virus mutated or something. But hey, what do I know. I'm nineteen."

Sam lets her head rest again. "Hm."

"It makes sense though," says Amy. "In med school, we learned about virus mutation. Even common ones like the flu do it. It's an evolution thing. And again—I'm only speculating here—it might be where the zombie virus itself originated."

"Yeah, I think I heard something similar on the news right in the beginning," agrees Bill. "Something about a kid and a seagull. His mom said he got way sicker in the hospital."

"Have you ever considered," Joaquin cuts in, "that it's not just a sickness?"

"What are you talking about?" I ask.

"All this." He waves his hand across the space in front of himself. "Zombies? The world? It was predicted."

"Oh yeah?" asks Sam, sitting up. "By who?"

"The Bible. I read the passages again the other day, in fact. One part, in Jeremiah, talks about eating the flesh of their fathers and sons, and another part, Revelation, I think? Talks about being unable to die, and about rising from the dead."

"Don't you think you might be misinterpreting? That seems awfully literal."

"I would have agreed with you before, but you tell me." Joaquin sits back, leaning on his hands. "The dead are walking, aren't they? Eating the flesh of their kin? This is punishment."

"Theirs," I ask, "or ours?"

Joaquin shrugs. "Either. Both."

"So you're righteous and holy, or you're a damn zombie?" Marco asks. "Spare me."

"Interesting word choice, Marco," Joaquin answers, a self-assured smile tugging at one side of his lips. "*Damned*, zombie."

"So if an innocent gets bitten, they're condemned, somehow deserving? Kids, babies?"

Joaquin shrugs. "In some religions, unbaptized people of any age don't go to heaven. Babies too."

"You're saying my babies won't go to heaven because they weren't baptized?" Calvin asks, squaring his shoulders. "That's not the God I know. My God wouldn't turn away an innocent. My God is merciful."

"Amen," says Jax.

"God punishes the deserving," Joaquin says.

"So anyone who gets infected is automatically damned, that's it?"

"What would you call it, Marco? Monsters who used to be people, walking on and on with no place to go, eating their loved ones, flesh rotting off their bones? Sounds like damnation to me."

"Or maybe a really bad sickness?" Sam says.

Marco slaps his hands on his lap, shakes his head. "You are literally saying people who get a sickness, one they can't possibly prevent, deserve it. That anyone who gets the smallest scratch is a damned soul. And why? Because they didn't adhere to the laws of one particular subset of a single religion?" He narrows his eyes. "What kind of bullshit God do you serve, Joaquin?"

"The right one, Marco."

"Growing up," David interjects, never taking his eyes off his hands, "I learned it's our lives here on earth, the deeds we do and the weight of each, that matters most. Eunice wasn't religious, never set foot in a house of worship as far as I know. But I don't think a woman as kind and giving as she was could be anywhere but heaven, if there is one. I don't know what to believe anymore, I haven't been to temple in years, but I think whatever God there is, they must care most about the condition of our souls, not the status."

"Not eating holy crackers and taking righteous baths, you mean?" Marco says.

"Marco," Uncle Bill touches his shoulder. "You don't have to understand it or subscribe to it, but you do have to be respectful. Joaquin's beliefs don't hurt you, do they?"

The silence only lasts a second before Marco is back at it. "So your belief, then, is that having this sickness, no matter how you get it, equals damnation, an unclean soul, end of? Are you saying HIV is damnation too? Or drug addiction?"

I haven't seen him so ready for a fight since Halloween night, two years ago, when he screwdrivered Mrs. Minkin in my back yard.

Joaquin is far more stoic. He talks down to Marco as though he's speaking with a petulant kid, goading him with the exaggerated calmness. "We're not talking about that, are we? We're talking about zombies."

"But you're saying if a person gets bit—anybody— they're going to hell for sure?" I ask. What I don't ask is, "What about me?" because in truth, I am a little afraid of the answer. I've been infected a total of three times now. I finger the scars on my wrist.

Joaquin locks eyes with me, and damn it, I blush. "I'm saying there's a reason for everything. Nothing is random. This isn't the first time humanity has met its reckoning either. This is worldwide, too, just like before."

Marco scoffs. "I can't entertain this garbage anymore. I'm going to bed."

"That's not a bad idea," agrees Bill as he stands and picks up Baby Maebelle and her blanket. "It has been one very long day." He hands the baby to Mel, brushes the grass off his pants. "Night, everyone. It was wonderful to meet all of you. Marco, wait up."

Around the circle, a contagious yawn jumps from person to person. One of the babies starts to whimper, so Mel and Calvin take them both inside. The other three kids follow, rubbing their eyes. Jax and Toby put the fire out, David and Ana collect cups. Amy and I wake the dogs, who have been sleeping since the moment after they finished their food, and we all migrate toward the cell house.

*

Hours later, an image of the little rooftop zombie plays in my head, followed by the other Abnormals I've encountered, every zombie I can remember, and more that I'm not sure are memories or composites of all the rotten, dead faces I've seen the last two years. My breathing quickens. What if they're coming for us right now? What if the cell house is surrounded by moaning hordes of the undead? My heartbeat thunders in my ears. I try to breathe deeply. In for four seconds, out for eight. It's still the only thing that helps when I feel this way. Sometimes, it doesn't.

I sit up, panting.

"Cate?" Sam is in my doorway. "You okay?"

"No." I can't say any more. I keep breathing. Slowing it down. In four, out eight.

"What's up?"

I don't know how to explain. In my head, it's zombies and tearing flesh and screaming. In my head, we're all going to die.

"Cate. Talk to me."

"Shh!" someone hisses from another cell.

Sam glances over her shoulder and shuffles to my bed.

"The Abnormal," I whisper when my head finally stops spinning. "The one Marco mentioned. We were on a rooftop, he and I, in a garden. It was beautiful. The zombie was crying like a real kid though." In four. Out Eight. "She asked me for help. That's where I got this." I hold up my arm. Even in the darkness, I know she can see the wide scars down the inside of my forearm and wrist and the black veins that surround them.

"What the fuck?" Sam grabs my arm.

"Will you shut it!" Murray shouts.

Chaz stops snoring and lifts his head. His big black eyes stare at us through the darkness.

"Can we walk?" I whisper.

Sam nods and walks back to her cell to get her shoes. Usually, I walk with Marco. As soon as we found each other, we slipped right back into the same routine. But Sam is here, and Marco is probably asleep anyway, and her reaction to my scars makes me think a longer conversation might be necessary.

The dog wanders out of my cell with me, but he turns the other way, toward Mel and Calvin's end of the row. Sam is waiting for me by the stairs. I try to get a read on her expression as we leave the cell block, but she mostly just looks tired. When we get to the outer door, I pick up the pace. I need to see the island, the grounds, and know we're safe. It's brighter outside, and nothing is out of place. Everything is as it should be.

"Slow down," Sam huffs, scrambling after me. "What do you mean the zombie did that? Wouldn't you have died, or needed to cut your arm off or something?"

I open my mouth, but I don't know what to say. Okay, yes I do, but all that comes out is air.

"Cate, what?"

"I'm, I'm immune. To whatever it is. I won't die from the infection, and I won't turn either."

"How do you know?"

"Because it happened before, the first night Mel and I were alone." I lift up my shirt, watching her while I do.

"Jesus, Cate," she whispers.

"I woke up to a zombie chewing on my hip. Mel cauterized it so at least I wouldn't bleed out, and, I don't know, I just didn't die." It's the same exact words I said to Marco when he first saw my scar a few months ago. How else do I explain what happened? A bite to the torso should have been lethal. I'd been so afraid of his reaction, but he said I had a superpower.

Sam's expression makes me want to run and hide. It's what I thought I saw before: disgust? She comes closer and reaches out to touch the scar on my hip but pulls back her hand when she gets within an inch of it. "Wow. It's awful."

Ouch.

"Thanks?"

"I'm sorry, but I mean look at it. It makes me sad, that's all. Those zombies ruined your beautiful skin."

"But I'm alive."

She tugs my shirt back down and wraps her arms around me. She's thinner than she was before, but aren't we all? I hold her tighter, trying to physically close this weird new gap between us. But the embrace feels superficial, and she breaks it off way sooner than I'd like.

We trudge back to the rec yard in silence. She doesn't reach for my hand, keeping her own in her back jeans pockets. I want to know what's in her head, but I'm afraid to ask. Is she freaked out by my scar, my immunity? It is peculiar, and, yes, the scars are ugly, especially the cauterized one, all gnarled and discolored. But after talking to Marco, it was hard for me to feel ashamed. I had begun to think of it as a strength. I can never be infected. If anything, that's something to be proud of. Isn't it? I can still die a thousand different ways, but I am safe from the worst kind of death, and when I die, I'll stay that way. Now, I feel shame creeping back in, burning my cheeks and stinging my eyes.

She opens the door to the cell house and holds it for me, smiling, but not quite making eye contact.

"I missed you," I whisper to her as we climb the stairs.

"I missed you too." She touches my hand for the briefest moment. "I'm tired. Let's go back to bed."

When I get to my cell, Chaz is back, curled up on the big pile of rags in the corner. I leave my jeans and shoes next to him, crawl into the tiny bed, and situate myself under the thin blanket. But I can't get comfortable.

Six: Switch

After spending the entire night going over my conversation with Sam—worrying about what it meant and wondering if it was really a great time to explain my immunity to her at all, having not seen her in over a year— I'm still awake when the others start to get up. First, the babies make their little noises, which prompts Chaz to stand slowly, stretch, and limp out to check on them. Shortly after, Mel and Calvin are up with the rest of the kids, followed by the earliest risers: Ana, Murray, and Joaquin, who is still in his cell when the rest of us are in the walkway nodding silent good mornings.

I debate whether I should wake Sam to start training yet. She has only been on the island a day, and after last night, I don't know how things will be with her. I'm lingering outside her cell when Joaquin steps out of his.

"Morning," he says as he approaches.

"Morning." My face burns, and I'm sure my cheeks are scarlet. I almost forgot—things are off with him too.

"You going to training?"

I shrug. "Yeah. Of course. I was about to wake up Sam." When I finish answering, I hear stirring in her cell.

Joaquin makes a face—is it disappointed, abashed?—and walks past me, down the stairs toward the rec yard. I consider running down to try talking to him, but David beats me to it, and they head out together.

I tap on the bars of Sam's cell with my fingernails. "Sam?"

She moves around a bit more and tells me to come in. She's sitting on her bed, clothes on, tying her shoes. "So," she says without looking up, "training?"

"Yep. It's harder at first, especially the getting up part. But it gets easier every day."

Sam yawns. "I hope you're right." She smiles at me as we walk outside together. It's an easy smile, one that suggests she was not up worrying all night like I was. "You're gonna help me today, right?"

"Of course!" I say with maybe too much enthusiasm.

Sam's eyes widen when she sees a few of the others sparring with their substitute weapons, which are all kitchen utensils. Murray swings a spatula at Tanya's head, and she ducks, barely in time for him to miss. She comes back up, holding her ladle handle-out, and pokes Murray in the temple.

"This is intense," says Sam.

"We won't spar today," I assure her. "No one expects you to be ready for that yet. We'll ease you into the routine." If we never talk about last night again, it's fine with me.

She stretches her arms over her head and gives one slow, catlike blink. "Ease is good."

"Cate! You two gonna stand around all day or what?" Calvin shouts across the rec yard.

"It's barely morning," Sam complains quietly, scrunching up her face. "What day?"

I roll my neck as I walk over and get into the last row. Sam moves to my left, making a spot of her own.

Ana and Calvin are at the front, indisputably the two best fighters we have. While Calvin starts shouting commands, Ana walks over to Sam.

"Good morning, Samantha."

"Morning. Sam is fine."

"Sam. How's your basic defense?"

"I, uh..." Sam glances at me, uncertain. "I know they need to be done in the head."

Ana frowns and hands Sam her wooden spoon, which is similar to the one I'm holding. "This is your weapon when you train. We use these in place of real knives for safety. You can keep that. Now, I'm a zombie."

Ana backs up a few steps and comes at Sam. Sam squeals and swings wildly at the air. She does hit Ana once, on the arm, barely. Ana's face doesn't change. "Okay. Cate, take her to the far corner. Catch her up."

"Am I that bad?" Sam asks, glancing over her shoulder at everyone else. "Did she really want me to hit her with this spoon?"

"Yeah, but I think she knew you wouldn't hurt her. You're not bad. Just new."

"She's kind of a hard ass, isn't she? Calvin too."

"They just know what you can come up against out there. From what you told me, you were pretty lucky. The rest of us saw people die, and almost died ourselves. Toby had two hands until the night we came here. An Abnormal came out of nowhere. And if I wasn't immune, I'd have died two years ago."

"And again, the island is safe, right?"

"Right, but you never know." I start to stretch without explaining myself, but Sam follows along fine. "I mean, the day before you got here, we ran into an Abnormal inside the library, which means it got all the way onto the island somehow, and then found its way into the cell house and to the library without anyone noticing."

"Okay, okay. I get it. So, catch me up."

"All right. We have this routine we use. It helps a ton, if you can remember to do it when you're up against an actual zombie. So, um, what you do is, you want to avoid the attack, right? Which for a regular zombie and most Abnormals is usually its hands, you know?"

Sam smirks. "Sure." Calvin did a way better job of explaining it to me, but she's getting it.

"So, you duck." I show her. "Like this. Easy. Feet apart, maybe a little staggered, and then you go down. As if you're sitting on a bucket."

Sam ducks.

"Perfect. Then you want to roll. Watch." I demonstrate.

Sam tries but ends up falling over. When she gets back up, her expression is dissatisfied. "You make it seem a lot easier."

"You should have seen my first few rolls. Try again."

"I feel ridiculous, Cate," she protests. "Does everyone have to be a badass zombie slayer?"

"No," I say, keeping my voice gentle. "But it helps to be able to handle yourself. What if you came up against a zombie, what would you do?"

Sam crosses her arms. "According to you, it's highly unlikely unless I leave, and I don't plan on doing that."

"You're right, but, hey. Try for me. It can be fun, once you get it down."

She does way better the second time though she's huffing the whole way through. Almost makes it onto her feet.

"Okay, good! See? Now, try to duck and then roll."

She does both and comes up into a wobbly standing position.

"Awesome! Oh, I forgot to mention. When you come out of your roll, you want to stay low, in a crouch."

"This is a whole thing, huh?" She does it again, coming into a very uncomfortable-looking crouch where all of her weight is forward.

I try to be encouraging. "Kind of, but more like—" I do it again, sticking out my leg in a swing automatically.

"Okay, well, you didn't tell me about the kicking thing." Sam puts a hand on her hip. "Is that all of it? You duck, you do a Bond roll, you come back up and kick 'em in the knees?"

"Yep, that's about it. Well, less of a kick, more of a swinging of the leg. Your goal is to knock them off balance, to—"

"Sweep them off their feet?" She smirks and wiggles her eyebrows at me.

It's nice to see her smiling again. My shoulders drop the smallest bit, releasing some of the tension I kept with me through the night.

"Yeah, exactly. And then stab them in the eye while they're down.

She looks surprised, but she's giggling. "Whoa, mood ruined."

I laugh with her. "Come on, we'll do the form together. I'll go slow and count it out. Ready? One...two...three...four."

I do a few with her until she can at least get to three without tripping herself. Then, while Sam is practicing, I watch the others. Mel isn't training, but she usually doesn't. Everyone else is doing the same form, but faster. Joaquin is in his normal spot, down the row a few spaces. He catches my gaze just before he rolls.

"Hey, I basically did it that time! Cate?"

I turn back to Sam. "Great job!"

She pouts. "I finally got it, and you weren't even watching."

"Sorry."

"Are we done soon?"

"No. In a second, we spar, then we stretch again, then we're done."

"I didn't know I'd joined the Marines," Sam mumbles.

"Oh, hush," I say, wrapping my arms around her for a second. "Just a little longer, then we eat. After, we can do whatever you want."

Sam grins as I let go. "You had me at 'eat.'"

"Pair off!" Calvin shouts.

"Now we spar. Or, we would, but I think I'll stay with you to—"

"Cate!" Calvin interrupts, jogging over to Sam and me. "I know you heard me."

"Yeah, but I thought you'd want me to stay with Sam."

"Nah. I've been watching her. Sam's doing fine. Better than you did on your first day." He gives Sam a wide, encouraging smile. "You go spar, Cate. I'll stay with her."

"Hey, do you know where Bill is?" Sam asks Calvin as I turn to leave them.

"Bill is with Melody. She's got him gardening. Don't worry; I told her he's ours tomorrow."

I can practically feel Sam deflate at the idea that while Bill gets to spend time with kids and dogs in the dirt, she has to be here with us, sweating and panting her way through Calvin's form. She'll get used to it. It's only hard at first.

By the time I get to the group, Joaquin is the only one left without a partner. He waves as I approach, glancing behind me at Sam and Calvin.

"Your girlfriend not joining us?" he asks as we take position.

"No. Calvin is catching her up. Am I the zombie first, or are you?"

"I'll do it."

He sets his spatula on the ground and makes his hands into claws. I duck as he comes at me, don't bother rolling, and stab his temple gently. We switch, and I advance on him.

Joaquin is usually great in training, but today, he's less so. He's watching me, so I know he sees the attack coming, but his duck is too slow, and he fumbles on the roll. When he comes back up into his crouch, I touch his neck with my fingertips.

"Got you."

Joaquin touches the spot I clawed; his jaw muscles flex.

"You okay?" I ask, picking up my spoon.

"I'm good. It's nothing." He puts his hands up.

I lower my spoon. "What is it? You can tell me."

Joaquin looks right at me. He runs a hand through his hair. "I don't know, Cate." He glances behind me. "Never mind."

"Joaquin. Talk to me." I'm getting the feeling I know where this is going, but I don't want any more weirdness with anyone else. There's no point keeping secrets if there's a chance it'll screw things up later. And judging by the way he's sparring, I think things are already going that direction.

"In the city yesterday, when we were in the apartment building together?"

Here we go. I glance back at Sam. "Yeah?"

"I guess, for a second, I felt, I dunno, something. About you. For you. And I thought maybe you did too. But I didn't know you were, you know, like that."

Even though I was sure I knew what was coming, I was only half right, and the words take the wind out of me a little bit.

I want to ask what he means. "Oh," is all I can think to say.

"And I know that her showing up changes things. I'm not the kind of guy to try and come between you and your girlfriend or anything."

"I know."

"So, yeah. There it is. It's no big deal, though, really. I thought you were into me, and then all at once, you—"

"Switch partners!" shouts Ana, and before I have a chance to say anything more, Joaquin sprints away to pair with someone else.

Seven: Balance

1 year, 9 months ago

I wandered aimlessly for weeks, sleeping in empty houses, cars, and convenience stores, scavenging what meager food and water I could find. More than once, as I lay my head down to rest, I contemplated simply not getting up. But every morning, for no reason other than my stubborn unwillingness to die, I got back up and kept moving. Which direction, I had no idea. It didn't matter anyway.

As I neared a small town in what I later found out to be southern Washington, I saw a guy, a lady, and two kids walking up the road a hundred feet or so in front of me. Well, first I heard them. They sounded normal enough, but I jogged between the abandoned cars that littered the highway anyway, trying to stay off their radar. They seemed not to know what they were doing. The younger one was asking random questions at full volume, and mom and older brother were indulging him and reminding him to use his inside voice. They were all talking way too loudly. The man shouted (yes, shouted) something about some damn peace and quiet and how they were going to get him killed with their yapping. Guy was a complete tool.

I scurried past, keeping away. When I was a healthy distance ahead of them, I slowed to a walk to catch my breath, and I heard the sounds of panic behind me.

"Dean, what do we do?"

"Mom, there's a lot of them!"

Zombie noises. Fighting sounds.

"Dean, where are you going? Dean? Dean!"

I turned my head but kept moving. The guy was booking it in my direction. He passed me, giving me barely a glance, and kept on going. Was he really abandoning his family?

"Come back!" cried the mom. "Please!"

I walked on. They could run if they needed to. No reason to trust anybody, especially strangers. Look what had happened last time I tried. I'd almost been shot by a bunch of churchgoers for a damn scratch on my leg. A benign scratch, by the way. I kept going, but I'd slowed my pace. Something felt wrong about walking away from actual people who I might have been able to help.

When the kids started sobbing, I turned back to try to help them. But it was too late. They were done for. Just some more zombies in the making. As I got up close, I tried not to look directly at any of them. You'd think, having consumed as much horror as I had in the form of movies and comic books, that I would be more stoic, more desensitized. But my stomach lurched and squeezed at the sight of all the blood. I dispatched the zombies still chewing on the family. It took me less than a minute, partially owing to the fact that they were all still nose-deep in warm guts. But there were only three of them, which meant if I had turned around, if I had helped, these people might have lived. But where would helping have gotten me? Responsible for more ignorant people who couldn't take care of themselves? Still, they would be alive.

I had to make sure they wouldn't come back and do to another family what had been done to them. Because all said, every dead zombie was a zombie that couldn't hurt anyone else. It would have been pretty sweet justice for one of the zombie kids to run across their dad and infect him though.

Oh, well. The coward would live to see another day. Maybe.

I put my knife into the back of mom's head, staring at the ground as I did. A tiny pair of cracked, bloody glasses lay at my feet, no doubt belonging to the smaller child. I gazed past the dead siblings and let my eyes unfocus, as I considered what I was about to do. I hadn't come across any zombie kids yet. If I took care of it quickly enough, there would be no zombie kids to speak of. If I did it right away, the kids would never turn. Wouldn't hurt anyone else.

Every dead zombie. I repeated it inside my head, my own macabre personal mantra.

Every.

Dead.

Zombie.

One of the siblings started to twitch back to life. The fingers closed; the jaw opened. I sucked in a breath, steeling myself, and I did what had to be done. Physically, it felt the same as with fully grown zombies. But mentally? I knew I would have nightmares. The oldest was barely younger than me. His bloody, dirty face looked so scared, even in death. My chest got heavy. As if zombies in general wasn't terrible enough.

I stood and wiped my blade on one of the backpacks. I tried not to retch at the tangy smell of blood, the carnage splayed out in front of me, and my own disgust with what I had done.

Their backpacks were pretty full, though, and they wouldn't need any of it. I deliberated for about a minute before I started sifting through their shit. It felt more like thievery than I expected, and more than once, I turned to glance at them. Still dead. Was this what I'd been reduced to? Scavenging supplies off the corpses of women and children? But still, I had to live, right? I came away with some clean socks, water, and two packs of crackers. I supposed it was one for the win column. Sort of.

As I was getting ready to leave, a faint sound came from under the woman's face-down body. A tiny hand reached out. A baby's hand. I rolled the lady off the infant. *Oh god. How am I supposed to care for a baby?* But when I crouched over it, I knew I wouldn't have to. One tiny scratch on the baby's pudgy little cheek, one single nick of a fingernail, presumably, had been this child's demise.

The baby looked through me with those pale, dead zombie eyes. A piece of hair came loose from my ponytail and dangled in the space between us. The little zombie reached out, grabbed my hair, and yanked hard.

"Shit!" My voice squeaked as I scrambled back and fell onto my ass. The zombie was unfazed, of course. It continued to claw and chew the air with a few strands of my hair caught between its fingers.

I sat there, in the middle of the street, staring at the baby. Was I really supposed to off a newborn? Okay, it wasn't full-on murder, but still! The prospect was...pretty messed up. Even if the thing was technically already dead.

Did I have to do anything though? I stood up, dusted off my jeans. On one hand, every dead zombie and all that. See also, the reason I had just made myself knife two kids? But on the other hand, what was this particular little terror going to do, gum somebody to death? Those little fingernails were sharp. I'd been around enough babies in foster care to know that. But this one was attached to mom with one of those baby harnesses. It couldn't even crawl or pull itself around on its belly. Which was better, because that would make the whole thing exponentially more horrifying.

The baby gurgled. It almost sounded human.

I flicked open my knife, and pretty much instantly, my eyes filled with tears, and my face contorted. It was just a baby, right? I didn't have to kill it. It would rot soon enough. It didn't feel anything. It couldn't crawl. Couldn't even move. You'd have to get really close to get fucked up by a newborn.

I turned and started walking away from the baby. The zombie baby. Zombaby. I let out a weird sort of laugh. Was that what people meant when they said "gallows humor"? Ah, to have the ease of a search engine. Hell, a dictionary.

I wasn't sure which direction I was moving in. It didn't matter, though, did it? Cate and Melody were still long gone. *Hello, Marco. Welcome to your life. You're alone.* Assuming they'd been able to stick to the planned roads, which was clearly a pretty naive thing to assume, I was way off route. I had also lost my map when I lost Bill in Connell, and on top of all that, I knew I'd never make it to Alcatraz on my own. I was free to go anywhere I wanted, which was in no way liberating.

I supposed south was as good a direction as any. Winter would not be friendly up north. But thick, gray cloud cover blanketed the whole area, meaning there was not one single shadow to tell me which direction was south. So I just sort of meandered, up and down the streets of what appeared to be a smallish community well into the gentrification process. There were some little shops, novelty and artisan stuff, a few normal yuppie places like Macy's and Starbucks, and an absolute fuckton of wineries. Or tasting rooms? What was the difference? I'd never have to know, would I? Not like I would be going on my twenty-one run. Not that I ever would have anyway. Alcohol had never really been my style. Cigarettes, on the other hand?

I would have killed for a cigarette.

But no such luck. Not one measly cigarette to be found in any of the stores I checked out. I only had to deal with a few zombies in all that time, nine exactly. Each encounter was multiple minutes apart, none in groups of more than two. That suited me fine. Every time I saw a new zombie, I thought of the baby, and my insides felt like they were being wrung out. When I came across one that didn't see me, I would skirt around it or make a random turn to get away. A small voice inside me chastised me for being a chicken, but I couldn't help it. The last thing I wanted was to fight with a zombie.

After I passed the same funky music shop three times, I figured I might as well explore. I had time to kill. Time was all I had, in fact. At least the windows were covered. If I chose to stay, I would be invisible to anybody—alive or dead—passing outside. It was a nifty, cluttered space filled with all kinds of stuff: music, incense, some glass pipes, shirts, and a stack of weird, artsy postcards.

I perused the aisles a while, fingering through the music and wishing I had something to play it on. I picked up a few CDs, in case I ever found a means to play them. On a whim, I wandered behind the register. Boxes of all kinds of cool stuff were stacked up on the floor. And somehow, sitting in plain view was a portable CD player a lot like my old Walkman, and big, expensive-looking headphones. I gingerly picked up the player. The opening mechanism was a little sticky. It had no music inside, no batteries either. Oh, well. I had music in my bag already and finding batteries would be a cinch. I hoped it would anyway. I put the Walkman and headphones into the flat front pocket of my backpack. They fit perfectly.

As I reached for the door, something clattered near the back of the store. A zombie wearing a band shirt came wandering out. It didn't seem to notice me; if I hadn't known better, I'd have thought it was straightening something on a shelf. I crept a few steps toward it, hand on my knife, but stopped and watched it again, rationalizing a decision I wasn't aware of making at first. It was stuck in a building, alone, and somehow, it still hadn't acknowledged my presence. Basically, it was about as dangerous as the baby. I swallowed the bile that came up at the thought of those tiny hands and wide, milky eyes. If I didn't need to kill the little zombie, why did I need to kill this one, or any zombie, if it wasn't a direct threat to me? Until the baby, I had operated on the principle that every zombie I killed was one less for the world to deal with. But the zombaby encounter had lessened my willingness to kill them indiscriminately. Or, it had changed my perspective on the idea. I slid my knife back into my pocket and slipped outside, letting the door swing shut behind me.

Outside, a chilly wind had started up. It flung my hair in every direction, into my eyes and mouth. I hastily tucked it behind my ears and pulled my hood over my head.

Over the sound of the wind and through my hair and hood came a weird scraping sound behind me. It was close, close enough that when I turned to see what it was, I also pulled my knife out and raised it. The noise persisted and was accompanied by another, but I couldn't see anything. I pulled my hood back from one ear and followed the sound to its source.

In the space between two buildings, a big black dog was struggling to move. It would take a step or two at a time, but its leash was attached to a metal chair, which the dog was dragging, resulting in the scratching sound. When the dog saw me, it barked once, a short and not uninviting sound, and tried to get to me. This of course made the leash situation worse, and the dog tripped and face-planted. I couldn't help laughing at first, but the pathetic face and whining made me stop and crouch to try to untangle the poor beast.

"You gonna bite me if I try to help you?" I asked, shuffling closer on my knees. I told it to sit on the off chance it might.

The dog sat and stared at me.

"Okay, cool. I'm gonna undo your thing here; hang on." I wasn't sure why I felt the need to converse with it.

I made slow movements toward the leash. The dog didn't seem perturbed, in fact it seemed at ease. It had to have belonged to someone at one point.

The dog sat still as I unhooked its leash and collar, and when I tossed them aside, the big furry thing immediately flopped over and exposed its belly. I reached down and gave it—or, her—a little scratch. When I stood back up, the dog did too. She followed me at a distance as I walked back toward the street.

"Go on, dog," I told her.

She took another few steps.

"Sit. Stay."

The dog sat, and I turned my back on her. Last thing I needed was a dependent.

If I hadn't almost walked into the understated sign advertising a bike shop, I would have walked right past it. The big front window was broken though, of course, and there didn't seem to be a single bike left in the whole place. I stepped over the glass, my hand on my knife. If there was a bike, it would be worth fighting a zombie or three to get it.

The shop had been ransacked. Somehow, it surprised me I wasn't as original in my bike idea as I'd thought. Seemed like bikes were a hot-ticket item.

"Damn it." I scoffed as I lifted a perfectly good frame that had been relieved of its wheels and seat. One normal-sized wheel sat propped up in the corner and a miniature one lay at my feet. In other words, I'd be walking a while longer.

A door squeaked on its hinges at the back of the shop. Two adult-sized zombies crowded out toward me. They were too close for me to get to the front door in time, so I pulled out my knife even though there was a heavy pit in my gut.

"Fine," I said to them, myself, and no one.

I raised my knife and ducked out of the clutches of the first zombie just in time to throw it off balance. I came up behind it, spinning, and buried my knife in the base of its neck. The knife, with its serrated back end, wasn't so easy to dislodge from vertebrae. So I left it where it was and jogged a few steps away from the second zombie. Just far enough to pull out my axe. I swung once, and the zombie went down. But I realized it had only fallen from the force, not because it was dead. I had to hit it once more before it stopped reaching for me.

My mouth filled with saliva, my upper lip sweaty. I bent down, expecting to retch, but after I stood there hunched over like a jackass for a minute or two, the feeling passed. I straightened up, retrieved my knife with some effort, and left the picked-over bike shop.

So I hadn't lost my ability to end a zombie, after all. I had simply discovered my line, my threshold. The baby and the dude in the record shop weren't threats to me or anyone else. So they were left to their fate, whatever it might be. The two in the bike shop, coming right at me, and me with no easy escape, added up to two dead zombies. Two spared, two slayed. A weird sort of balance.

The dog was still sitting at the corner of the building. As soon as she saw me, her tail started to wag wildly. She yipped but stayed put.

"Go on," I told her.

She pinned her ears back, whined, and stared me down.

"I'm no good with dogs. I've never had one. You're better off on your own. Get out of here."

The dog didn't budge. So I chose a direction—left—and started walking.

She followed, staying a good length behind me. She kept pace as I sped up, and every time I turned around, there she was, with her hopeful eyes and wagging tail. I had tried, hadn't I? If she wanted to follow me, there wasn't a lot I could do. At least she wasn't a person.

We arrived at the Washington-Oregon border around midday.

"Last chance to go back, dog."

She watched me, intent. I'd forgotten to check for a name on her collar before I threw it away, or rather, I'd assumed I didn't need to since I never expected to see her again. Oh, well, names were like manners in the zombie apocalypse—maybe socially expected, but not wholly necessary.

She sniffed at my shoes and head-butted me in the knee. I scratched her ears. She seemed to enjoy it. "Okay. Guess I have a dog now. You a good guard dog?"

I got no answer, because I was talking to a dog. Might as well have been talking to myself. Good, Marco. At least she would keep me warm, and maybe I'd get lucky and she would hunt some food for us or something. She did look vaguely wolfy. I ruffled her neck fur. We kept walking south, into Oregon.

Eight: Weight

I'm in a car with my mom on a pretty highway in the middle of nowhere. I have a package in my hands, no bigger than a kitten.

My mom gazes at me and smiles. She says something normal. I say something back. She laughs. None of this matters. The sky is darkening. There's something in the road.

"Cate."

But her smile is so pretty. Her hair, more silver than I remember, blows across her face. When it blows back, just for one second, her face is changed. Absent. Gray. Before I can scream, she's my mom again. Beautiful and vibrant. Thin wrinkles surround her blue eyes, the kind you get when you smile a lot. I never noticed them before.

"Because I didn't live long enough to get them," she says, but her mouth doesn't move.

The package in my hands is warm, and...wet? Blood. It's blood. Leaking all over my hands.

She disappears from the driver's seat, and I'm alone.

I unbuckle my seatbelt with shaking hands. Scramble into the driver's seat. The car swerves. The thing in the road is a man. A big man with a blond beard.

My foot can't find the brake! I can't stop. I throw my hands in front of my face and squeeze my eyes shut.

"Cate!"

I open my eyes.

Sam is in my cell, sitting on my bed, shaking me. "Cate," she whispers. "Cate! Hey."

I'm crying and I can't stop. My heart is thundering. My face is hot, and my hands are cold. I am shaking. I can't breathe, can't, can't breathe!

Sam stares at me as though she's worried. "Bad dream?"

I nod. Shake my head. It was, but this is not that anymore. I did something awful, didn't I? Something unforgivable? What have I done? My body feels like it might fly apart, and maybe it needs to, but the walls of my cell are pressing in, preventing it. I count my breaths. In four, out eight. Tears soak my face, my neck. This isn't working. I can't breathe. I feel like I need to claw my throat open. I shove the covers off, sit up straight, hug my knees to my chest, and heave, trying and failing to get the air where I need it to be.

"Hey, stop!" Sam wraps her arms around me, tight. "You're fine now, it was a dream. Calm down."

I can't! I want to tell her. All I can do is shake my head and push her away. She has seen this happen, why won't she back off?

She holds tighter. "Cate, come on."

"Please!" I almost shout, scrambling off the bed. The dog lifts his head and watches me. "Please don't touch me."

"My God, Cate. I was just trying to help." Her voice has such venom in it. She gets up off the bed and leaves me alone in my cell.

Don't hate me, please. I want to say it, but I can't. My heart is still pounding, in my ears, my throat. My vision is black and sparkly at the edges. I'm dizzy. More tears. In four, out eight.

Once I catch my breath and the ringing in my ears quiets down, I get up, wipe my face on my shirt, and the dog and I go outside.

It's cool and foggy, and the sky is still inky blue. The boxer shorts and oversized T-shirt I sleep in don't do a lot for warmth, but the cold is calming. It makes me feel more real, more solid. It's easier to breathe, too, out in the open air. I could fall into a thousand pieces out here and put myself back together as slowly as I want. But I don't need to anymore. Mercifully, the panic has passed. I suck in deep breaths until my lungs are so full they start to hurt.

Chaz follows me until we walk through the door at the other end of the rec yard. When we get to the bottom of the steep stairs, he shuffles off to do his business. Someone will let him back in soon enough. The sun is coming up, and people will be waking up anytime. I keep a slow pace walking around the main structure. I'm not ready to go back in yet.

"Cate?"

I whip around, even though I know who I'll find. He's out here more often than not. He smiles and catches up to me.

"Couldn't sleep?" Marco asks.

"Bad dream."

"Apparently." He squints and regards my disheveled features. I'm sure I look a mess, with my snotty, tear-stained shirt and my dirty bare feet.

"I woke up weird. It was bad, I panicked. And Sam..." I don't know how to finish the sentence.

"Sam?"

"I think I upset her."

"Ah. Want to tell me about it?"

"Panic attacks?"

"Well sure, if you want. I meant the dream though."

"Would if I could."

"I hate the ones I can't remember. They leave you with a feeling, and not a good one, but you can't pin it down."

"I can pin them down, but not all at once."

"So start with one."

There's guilt; I'm pretty sure the dream had something to do with Toby. Or my mom? Either way, guilt. I suppose I don't know quite what to think about Sam, but it has thrown me off balance. Now that I'm looking at Marco, my usual worry and slight resentment about his absence from training rear their heads as well.

"I think things are different with Sam and me," I blurt out, mostly because that one is easier to talk about without risking an argument.

"Why?"

"I don't know. She seems different."

He chews on what I said for a second. "Okay. But aren't you different too?"

"I guess so. When I saw Bill and Sam again, I thought at least something might be the same as before."

"Well. Bill's basically the same. Few pounds lighter, maybe. And his glasses have seen better days."

I let myself smile. "Yes, I suppose that's true."

"Have you tried, I don't know, talking to Sam about it?"

"You would come at me with the obvious answer."

He bumps me gently with his shoulder. "Am I wrong though?"

"No, and it's obnoxious. You're so cool and confident, and somehow you're always right."

His voice gets quieter, deeper. "I am none of those things, Cate. I'm scared a hundred percent of the time, and I've only been right about the big stuff."

"You got us here, Marco."

"Not all of us," he whispers, kicking at the ground as we walk. He won't meet my gaze.

All at once, I see what I saw on the boat when we left the city three months ago, what I somehow stopped seeing: the weight of everything our people have lost—of the last two years—sitting on the narrow shoulders of the person who led us here. And it seems too heavy for one person, even someone like Marco who you'd think at first glance is all self-reliance and grit.

"Nobody blames you for anything," I say, holding onto his arm.

He peers down at me. "It doesn't matter. I blame me."

"I know, and I can't stop you. But you got us here, where we have a shot at an actual life. That's pretty huge, you know."

"I guess."

"At least you didn't directly mess up someone's whole life."

"What do you mean?"

"I cut off Toby's arm, Marco. Myself."

"You saved his life, Cate."

"Maybe. How do we know he's not immune? Anyone could be."

"You know the chances of that are slim."

"He worked with his hands, and he loved what he did. Before we left the city, I heard him talking to Jax about things they could build on the island to make it better for all of us. I ruined his life."

"Did you stick him at the edge of the dock?" Marco asks.

"Well, no."

"Did you somehow send that random Variant after him?"

"No."

"If you could go back, would you really wait around to see if he might be immune? Toby is still having a tough time coping with this. Because you're right, it is a big change. Especially nowadays. You did it to save him, though, right? So accept it, and move on, Cate. Like Toby has to."

I pick up a small stone and toss it halfheartedly at the plane as we pass it. They aren't the encouraging words I might have hoped to hear. On some level, I kind of wanted to be coddled. But Marco is not the coddling kind. He does speak the truth, however. If I can push aside the guilt that feels more like self-pity all of a sudden, I know it's not my fault. I'd done what any one of us would have. I just happened to be closest. I may very well have saved his life, even if the circumstances were the polar opposite of ideal.

"Okay, Marco. You're right. Thanks."

His smile is sincere. "I know."

We walk in silence for a time. It feels good, and easy. By the time we've circled back to the rec yard entrance, people are filing out into the gray morning light. The dog waddles over when he sees us, licks Marco's hand, and changes course to join Mel and the kids.

"You gonna talk to Sam before training?" asks Marco.

"She's not training today. She wanted to split her time between that and gardening with the kids."

"You didn't answer my question."

"I'll talk to her soon. I need some time to figure out what I'm going to say. What about you?"

"Me?"

"Are you going to train with us today, or what?"

"Tomorrow, maybe. Leg's still healing."

"Okay, but I'm holding you to it."

He grins. "I wouldn't expect anything less."

Nine: Cooperation

1 year, 8 and a half months ago

"Come on, come on."

I twisted two stripped wires together. Two more. Nothing. I tried a combination I hadn't yet, and jumped back when a spark flew out of the entwined pair.

"Nope." I rubbed my hands together. A little shiver snaked up my spine into the fine hairs on the back of my neck. It hadn't been that big a shock. Calm down, Marco.

I didn't even know where I was. Still in northern Oregon, probably. I hadn't found a bike since the church. Between having that gun pulled on me, the subsequent pity party, and the zombaby incident, I hadn't put much effort into acquiring one. I had nowhere to get to in a hurry, and I wasn't sure the dog could keep up anyway. But when I spied an old station wagon parked on the side of the road, I figured I'd give it a shot. Apparently, hotwiring a car was not as easy as they made it look on TV.

"Dog!" I called and studied my surroundings while I waited for her.

The scenery was monotonous: a sea of grass and neglected crops, a lot of dry brush. The hills were cut in curving patterns, as if by rivers. I wondered what it all used to look like, not before the horizon was peppered with zombies, but even earlier than that. Before people.

Dog came trotting up with bloody jowls and leaned her head on my leg, leaving a red smudge on my jeans.

I'd had no clue how much to feed her and had no dog food anyway. So, I let her self-regulate with hunting and foraging because what did I know about dogs? The first night, she ate a rodent and some grass. This was about the third time she'd caught something in as many days. She seemed fine, and what else was I supposed to feed her?

Before we had gone very far, two zombies, both smelling many days dead, wandered around the corner of a gas station. I ran up, ready if not eager, for some practice. I put my axe in the first one's face. It made me feel differently than it had before. Guilty? That couldn't be it. But as I was attempting to yank my weapon out of the first zombie, the other one grabbed my arm. I tried to elbow it off and get my axe free at the same time, succeeding in neither. With a loud, low growl, Dog sank her teeth into the second zombie's rotten leg and pulled it off me, giving me a chance to cave its head in with the back end of my finally freed axe. It took three good whacks. After, nausea turned to dread as I remembered who had just effectively saved my bacon.

"Dog!" I croaked, my voice cracking. She had definitely gotten some of that thing's—ugh—fluids in her mouth. I squatted and buried my face in her soft black-and-brown neck fur. I hadn't thought I'd get attached to a dog, of all things, but there I was, clinging to her like she was the last friend I would ever have. Hell, she probably was. She licked my face as if to reassure me. The slobber on my cheek turned freezing cold as soon as I stood up. I wiped it with my sleeve and stared down at her. She sniffed the air, moving her head back and forth.

"I don't know what happens now," I admitted. Would she turn? Did that happen to animals? Some animals? The seagulls seemed meaner, but maybe I was imagining it because of all the news coverage of the kid in Arkansas who'd messed with the wrong seagull and started the actual apocalypse.

Damn sensationalist media.

The wind picked up, biting and painful. I zipped up my jacket. Soon, it would be too cold to sleep outside. Soon, it would be freezing. Bad for zombies, probably, but also bad for me.

I wondered how Cate and Melody were doing—if they'd found Bill or anyone else. Had they sought shelter? Were they alive?

Dog whined, long and high. Thick fur covered her, but her paws had no protection against the chilly ground. If my socked and booted feet were cold, hers had to be.

"Okay, Dog." Time to find a place to spend the night. It was getting dark, and street lamps weren't a thing anymore.

I scanned the highway, hoping for any sign of a city or a building. You'd have thought there'd be another town already. But no, that would have been too easy.

Grumbling to myself, I trudged off the road and into the truck I had unsuccessfully tried to hotwire. Once we'd climbed onto the bench seat, I locked the doors and wrapped an arm around Dog. The windows were cracked, and I couldn't roll them up because the operation was electric. Some shelter. She settled closer to me and let out a short huff. Was she getting warmer? Was it a fever, or was she always so warm?

She fell asleep fast. She didn't seem restless the way people got before they turned. The sky darkened. Maybe dogs didn't turn. I let my eyes close and my breathing slow to match the pace of hers. Maybe she would be okay. Maybe we both would. It was really cold though. I cuddled closer to her. The wind outside whistled across the open landscape, and every once in a while, it shook the truck.

I woke up to Dog whining and pawing my arms and legs. She wasn't a zombie dog either. Score. But the air was thick and foggy. I sat up and immediately got dizzy and started coughing. It wasn't fog, I realized as I hunkered back down.

Smoke. There was a fire nearby and smoke was pouring into the cracked windows. Dog was barking and hacking. I inhaled reflexively and was met with a furious coughing fit. I pulled my sweatshirt over my nose and mouth, put on my backpack, and gave the dog's neck a little reassuring rub.

"We're gonna get out of here," I told her.

I grabbed the metal door handle and pulled. Nothing happened. The door was locked. I had locked it. The smoke was making me dizzy, even with my makeshift mask. I reached for the lock, but the air was so hazy by then I had to keep my eyes closed, reduced to feeling around for it. Dog had been going bonkers a second before but now whined and lay down on the floor of the truck, heaving.

My head felt so heavy. In a second of complete clarity, I understood that I was about to die. I had always assumed I would accept death when it came, or maybe die fighting for something or someone, a hero. But I wasn't going to die in any kind of noble way. I would choke to death, trapped in some truck on some highway in Oregon. Alone, but for a dog I'd led to the same grim death. I slumped over on the seat. Shut my eyes. *I'm sorry, Dog.* My throat was too raw to speak and I was still choking.

I'm so sorry.

Banging on the window. The truck shook. Outside, a voice.

"Hey, kid! You alive?"

Another.

"He is!"

I gazed up through the smoke in the cab, and the first thing I saw was Dog. She was staring at the people. Two of them, their faces obscured by smoke and shadow.

"Back up!" called the tall one. She busted the window, threw the door open, and held out a hand toward me. "Come on; let's go!"

I took it. My legs like jelly, I barely remembered stumbling out of the truck or away from the burning bushes. I didn't register how we did it or how long it took us as I stood on the quiet street with Dog and two women in the hard and heavy rain and freezing cold. The rain was already most of the way done killing the fire.

"Are you all right?" asked one of them. But she wasn't asking me, she was talking to the other woman. She reached up and touched the shiner on her friend's tawny face. It looked a day or two old, at least. "You were amazing!"

"I'm okay. You?" The shorter woman nodded. "What about you, kid? You all right?"

I gave myself a cursory once-over. I didn't feel any pain except in my throat and eyes. "I think so."

Dog sat on top of the shorter woman's feet and leaned against her legs. The woman scratched Dog's ears and adjusted her hat over her short black hair. "You're lucky neither of you died of smoke inhalation."

"I thought I was going to die," I admitted. But the vulnerability of those words made my muscles stiffen. Who were these people? They had helped me, sure, fine, but they were still unknown. Still not to be trusted. I clamped my mouth shut and chastised myself. Had I learned nothing?

"I'm Tanya," said the big one with the black eye. "This is my wife Amy."

I almost put my hand out to shake, but I was a good six feet from them and probably shaking hands wasn't a thing anymore. Politeness was dead, after all. Good riddance. I dipped my head once instead. "Marco. Thank you for your help. We better be going. Dog?"

Dog glanced up at me, whined, but didn't budge. Great.

"What's your hurry, kid?" asked Tanya. "You got a pressing engagement?"

"I...no."

"It's not a great idea to stay anywhere for too long though," said Amy. She widened her eyes at Tanya, making it obvious she was saying something without saying it. "We should move on as well, don't you think?"

Tanya got it, apparently, because she hiked up her jeans and said, "Right."

"Right," I echoed. "So, uh, thank you for, y'know, saving my life."

"Of course," Amy said, smiling with only her eyes.

"So, where are we going?" asked Tanya.

"We?"

"Yeah, we. Amy and I saved your ass; you said it yourself. And we find ourselves in need of a quick escape. So, since you clearly have a direction in mind—and our only direction at this time is 'away from here'—where are we going, Marco?"

"Listen, I don't want to be rude, but—"

"So don't be."

A noise in the near distance made both women perk up. Amy gasped, and Tanya grabbed my hand and yanked me toward the side of the road. Dog followed unhurriedly. Once we were off the road, Tanya shoved me down behind the truck. It still stank of smoke. As soon as we were hidden, three men came into view. Their clothes were dirty and they were coughing like an anti-smoking ad.

"Why are we hiding from those people?" I whispered, taking context clues from the aforementioned yanking and shoving.

"Where's Kenny? Tom?" Amy whispered in lieu of an answer.

Tanya shook her head. "Probably died in the fire. Pity it didn't take them all."

So we didn't like these people.

We sat still, silent as the three burly men walked past, talking between gross coughs about "finding them soon," and "they couldn't have got far." I figured the "they" these men kept mentioning might be Tanya and Amy, with the hiding and all. We stayed crouched down until they were long gone, and for a while after. Dog was the first to run back out into the street. Amy made a noise of protest and reached after her, even though the men were clearly not around anymore.

"I think it's okay, baby," said Tanya at normal volume. She kissed Amy on the forehead and stood.

"So, when you said you were trying to get away," I said, "you meant from those guys, didn't you?"

"Yes," said Amy. "When they started the fire, we knew it might be our only shot. So we ran right through it, back the way we'd come from."

They had to be some kind of awful for Tanya and Amy to want to jump through flames to get away from them.

"They do that?" I asked, indicating Tanya's bruised face.

"That's the least of it."

"They are not good people, Marco," said Amy.

I didn't say the first thing that popped into my head. I had no way of knowing whether these two were good people either. How could I? I had thought the pastor and his people were okay. Mistake. But these women seemed scared; like they urgently needed to get out of whatever situation they'd been in. Tanya's bruised face, for a microsecond, reminded me of my old foster mom, Cindy. If only she'd gotten away from her shitty situation, she might still be alive. If only I'd been able to help her. But I could help these two and hope they wouldn't turn around and screw me later on. I figured I could always leave them somewhere once we were far enough away from those people.

"So, uh, I was sort of heading south, I guess."

The women looked at each other, at me, at Dog, whose butt wiggled every time Amy even glanced at her. She would probably end up staying with Amy once we parted ways, which was fine. I was better off alone.

"Okay," said Tanya. "Let's go."

"So you really had no clear direction?" Amy asked as we marched through the rain. "Just south?" The way she stared at me made me think she knew there was more.

"Well, no. I did have plans, up until recently."

"What happened?"

"I got separated from my...uh, the people I was with. Two of them survived, as of a couple weeks ago. But I didn't get to them in time to leave with them. They drove away without me." A pit formed and dropped in my stomach when I remembered the sight of those taillights shrinking into the night as Cate and Melody made their getaway.

"They didn't wait?" asked Tanya.

"They did, for a long time. I got caught up. I wasn't fast enough."

"Are they still going to go through with the plan?" asked Amy.

"I guess so. Probably. It is a good plan."

Amy veered closer to me but kept a good few feet between us. "Then why have you given up? You're still here; you're alive. They may be waiting for you right now."

"I doubt they've arrived yet."

"Where are you supposed to meet?"

"Alcatraz."

"The prison?" asked Tanya, smirking.

"It's a park now," Amy said. "But it has at least basic first aid, doesn't it, being a national landmark?" Her eyes lit up as she started counting on her fingers. "And security, water, and space to grow food... Marco, that is an incredible goal. Why did you ever give it up?"

"Because how the hell am I supposed to get there on foot?"

"Who says you have to go on foot?" asked Amy. "Can't you drive?"

"I never learned. That's not to say I wouldn't attempt it. I was trying to hotwire the truck you found me in."

Tanya arched her eyebrows. "But it's possible to walk there, isn't it? At least until you need a boat."

"I mean, yeah."

"Are we thinking of trying for Alcatraz?" asked Amy, her eyes twinkling. "Not going north?"

Tanya grinned. "Do we have any legitimate reason not to? What do you think, Marco?"

I didn't know what to say. These women, who had obviously been through some shit, were so ready to jump on the Alcatraz bandwagon. Why had I given up so easily? Being alone had helped me along in that decision, for sure. Had I let my disappointment and fear get the better of me? There were so many reasons it could go horribly wrong. Exposure, for one. Winter was shaping up to be cold and wet. Starvation, dehydration, zombies. So many zombies. Not to mention a lot of apparently terrible people. But even so, I felt the stirring of a hope I'd actively been suppressing. Alcatraz could still work. There was still a chance.

"Why were you headed up north in winter, anyway?" I asked, deflecting to buy time. Maybe to glean a little more information about the two of them.

"The guys had heard about a compound up there— safe, sickness-free. I still wonder if it wouldn't be a better plan, except that's where they're going."

"If they make it," said Amy. "What if they don't? They almost ended their own miserable lives play-fighting with flaming sticks. There's a good chance we can start over in Canada."

There it was. They had been drawn to the shiny new idea of Alcatraz, but I knew they would default to their original plan, however ridiculous it was.

"Are you kidding me, a compound?" I asked Amy, point-blank.

Amy tilted her head prettily. "What do you mean?"

"Have you ever seen a zombie movie?" I scoffed, crossing my arms, feeling superior. "Either they're all dead when you get there, or someone gets bit and you all die together. Or, my favorite, you get all the way up there and it turns out it doesn't exist. Then you're up in bumble-fuck Canada in the middle of winter." At least my plan was legit. Unlike the so-called compound, Alcatraz was, in fact, a real place. A secure place.

"You know what—" Tanya began.

"I think he's right," said Amy. "Alcatraz is a better plan."

Amy's expression was so sincere. I had thought they were instantly going to go back to their terrible Canada plan. But they wanted to go to Alcatraz. With me. It was possible I didn't have to be on my guard one hundred percent of the time. Like the zombaby and the guy in the record store, not every person was a threat. Statistically, being a black belt, I was bound to run into some people who wouldn't be threats, or who I could at least take on physically if they decided to try anything. I wasn't about to trust Amy and Tanya outright, but there was a possibility, a potential for cooperation, at least. If nothing else, I could always ditch them if I had to.

Tanya snapped her fingers. She was facing me again. "Marco. Hello? We going to Alcatraz or what?"

"We are. But if you're joining me, we're doing things my way."

Tanya clicked her tongue. "We'll see."

"What if there are already people there?" Amy asked before I could argue.

"Like who?" asked Tanya.

"Well, I've thought about that too," I said. "A bunch of people visit there every day, so some of them may have either got stuck, or went there for the same reason we're going."

"Yes, maybe. But I once heard that Indigenous activists reclaimed Alcatraz," said Amy. "Back in sixty-nine, I think."

"I read about that when I visited a few years ago," I said. "It lasted over a year, didn't it? Federal marshals went in and forced them out."

"Same story, different century," mumbled Tanya.

"There's still a reserved sunrise thing on the island," I said. "Or, there was. You know, before."

"So, what if we get there and the island has been reclaimed again?" asked Amy.

"Well, we can ask if they're willing to share," I suggested with a shrug. If anyone was still alive, which was a long shot in itself.

"And if they're not down with sharing?" asked Tanya, eyeing me.

"We'll find someplace else to go. We're not going to recolonize it, for shit's sake. Alcatraz is a damn good spot. But it can't be the only good spot left in the country."

"Fair enough. Should we come up with a contingency plan, in case the island is populated?"

"Are there other nearby prisons we could try?" asked Amy. "They would have similar facilities, wouldn't they?"

Tanya snorted. "If this country has plenty of anything, it's prisons." She wasn't wrong.

I shook my head. "They're all on the mainland. Not a good option."

"Why not?" asked Tanya. "They're still secure, have medical wings, maybe food. What's wrong with that?"

I scoffed. "Seriously? Easy as shit to infiltrate, for one. Alcatraz is a dead prison, a national park. There are no prisoners. Every other jail and prison will be packed with inmates, or inmate zombies. I seriously doubt the guards made it a priority to save the people inside. That means food and meds will have run out ages ago. But hey, you want to try it? You go on ahead."

Tanya planted her hands on her hips. "Okay, can the bullshit, Marco. I asked a simple question. No need to be a prick about it."

"Listen, lady, I've done a lot of research about this"— okay, not a ton, but obviously more than her—"and I know what the hell I'm talking about. When I said you should listen to me, I wasn't kidding. I know my shit, and I haven't been wrong yet. The last people I was with all died or got separated because they didn't listen. You want to live? You'll do what I tell you."

"Do what you tell us?" Tanya repeated. "You, a child?"

"I'm not a child. I'm eighteen."

"My point exactly, you're eighteen. What the hell do you know?"

"I know Alcatraz is the best plan we've got, and who came up with that plan? Oh yeah, it was me!"

The dog growled.

"Tanya?" said Amy. She pointed across the highway at two fresh zombies coming our way.

Tanya stepped between her wife and the zombies. "Back up, baby. I've got this."

Yeah, right. She would get herself scratched or worse. Her tiny pocketknife wasn't going to do shit. I jumped in front of her just in time and kicked the closest zombie, causing it to stumble backward. The second one grabbed for my sleeve, and I waited until it leaned in for a bite before I buried my knife in its eye. As soon as the other got up, I ran behind it and stabbed it in the base of the skull.

"I could have handled it," said Tanya, slipping her knife back into her pocket.

"Don't you mean thank you?"

"I mean what I said. We don't need saving. We can handle ourselves."

"Is that why you're tagging along with me instead of following your friends or going off on your own?"

Tanya shook her head and put an arm around her wife. "You don't have a clue what you're talking about, Marco. I would advise you to shut your mouth."

"I obviously *do* have a clue what I'm talking about. Like I said, I haven't been wrong yet."

"Well, congratufuckinglations," Tanya snapped. "You're right all the time, and you're a rude little shit."

As she and Amy hurried ahead, she mumbled, "Better hope there's nobody to try and negotiate with when we get to that island. Marco will have them ready to shoot us all."

"At least I can get us there alive," I called, loud enough to make sure Tanya heard it.

"I suppose," said Amy, glancing back at me and touching Tanya's arm, "the best option is to see what we find when we arrive. Isn't it?"

Tanya glared at me and let out a big sigh. "You're right, Amy."

Amy leaned into her wife. "I know."

Both women glanced back at me, waiting for confirmation that we were all on the same page. I wasn't sure we were, but I kept it to myself.

"Sure. Fine."

They stayed ahead of me for a good, long while. Occasionally, I would catch one of them peering at me. After a mile or two, Amy slowed down until I caught up with her.

"We get it, you know," she said. "You've probably lost a lot of people, and you're afraid it could happen again."

I didn't answer, opting instead to stare at the ground.

She continued. "The thing is, acting the way you did will lose you more people. I think you do care, whether you admit it or not."

"Your plan is a damn good one, and we're happy to follow it with you," Tanya said, hanging back so we all moved as a group. "But what just happened could easily get someone killed. Nothing is worth that, least of all your ego."

My face burned. I bit the inside of my cheek.

"We've seen smaller noises bring on larger groups of, um, aggressors," Amy said.

"Me too." I didn't elaborate; I didn't want to tell them about the way Gary had brought on an entire horde of zombies by breaking a single window. He was a tool with no self-control, but he also hadn't understood the scope of things at the time. I knew what was happening, and what zombies could do, especially in groups. I'd seen it over and over.

"So, what happened back there?" asked Amy.

I shrugged.

"You seem to know what's going on, and you insist you're not a kid, but then you go and do something like that. Why?"

It was a good question. What the hell had I been thinking, shouting at Tanya in the middle of an open road? I'd been right, of course, but it wouldn't have mattered if one or all of us had died. So, what was my problem? What kind of person would lose their temper when it was literally life or death?

"I'm sorry," I said, not meeting either of their gazes.

Tanya touched my arm. "We're on your side, Marco. We're a team now. So don't fuck it up, okay?"

I glanced at her, ready to see anger and disappointment etched all over her face. But instead, she wore a playful smile.

Tentatively, I smiled too. "Okay."

Ten: Team

1 year, 8 months ago

On the second day after we met Tanya and Amy, Dog became Duchess. Tanya was adamant that everyone deserved a name, and although I pointed out that, one, she was a dog, and, two, she came to "Dog" just fine, Tanya wouldn't have it. The dog didn't seem to care (because of course she didn't), but she had bonded to Amy, so it felt right to let the two women name her.

For days, we hiked a winding path that we hoped was south, sometimes chatting, sometimes falling into hours of silence. Tanya and I argued two more times about minor things over the next week. Both disagreements ended with Tanya telling me the quiet was preferable to what she called my "shitty juvenile attitude". She only disliked my attitude, I countered, because I was right. She reminded me that one could be right without being an ass about it, which made Amy laugh. The last time she said it, I figured she had a point.

The wind blew harsh and cold every day. Even when our route took us through small towns or forests, the bone-chilling air currents found a way. It was worse on those roads. Somehow, with trees or buildings on both sides, it howled as though we were in a tunnel.

"Funny," Tanya said as we all zipped up our jackets against one particularly angry gust. "I thought going south would mean more temperate weather."

"I have a feeling this is going to be one hell of a winter," I muttered.

The temperature had dropped noticeably over the last week. Snow had begun to fall from time to time, and though only delicate little flakes, it was sticking.

"Gonna have to find some kind of longer-term shelter if it gets much worse."

"At least the danger of contamination is drastically decreased," said Amy brightly. No matter what she said, her voice sounded cheerful and pretty. "I haven't seen much movement all day."

"You mean zombies?"

"Zombies?" Amy tilted her head and almost, *almost* smiled.

"Yeah?"

Tanya clicked her tongue. "Marco."

"What?"

"Is that really what you've been calling them?" asked Amy.

"I mean, they do eat people. What else do you call it?"

Amy shrugged. "Sick people."

"Okay, sort of, but they're dead."

"I don't know that. I've never been close enough to check for myself."

"I have. The people I was with before, they knew this old lady, their neighbor. She died in their house and came back after they put her in their yard. I checked the pulse, so did Cate's sister Melody. A nurse."

"I believe you, Marco," said Amy in her even tone. "But I'm a doctor. I have to see them as people, and maybe one day, someone will figure out a way to help them. I'm betting Cate's sister Melody didn't believe their neighbor was dead at first either."

"She did, but as soon as the lady came back, Melody was sure she'd never died at all. You're a doctor?"

"I was a surgical intern, when—" She looked around as if to say "you know."

We all knew.

Amy got quiet again, her gaze glassing over the way it often did. Tanya, who could apparently feel the changes in Amy's demeanor, put an arm around her wife and squeezed. I had not asked any more about their story, and they'd neither offered any more information, nor asked me for mine. But I suspected while my end-of-the-world experience was about the same as could be expected, in other words awful, these two had had it worse. I didn't lose much when the world went to shit. I had no family, really, no permanent home, no real friends. Except Cate. But then, that happened postapocalypse, so for a minute, I had actually gained something valuable. Sometimes, I forgot a lot of people had lost way more than me. In a way, I guess I had it easier.

Duchess trotted to Amy's side. She pressed her big black head on Amy's leg as we walked, peering up at her every few steps. Somehow, she could sense Amy needed her. Tanya said it was unusual behavior for the breed because Shepherds were often one-person dogs. To which

I had replied that Amy was her one person. I had been a stand-in, which suited me fine.

"I've missed this," Amy said quietly, studying the snowy trees and rooftops. "So pretty. You almost forget what's underneath."

"I always liked the quiet before the world went to shit," I answered. "I used to draw when the weather got like this. I'd bring my sketchbook out to whatever yard or porch my foster family had and draw until my fingers were numb."

"You were in foster care?" Amy looked right at me as we wove through the many abandoned and not-so-abandoned cars.

"Yeah."

"Me too, until I was about three. You?"

"Twelve on up."

"That's rough."

"I guess."

"So, you draw?"

"I did."

"Why not anymore?"

"I don't know, it just doesn't seem important these days." Actually, I had lost all of my stuff in Connell. Everything I had ever drawn was still sitting in that damn church.

"If you ask me," Amy mused, "I would think doing things you love would be even more important now. Maybe you'll draw again one day."

"Got one over here," said Tanya, pointing to a cluster of buildings off to one side of the highway.

"More than one," I said as four more zombies wandered around the same corner.

We took out our weapons: me my axe, Amy her knife, and Tanya a hammer we'd found her a few days before. It was obviously still new to her. She clutched it, changed her grip, changed it again.

"Just stay focused," I reminded them. "Five isn't a big deal if we're calm and we stick together." Still, five at a time was something I had not experienced with them. I hoped they were up to it. I could take five on my own, but it would suck.

As the group of living dead approached, arms outstretched, I crouched and kept my knees loose. I used the back end of my axe, the blunt end, to knock the first one down. It wouldn't incapacitate it for long, just long enough. I yanked my knife out of my pocket and drove it into the zombie's eye as it began to pull itself up. I remembered from my recent showdown with the granny zombie in Connell that the knife was easier to get out of a skull than the axe, as long as I stuck to the eyes.

Next to me, Amy was having trouble. Tanya stepped in, shoving and then whacking the closest zombie with her hammer. It was enough to, again, knock the thing over, but Tanya wasn't as quick as me with the follow-up, so the zombie rose with nothing but a gross new wound.

"Marco!" called Tanya.

I turned to help her with her zombie, but at the exact moment I turned, one of the others—the last one, I was pretty sure—caught my ponytail mid-swing and pulled me off my feet. The pain in my scalp was sharp and unexpected. I almost lost focus. Almost. Tanya had finally taken care of the one zombie, and I used my captive hair as leverage to get number five, grabbing its wrist, pulling it to the ground with me, and straddling it, keeping my face out of clawing range. As soon as I was on top of it,

Tanya rushed over and hammered the thing in the face several times. It was dead before she finished, but I appreciated her spirit.

"Thanks," I said as she helped me up. I didn't mention I basically had it by the time she came over, could easily have done it on my own, and more efficiently.

"We'll need to do something about that hair," Tanya replied, pursing her lips.

"Yeah, maybe." I ran a hand through my messed-up ponytail. I'd thought about it but never enough to do anything. The truth was, I liked my hair, so the idea of cutting it off was kind of a drag. "Not like there's a barber shop open anywhere."

"You're looking at her."

"You were a hairdresser?"

"I was a professional artist and mistress of many mediums, including hair."

"She was putting herself through fashion design school," Amy added, giving a rare smile to her wife.

"Not anymore. Oh, well. Cutting hair is more useful now than fashion design anyway. Not a lot of people going for apocalypse-chic on the runway these days."

"That's not true at all," I said. "A lot of people can't sew. I can't. Your skillset can keep the clothes on our backs a lot longer. Holes happen. Look at my jeans."

Tanya smirked and tilted her chin up. "You know, Marco, you're right. You're pretty astute when you're not putting up the tough-guy front. Tell you what. You teach me to fight, and I'll teach you to sew."

I hardly had to consider. She wasn't too shabby with her hammer, so it wouldn't be hard to teach her. And then, if I did end up going my own way—which seemed less likely every day—at least I would have acquired a useful skill. "Okay, yeah. Deal."

"So?" Tanya linked arms with me as we walked away from the macabre scene we'd created. "What's my first lesson?"

"What—now?"

"Do we have anything else to do?"

A smile crept over my face. "Sure, okay. First lesson, head shots only. No. First lesson, you don't always have to fight. If we can run, we should. Second lesson, head shots. Soft spots are temples, eyes, and back by the neck. Get 'em fast and hard. Also, duck."

Tanya chuckled. "Run. Heads. Duck. Got it."

"It's easier to use the blunt end of your hammer. The claw seems like it would be good, but it'll get stuck, and then you're screwed."

"I hadn't even thought to use the claw, but okay."

"It's all about momentum. Throw your weight behind it."

Tanya took a handful of snow and cleaned the goo off her hammer. "If your scrawny self can take on a—" She paused and shook her head. "—*zombie*, then I'm sure I can manage."

"You'd be surprised, though—"

The dog growled, low and menacing.

"What's up, Duchess?" I asked, petting her neck. Her hackles were raised, and her body was rigid. The growling got louder as several people appeared on the other side of the road. I pulled out my axe in as obvious a way as I could.

A woman with jet-black hair stepped to the front of the group. I sized her up, hoping I wouldn't have to fight a lady. Was that sexist? But she put her hands up, weapon-free. "We don't want trouble. We thought we heard shouting." She regarded all the dead zombies behind us. "Looks like you got it though."

I lowered my axe a fraction of an inch.

Tanya moved closer to me, putting herself in front of Amy, gripping her weapon. "Yeah, we got it."

A man stepped forward, built like a linebacker with a bushy blond beard. I could take him on my own. Probably. He didn't have a weapon in his heavily tattooed hands. He did have a big wrench, but it hung in a utility belt.

I let my axe-holding hand fall to my side.

"You all headed north?" asked the woman. "We can join up. It's safer with a group."

I exchanged a quick glance with Tanya. Joining a bigger group would be safer for her and Amy. I wouldn't even hold it against them if they took the dog and left.

Tanya answered curtly. "No thanks. We're going south."

Unexpected relief washed over me. They weren't leaving.

"There's nothing for you south," said a smaller blond guy with a ponytail as long as mine.

"It's a shitstorm down there," continued the big bearded one.

Little guy nodded. "We came from a ways south. It's all gone to hell."

Amy stayed quiet, but I felt her move closer to Tanya.

"We heard it's not as bad up north," said a girl about my age. She had a huge scarf triple-wrapped around her neck so only the top half of her face was visible. Her voice was muffled through the scarf. "You know anything about that?"

I almost asked her why the hell she thought anywhere was better, and had she ever heard of a thing called the apocalypse, but I recalibrated, trying to implement what Tanya had been badgering me about. "I think it's bad all over. Sorry."

The girl dipped her head, staring at her worn-out tennis shoes.

"You headed south for a reason?" asked the linebacker.

"Marco got separated from his people a while back," said Tanya.

I opened my mouth to ask why she was volunteering information to strangers, and then she volunteered even more.

"We're meeting them on Alcatraz Island."

I tried to give her a look, but I was pretty sure she was deliberately ignoring me. Was she hoping these people would join us? Last thing we needed was more people we didn't know if we could trust.

"Alcatraz?" asked a round woman with gray-and-white hair and a bandaged leg. She exchanged a look with a man who, for a moment, sort of resembled a younger Bill.

"Yes, why?"

"There's something going on in San Francisco. Around it too. The dead, they're... Just watch yourselves, the closer you get."

"That's all we've been doing," said Tanya.

"Can we come with you?" asked the smaller blond guy. He glanced at the big dude, and they seemed to be having a conversation with only nods and hand gestures.

"Jax, Toby," said the man who had issued the cryptic warning. "You don't have to go. We're still family."

"We appreciate that, Maurice, and everything else. But we were only going north because Lily wanted us to, and she's gone now. And the kid's right. It's not going to be better anywhere, and we'd just as soon go somewhere warmer."

"Hang on a minute," I said. Every one of them turned to me. "We don't need any more people."

"Are you sure?" asked the ponytail.

"We're real good with our hands," added the giant. "We can build and fix damn near anything."

"We fight good too," said the other one.

"Sorry, man," I said, shaking my head. *Don't be a dick, Marco. Assertive, not abrasive.* "I mean, go south if you want to, but we're not taking anyone else on."

"Marco, a word?"

Oh, finally, Tanya was looking at me.

She turned so her back was toward the others and jerked her head to indicate I should do the same. "What are you talking about, child? More people means more defense. More chance of success."

"We don't know them."

"You didn't know us."

"You literally saved our lives."

"They might one day too."

I glared at her. She glared back, challenge in her eyes. Why did she think she had a say in who we took on? *But hang on*, said another voice in my head, because why did I think she didn't? I was no leader, and the way she bossed me around, it was entirely plausible Tanya was more in charge. Or more accurately, we were just three people and a dog with no need for a hierarchy. But it was my idea! Alcatraz was mine. Well, it was a national park and at one point had been reclaimed by its original inhabitants. So, not mine.

"Fine." I closed my eyes, took a breath. More people.

Tanya eyeballed both men, arms crossed, sizing them up. She stepped right up to them, looming over ponytail and staring up into the big guy's eyes.

"Gentlemen. We've decided to allow you to join us on a trial basis. If you ever touch me or my wife—any fuckery at all—I will feed you to the next zombie I see, feet first. No qualms." She let her words hang for a minute, narrowing her eyes. "Got me?"

"Gotcha," said the bearded one. No hesitation. "I'm Toby."

"Jax," said the smaller guy, waving.

"Tanya, my wife Amy. This is Marco."

"And who's this?" asked Jax, crouching to Duchess's level.

"Duchess, our vicious attack dog," I said.

Duchess examined Jax, sniffing him up and down. When she was done, she gave his face a little lick.

"We get the apprehension, Marco," said Toby.

"We appreciate the faith," Jax added, standing back up.

Toby turned toward the others. "I guess this is it."

"You sure about this?" asked one of their people. "Really sure?" His eyes flitted over to the three of us and Duchess.

"It feels right," answered Jax.

"Gotta go with the gut," said Toby.

Not-Bill stretched out his arms and embraced Toby, clapping him on the back a few times. "See you on the other side, brother."

Toby squeezed into the hug before letting go. "Lily was lucky to have found you, Maurice."

"Bye, Maurice."

"Bye, Jax."

"See you, everyone. Stay safe. Maybe we'll see each other again when this is all over," Toby said.

Over? Was he serious? Worse than dangerous predators, we had somehow linked up with optimists. Those were always the first to chicken out, and the first to die, or get people killed. They wouldn't take us down with them. I wouldn't let them.

"Let's get going," I said, hoping to bring the extended goodbye to a close. They were either coming or they weren't. Sitting in the open was just asking for trouble.

"You're brothers," said Amy as we finally got a move on, plus two people.

It was sort of a question, but not one that needed to be asked. Duchess wove between the legs of the newcomers, smelling and wagging her tail before returning to her Amy.

"Yep."

"Sure are."

The groups passed one another, waving, probably because it was less weird than silently filing by one another. I was in the back, and when I passed the old woman, she touched my arm.

"They're not normal, the sick ones in the city," she said. "They're different. Changed. You'll be fine; you look like you'll be fine. Just keep your wits about you." She squeezed my hand before turning to catch up with her people.

"Well that's not ominous," grumbled Tanya.

"What was she talking about?" asked Amy.

"She's exaggerating," said Jax.

"The, you know, the sick ones. They're just different in the city," Toby clarified. "We assume so, anyway. We skirted around it, but the closer we got, the more there were."

"More what?" I asked.

Jax shrugged. "They're still, you know, sick. But they're a little bit more..."

"Agile?" suggested Toby.

"Smart?" added Jax.

Toby grunted in agreement. "But Agatha is kinda weird. Sweet, smart, helluva shot. But weird as the day is long."

"Are you going to miss them?" asked Amy.

Jax seemed sad suddenly. "Yeah. Maurice was our sister's husband."

"Would that be Lily?" asked Tanya.

"She was a few years younger than us. Married Maurice when she turned eighteen. But it worked. They were happy. When all this happened—" Toby waved a hand at the landscape. "—she begged us to come north. We were thinking about heading down to Mexico. Sunshine, clean water for fishing, you know? Build a place up, survive."

"But you went with your sister," I said.

Toby hung his head. "She died early, days before we passed Frisco. After, we stayed with Maurice and his kid sister. Found others. What else were we gonna do?"

"Makes sense," said Tanya. "You already had people. Safety in numbers, et cetera."

"Exactly," said Jax.

"So, why'd you leave to join a smaller group?"

Jax and Toby made the same face, eyebrows up, mouths down.

"Felt like it was time," Toby answered.

An hour or so later, we crossed the California border. The cold didn't let up at all, and in fact, the later it got, the heavier it snowed. We weren't moving south fast enough to outrun the winter weather, and I suspected we wouldn't escape it anytime soon.

"I think we need to find some kind of shelter," I called over the wind. My hair flew right into my mouth, and I choked on its unpleasant, stringy texture. Maybe I would let Tanya cut it.

"Marco is right," said Amy. "I'm freezing. Even Duchess is shivering."

We tried out three places before we found a decent spot, a house at the end of a private road with old-school wood paneling on the interior walls, flowered eyesores for furniture, and carpet the color of snot. There was some food in the pantry and several of those five-gallon water jugs in the garage. Everybody took their shoes off the first night. I kept mine on.

The weather lasted a lot longer than we expected. When the second week went by, we started to move in. We unpacked our stuff, sharpened our weapons, and washed what we could by using melted snow, and hung the clothes to dry in one of the bathrooms. I taught Tanya and Amy more about defensive combat, and Tanya taught Jax and me to patch holes, hem things, and repair buttons. Amy and Toby exchanged recipes that could be made with the limited supplies we had.

Sometime during the third week, Jax convinced Amy to help him pierce his ear. He had found some earrings in a jewelry box in the big bedroom and excitedly waved a small silver hoop at her, saying he'd always wanted to do it and who better than a doctor to assist?

"Better not pierce the gay ear," Toby chuckled.

Tanya leaned forward, hands on her hips. "The what ear?"

"It's a joke, Tanya, jeez."

"Explain it to me then."

Toby's face got red.

"It's homophobic as shit, is what it is," Tanya said. "You owe us an apology."

Toby tucked his chin. "Sorry, Tanya. Amy. I didn't mean anything by it."

Tanya sat on the hideous floral couch and made an *I hope you learned something* face at Toby.

Jax pounced on the silence and started begging Amy again to pierce his ear. "Just one little stick between friends, is all." He wiggled the hoop next to his ear. "Come on, doc, I've always wanted one. Pretty please?"

When Jax walked out of the bathroom with his new piercing, and for the next three days or so, Toby called him Captain and told him to walk the plank at least a dozen times.

After I got my hair caught on a hinge in the bathroom door, Tanya finally got me to sit for long enough to let her cut it. When she was done, I felt equal parts nostalgic for my lost locks, and optimistic. No zombie could use it against me anymore. Amy said it looked dashing and compared me to a famous person I didn't know.

After eight weeks, the snow finally stopped long enough to begin to melt. As soon as the roads were clear a couple of days later, we all agreed it was time to move on, hopefully far and fast enough we wouldn't have to endure another such winter before we reached our destination. It was still brutally cold some nights, but we had a long way to go, and none of us wanted to stop until we got there.

Eleven: Compromise

Why did I think it would be a good idea to try talking to Sam right after training? I should have waited until after breakfast. I should have waited until everyone was off doing their own thing, instead of walking up and just telling Sam I wanted to talk to her. It seemed so much more pressing five minutes ago.

"I don't want to fight about it," I plead, keeping my voice low.

"About what?" Sam snaps. "The fact that you ran to *Marco* about me? Why not talk to me? What's going on with you two?"

"Nothing. We're friends!" I take a breath. "And I should have come right to you. But you went back to bed, and I was confused. You're different, we both are, and I was scared because I thought everything would be the same, that we would be okay."

"Well, I thought we *were* okay. I guess I was wrong." Sam stomps about ten feet away and turns back around. "And you know what, I haven't changed, not much. But you have. You're hardly the same person anymore."

"What's that supposed to mean?"

"I don't know. You're just different. You used to need me, or at least want me around. When Bill told me where to find you, I came all the way down here for you, and I feel like you couldn't care less."

"You have no idea!" I shout. "I thought about you every day, every single day for two years."

"Then why does it seem like you talk to Marco more than me, and now about me too? You told me he was weird when you first met him."

"That was years ago. I got to know him better. You could too, you know."

Sam makes a noise in her throat. "Pass."

"What is your problem?" I hear how loud my voice is, but I can't help it. Or, I don't want to.

"My problem is, you're all I have, but you don't need me because you have Marco!"

"You have Bill too. And what, am I not allowed to have friends? Marco was there for me when my mom and Andrew died. He helped me through the worst part of my life."

"So why would you need me, right?"

I don't know how to answer. Sam and Marco are two different people; they occupy two different spots in my heart. Why is it so hard for her to understand?

"I just do," I say after probably too long.

"That's not good enough, Cate."

Before I can formulate a response, she's walking away toward the garden where Mel and the kids are working. I follow. "Sam! We're not done talking."

"I am." Sam barely glances over her shoulder at me. "I get it. You're close with Marco. You've made it pretty clear exactly how close. But I don't think you know how that makes me feel. I don't want to talk to you anymore, Cate. Leave me alone."

I'm not ready to give up. It's unreasonable that she can just walk away mid-fight. "Sam—"

"Cate!" Adrienne runs over to me, carefully hopping over the plants. "Cate, I saw my mom."

Her face is bright and hopeful and covered in dirt from the garden. Did I hear her correctly?

"Did you say your mom? I don't think you saw her."

"Yes I did, and she's alive! I saw her standing over there on the path." She points toward one of the old abandoned buildings, one we checked in the first few weeks and found to be useless and in bad enough shape that it was dangerous.

"Adrienne, there's no one over there. It's not safe in those buildings. We checked before, remember?" And because I'm starting to understand kids, I add, "Don't go exploring anywhere without an adult, okay?"

"I saw! My mom!" Adrienne cries. She stomps her foot and crosses her little arms. Behind her, Sam is on her knees next to Francis, quietly pulling weeds.

Mel comes over and crouches next to Adrienne. "Sweetie, we talked about this. It was probably a dream. Sometimes I dream about my dad too." She smooths Adrienne's hair. "If she was alive, why would she be hiding? I know you miss her; I do too."

"People sometimes come back," Adrienne protests. "What about Sleeping Beauty or Snow White?"

"Adrienne, those are stories. They're not real. Remember how..."

I sidestep them and start to walk over to Sam, but when she sees me, she turns her back to me. I scoff, loudly enough for her to hear. Fine, then. We won't talk.

I don't see her all afternoon. Or, I see her, but she's obviously avoiding me. I catch her glaring at me a few times. I thought it would be better, taking Marco's advice, putting everything out there. Communicating. Seems like I've made things worse.

I move robotically through the rest of my chores, and by the time I sit down to eat dinner, Sam is done with hers. She leaves with Tanya and Amy, not even glancing back at me. When Marco sits across from me and gives me a *what's up?* type expression, I shake my head and look away. He can tell something is off, or maybe he heard us arguing. But I don't want to talk about it, especially not to him. When everyone else goes in for bed, I stay out. I walk toward the garden, because Marco doesn't usually go there at night, and I really want to be alone.

A fog rolls in, so thick I feel as though I could reach out and grab it. Through the mist, faint and distant, lies the city. Though I can't see it in the darkness, its presence is both comforting and haunting. It seems like a lot more than a couple of days since I was there, across the water, rummaging through the fancy apartment building with Joaquin. Were things easier then, before Sam came crashing back into my life? Easier may not be the right word. Living on a prison island and scavenging for supplies is not easy. Zombies, Abnormals, also not easy. Simpler, maybe. Yes. Less complicated.

A few times over the last two years, I've allowed myself to daydream, to imagine a reunion with Sam. I pictured the moment of recognition, the tearful hello, the first kiss. I never really made it past that fairytale moment. I never thought about what would come after, but I wouldn't have thought it would be this, this pain and discontent. I spent so long missing her, lamenting her absence, I didn't allow myself to fully appreciate what we had built in the interim. We all lost things and people. Every life in the world had gotten turned inside out during those first couple of months. But all of us here were so lucky to have found one another. Who would have thought that adding people we already loved would cause pain?

What would it be like, I wonder, to run away? To be the one who is lost? I stare at where I know the city is, where there are buildings upon buildings. There must be at least one place over there I could fortify, make a new life. The next time we go on a run, it would be so easy. I could just not come back. I'd do fine on my own. Or maybe I'd disappear, fade away...

I shake my head and walk faster to give myself something else to concentrate on. I don't know why I think that way. My old therapist, may she probably rest in peace, once called those thoughts intrusive. They're unwelcome, and they come out of nowhere. It's not that I really want to run away and live or die alone in the city. I have a good life here, considering. She also said I have a self-destructive streak at times. "Just have to recognize the patterns," she told me. I would never do such a thing to Mel anyway. Or Marco. Or Sam. Even if we're not going to work out, even if the changes in both of us are too big to accommodate what we were, I do love her. And I know, I think, she loves me too. But that doesn't mean we fit. Do we? Are we forcing this for the sake of our history, the "should" of it all?

"Cate, wait up."

I turn to find Ana jogging up behind me. "Hey, Ana," I call, letting my voice sound as weary as I feel, hoping she'll get the hint.

"You and Sam not doing so hot?"

"What makes you say that?"

"Well, I heard you two arguing. I think everyone did, to be honest."

Jesus. It's like high school, living in a group this small.

"It's nothing," I say. I know I'm coming across prickly, but in my defense, she's being kind of nosy.

"Exactly," she says, drilling a hole in me with her eye.

"What do you mean, Ana? And what business is it of yours?" I never would have said something so brazen in high school though. I more likely would have gone red in the face and escaped as quickly as possible.

"Okay, one," Ana snaps, "if you didn't want it to be public then you shouldn't have made it public. Two—" She stops us both walking, takes a deep breath, blows it out through puckered lips, and in a more measured tone: "—can I share something with you?"

"Sure," I answer, because saying no would be pretty rude.

We start walking again, away from the garden and toward the main path. "I met Rob after the world ended."

"After?" When I had seen them together, that first day in the woods after they rescued us, I would have thought they'd been married for years or something. They were so similar, and so clearly in love. When he died on the docks as we fled the city, even though I hardly knew Ana, I could tell it broke her.

"Way after. I was with someone before. Nothing serious. His name was Matt."

"Oh."

"He was gone months before we found you. He was my boyfriend, sort of. Not really. We were on a road trip when it all happened, some haunted house tour he didn't want to go on alone. It was maybe our fifth date? Matt loved Halloween. I could take it or leave it, myself. Don't like all that spooky stuff." She lets out a bitter laugh. "I was already thinking of breaking it off after the road trip. Then the world went sideways. We met Marco when he had already found a lot of others. Sylvia used to have three kids; did you know?"

"Yeah, Nick had a brother."

"Twin brother. Nate."

"And he died, right?"

"He did." Ana stops walking for a second, runs her fingers along the rock wall, picks at a loose pebble with her fingernails.

Another deep breath. "Matt and I were gathering sticks and ran into some trouble. Only three of them, but a lot more than I was equipped to deal with at the time. Matt, too, for all his love of dark and dangerous. Marco and the others heard us yelling and came running. Unfortunately, so did a bunch more of them. Zombies."

When I glance over at her, she seems to be looking all the way back to that day. She's certainly not here with me.

"There were about ten or so. Nothing we can't handle now, but back then—you know."

"Did Matt and Nate both die?"

"No, only Nate. I imagine Matt died soon after though."

"What do you mean?" I ask, my step faltering.

"So, I told you, Matt had no practical survival skills. Neither did I. And ten zombies were a lot back then, even for all of us. Especially with three little ones to protect. Well, we surrounded the kids when the dead surrounded us, but one of them came at Matt, and he instinctively dodged it."

"Oh no."

"You really can't call it anything else, can you? Instinct kicks in, fight or flight. In the absence of skill, flight is sort of automatic, isn't it?"

She's staring at me now, as if she wants an answer. Or some sort of absolution. Her eye is wide, and even in the blackness, I can see her normally super-pale cheeks are red and blotchy.

I don't know how to answer. I wasn't there, but it sounds pretty bad, instinct or no. "So, the thing got Nate?"

"Yeah. Barely. It only got one single scratch on him before Nate's dad got to it. One little scratch."

"But that's enough," I say, remembering how one tiny scratch on my uncle Frank's arm split up my whole family.

"Nate died quick. I guess he had already been sick. Heart thing. But Sylvia and her family didn't exactly understand the nature of the sickness, or maybe they were in denial. But the idea of their baby coming back, and what had to be done to keep that from happening, was especially traumatizing. In the end, Nate's dad was the one to—you know." She keeps her eye on the ground.

"Those poor kids," I mutter as much to Ana as nobody. And now they're orphans too. Like Mel and me, only much younger. I think of poor Adrienne in the garden today, her dreams of seeing her mother so real she was convinced she actually had. I've had so many of those dreams I lost count a long time ago.

"And after, the group voted to make him go. Matt. Or, the people who wanted him out were loud enough that no one put up much of a fight. I don't know why I didn't stay with him. I guess I knew I had a better chance with a bigger group. Maybe I was a little horrified that he had indirectly— I mean, I know he didn't kill Nate. But at the time, I don't know. We gave him the means to survive—food and water and a weapon—but he didn't know how to protect himself. He cried when we left. So did I. I wonder all the time whether we did the right thing, and I don't think we did. I don't think it's right to exile somebody in this world. It's a death sentence, ninety-nine percent of the time."

"You don't think he found people?"

"I don't. It was only a few months after the end. He was never going to survive; I think we all knew that."

"I'm sorry, Ana."

"It's done. Long done. We never should have made him go, even for something like that. I can't think of many reasons to exclude anyone anymore. He wasn't my person, but he was a person. Anyway, that's all beside the point. I met Rob months after we ousted Matt. And it was different. It was real. It felt like I had found the person I'd been waiting for. He understood me; you know what I'm saying? And we had a lot of days together, but not enough. And this is what I'm trying to tell you."

"I don't follow."

"I'm talking about Sam now. You loved her once, right? Was it real? Did you know?"

"I love her now. I think it's real. But I'm confused."

"Okay, then unconfuse yourself. Sam is one of us now. When she and Bill landed here, against some pretty stacked odds, they became part of this family. And on top of that, you love Sam. Nothing else matters."

"She thinks there's something up with Marco and me. And she thinks I don't want her."

"Do you?"

"Of course."

"If you love someone, you make an effort to demonstrate it to them, especially if they obviously need you to. The people on this island are our people. Our family. Sam is the newest. She's getting her bearings. Help her."

"I'm trying, but she's different. So am I."

"Everyone changed, Cate, we had to. And still, you love her. And still, she loves you. That's beautiful. Fight for it. There aren't a lot of beautiful things left."

I've never seen Ana look so earnest before. All her normal hardness is gone, leaving behind the face of a woman who has loved and lost and is trying to make sure I don't suffer the same. "Okay, Ana. I understand."

"Do you?"

"I do. You're right. I'll talk to her first thing in the morning."

Ana smiles. It's happy and sad all at once. And before I have time to register what she's doing, she reaches out and hugs me. It's a brief hug, not overly warm, and then it's over and she's hard-ass Ana again. "I'm tired. And you look like hell."

"Thanks a lot."

Another smile, a lot smaller and far briefer than the first. She opens the door to the cell house. "Get some rest."

*

I wake up to the sounds of movement. People talking, rustling around in their cells. Amy and Tanya shuffle down the walkway with Duchess close behind, her nails click-clacking on the floor. Chaz leaves my cell to do his morning rounds. Calvin tells me to get my ass up like he does most days as he and the others pass my cell on their way out to the rec yard for training. I rouse myself, dress, put on my boots. But I don't go outside.

Sam is still asleep in her cell, or she's trying to sleep. Her back is to the door, and she's curled up under her blanket.

"Sam?" I whisper.

She stirs.

"I don't want to fight anymore," I say, taking another step into her cell.

She turns over to face me. Her eyes are red and there are dark circles under them. But she seems at least tentatively happy to see me. "Me neither."

There's a lot to say. But I don't quite know where to begin, and all I really want is to be close to her. So I sit down at the foot of her bed. She lifts her head to watch me, then picks up the corner of the blanket. I accept the silent invitation, kick off my shoes, and crawl in beside her. We barely fit next to each other on the tiny mattress. My feet hang off the edge. Sam kisses my forehead, my lips. I twirl my fingers in her hair. Maybe we don't need to talk about anything right this second. Maybe things will figure themselves out.

"We should get to training," I say reluctantly. I start to get up, but she takes hold of my arm.

"Stay," she murmurs. When I lie back down, she wraps her arms around me, but it feels good and welcome, more affectionate, less suffocating than it did the other night.

"We have to go soon," I remind her. Even as I'm saying it, I'm thinking *do we though?*

Sam, as if she can read my mind, asks, "Are you sure? How long has it been since you've let yourself sleep in?"

"I dunno, before the apocalypse?" Or, probably a few days in that little brick house where Mel and I spent the first winter. Still, it has been a long time.

Sam huffs a little chuckle. "You train every day. You can be a few minutes late. Stay, Cate. Stay with me. I feel awful about yesterday. I missed you all day and night. I hardly slept."

I don't mention that it's supposed to be Marco's first day back. I don't want to ruin this fragile peace. It is tempting to stay here a while longer with Sam. Marco will still be there in a few minutes. "Okay. Just for a minute or two."

I let myself drift in and out of sleep. When I start to get restless, I gently pull my arm out from under Sam and check my watch. "Damn it."

"Mmm?" Sam opens one eye.

"We slept for two extra hours."

She smiles. Stretches without sitting up. "I guess I was right. We needed it."

I'm not sure if I agree, if I'm annoyed to have missed today's training, or what. I get up and pull my shoes back on. "I guess."

"Come on, Cate," Sam says, following me out of the cell. "It's one day. You're fine. It can't be the first day you've missed."

"It's the first in a while." And it feels weird. Not bad, not good. Maybe I did need a break. We step into the sunlight. It feels like my body is drinking it in. Normally, I would already be up and about my chores instead of wandering out of the cell house with sleep in my eyes.

"Oh hey," calls Tanya from the other end of the rec yard. "Catching up on your beauty rest, were you?"

"I don't know about beauty," Calvin chuckles. "Check out that bird's nest on top of her head."

"Shut up," I say, smacking his arm as we reach him. I unwind the green handkerchief from my wrist and wrap it around my head.

"It was beautiful after I cut it," Tanya teases. "I cannot be held responsible for the tragic aftercare."

"You missed training," Calvin says as if I can't tell. "Marco wasn't half bad, but he could benefit from some one-on-one if you have time."

"We took a break," says Sam before I can tell him, hell yes, I'll help Marco or ask for more detail about his first day back.

"Don't you have to work first before you can call it a break?" Mel asks, bouncing one of her babies up and down on her hip as Adrienne awkwardly mimics her with the other baby.

"I didn't sleep well last night," Sam says.

Mel rolls her eyes. "Try having twins."

Sam stifles a laugh. "I, uh, don't see that happening."

"No kidding," mocks Mel.

"So," I chime in, "what's for breakfast?"

"Nothing anymore," Mel snaps. "We ate right after training, same as always. The world doesn't stop and wait for your love life."

"You didn't save us any?"

"Of course we did," says Tanya, glancing sideways at Mel.

Sam and I follow Tanya to the normal eating spot, and she hands us each a plate. "Amy and I were on dish duty this morning, but since you two slept all damn day, you can wash your own." Quick wink. "Enjoy, ladies." And with that, she sashays back toward Amy, who appears to be deep in conversation with David and Toby.

We munch our breakfasts in silence at first. About halfway through, Sam asks me for the hundredth time why it's so important for us to train every single day, and if the island is so safe, why everyone needs to.

I repeat the explanation I gave her before, generally. We never know when something could happen, Abnormals are a thing, and we don't always stay on the island.

"Yeah, okay." She doesn't seem convinced. "So, what now?"

"Chores. There's always stuff to do. Upkeep, cleaning, patrolling. David has a list."

"So, why can't I contribute by doing that stuff? Why would I need to train if I never plan to go into the city?"

"You don't want to leave the island at all?"

"I mean, maybe one day. But I don't know; it's ugly out there. Here, it seems like everyone is safe and gets along. Why leave if I don't have to?"

"You mean, why train or go into the city if there are other people willing to put themselves in harm's way?"

"Jeez, Cate, you make it sound like that's not the way it has always worked. Societies are built on everybody doing what they can do. I wasn't going to be a cop or a firefighter before. I didn't want to join the military, but you never gave me any shit for it back then. What's the difference?"

I don't have a real answer to that, other than "everything has changed." But she's at least a little bit right. Back then, there was no way I could have survived without electricity and running water and grocery stores; I could never imagine putting my axe in a zombie's face. Now, I do all of that and more. I'm stronger, because I have to be. That's the difference. But Sam isn't, and it's frustrating.

"I get it," is all I say.

"So, try taking a break from training," Sam pushes. "You were fine two years ago with only exercising, like, once a month. In fact, we found ways to get out of gym class more than we went. Find some other stuff to do. You don't have to go on every trip into the city, do you?"

The thing is, I enjoy the trips in. They help release the tension constantly building inside me. It's such a relief to have an outlet for the buzzing in my brain. The fear and exhilaration, the triumph of a narrow escape or a pile of dead zombies—it's something I've come to look forward to.

"Cate?"

"Sorry, what?"

"Take a few days off. From training. Be with me."

"Why can't you just try training?"

Sam makes no effort to hide her disappointment.

"What?" I ask.

"I came to this place, this island, this literal prison, to get to you. You know? I've never been this far from home. I left every single piece of my life behind to find you. And you can't compromise, take a few days here and there to be with me?"

We stop walking, and I stare at her. My Sam. She's right. She did leave everything behind. But so did I. I guess the difference is, I did it to keep my family, and she did it because she'd lost hers. She ran to my house on the off chance she would find me, and—lemon juice in that paper cut—she didn't find me for two years. She came all this way for me. There is a familiar fullness in my chest, and I suddenly have the urge to kiss her, so I do. I wrap my arms around her and let the relief and joy and gratitude that she's even here replace the doubt and confusion I've been carrying around.

"Okay. A few days. And sometimes, you'll come to training?"

She agrees to train with me once a week to start and promises she'll try to come more as time goes on. And we have a lot of time. So I don't push it for now. I'm not sure how I'll feel about skipping out on training, if it will get easier or if it will always feel strange, and I have no idea how Calvin will react. Will he kick me off the missions into the city, say I'm too soft and unreliable? I hope not, but for now, I'm just happy to have Sam back.

Twelve: Disarm

1 year, 5 months ago

"Tanya. You have to open your eyes."

"I know that, Marco, but tell it to my reflexes. Do I want to get corpse gunk in an orifice? That's how you get infected." She crossed her arms and relaxed her stance.

"It won't hurt you," Jax said, tiptoeing toward us. "I got some in my nose a while back. Right up there. They quarantined me and everything. I was sure I was gonna die."

"You should have seen him though." Toby giggled. "Trying to dislodge the zombie stuff. I'm gonna go write my name in the snow."

"Point is," Jax said, glaring at Toby's back, "I'm okay. I think it's only in the bloodstream that does it."

"And I know tree bark won't do it," Toby called over his shoulder.

"Just try, Tanya," I said, trying to be patient. We were dealing with the realest kind of life-and-death situation, but somehow, everyone seemed to be annoyingly cavalier.

"This isn't even a real zombie. You don't have to look right at them, if it helps. Turn your head, fine, but if your eyes are closed, how do you expect to hit a target one-sixth the size of the whole body?" I swung my axe at the tree we were using for practice, turning my head to demonstrate. "See? Try."

"Can I try?" asked Jax, stepping up.

"Uh, sure."

His accuracy wasn't bad. He hit the side of the face I'd drawn to represent a zombie head. It took him a second to get his knife out of the tree.

"Okay, okay. I got it this time," said Tanya, wiggling her hips and shoulders like a cat about to pounce. She licked her lips, swung her hammer back, and rushed the tree, getting a clean hit right in the center of the face. Bark went flying, none of it in her eyes.

Jax whooped and held out a hand for a high five. "Tanya, you powerhouse!"

"Better," I said. "Now do it about a hundred and fifty more times."

Tanya and Jax ceased their high-fiving and stared at me.

"Kidding, jeez." I said, holding my hands up. "That was great, Tanya. You're getting better. Amy, you want to try?"

"Ladies and gents," said Toby, shuffling through the thin snow toward us. "We've got company."

"Far enough to run from?" I asked.

Toby scrunched up his face. "Run?"

"Why fight if you don't have to?" I started gathering my stuff, but it was definitely too late: six zombies staggered from the direction Toby had just come.

I dropped my bag and yanked my axe out of the tree.

"Nothing like a little real-life practice, hey, Tanya?" asked Jax.

Tanya placed herself in front of Amy and glanced from me to the zombies to me again. I nodded, hopefully in an encouraging way.

We'd made a surprisingly good team so far. Of the three major encounters we'd had over the three months since Jax and Toby joined us, they'd proven they could at least handle themselves.

"Jaxon?" said Toby.

"Got it," said Jax, using an inefficient sort of haymaker maneuver to stab the first zombie in the temple. It crumpled to the ground as two more came.

Tanya smashed one in the forehead with her hammer. Her eyes were open, but the hit wasn't hard enough. It would have broken bark, but not bone. She finished it off with one more good whack.

I'd been watching her, making sure she and Amy were good, and I'd let the third one get way too close to me. I raised my axe to kill it, but there was no way I'd get a good enough hit at that distance. At the last second before it closed in for a bite, my arm was yanked practically out of its socket, and I was three feet to the left. Toby stood in my place, and with his huge wrench, he caved the thing's skull in with a single well-placed hit.

My heart hammered in my chest. "Thanks, Toby."

Toby dipped his head. "Gotcha, man."

As Jax killed number four, with a little extra effort, number five came at Tanya. She and Amy backed up a bit, but Tanya shouted at Amy to duck, and as soon as she did, Tanya leaned back and delivered a wicked kick to its rotten gut, sending it fumbling backward. She was on it before it had a chance to stand.

"Way to be, Tanya!" shouted Jax. Then, immediately after, "Toby!"

The sixth zombie, the last one, was behind Toby, its jaw inches from his arm. I was in just the right place to shove it away and swing my axe at its head. I missed, but only because the zombie happened to wobble the exact right way, so it sort of looked like it dodged my hit.

Duchess came at it, her jaws gnashing, and she grabbed it by the shirt sleeve. It almost seemed like the zombie peered down at her, the way its head rocked to one side. It was clearly the momentum or something. For a second, a flash, I thought I saw blue eyes. It was only the winter light, of course. That was what I told myself.

When the zombie came back at us—Toby and me—I was ready with my axe. But Toby punched it in the head, a surprising move considering the risk of splitting his knuckles and getting infected without even being bitten. He and I swung our weapons at the exact same time, so as its head bounced off Toby's wrench, it hit the back of my axe. But by then, it was already dead.

It was totally quiet. A bunch of dead zombies lay around our campsite, our stuff miraculously clean of any gore.

"Man," panted Toby, "I thought I was a gonner."

"We could have amputated," suggested Amy, who was still shaking. Duchess sat on her feet.

"We got what we need for that kind of procedure?" asked Jax.

Amy's shoulders rounded. "No, not even close."

"Might be something to think about though," I said.

Toby massaged his hand, the one that had almost been zombie food. "No biggie. I'm good. Thanks to you, Marco."

"Just returning the favor."

I bent down to examine number six's face, not really sure why I was doing it. When I saw it, though, I did know. The eyes—they were blue.

"Guys?" I wasn't sure why I was whispering.

They crowded around, stared at the zombie I was kneeling over.

"What?" asked Jax.

"The eyes." Amy sounded almost reverent.

"They're white, usually, aren't they?" Tanya went to another of the recently slain zombies, another, a third. "These ones all have pale eyes."

"It seemed as though you were having more trouble with that one, as well," Amy observed.

"I guess I was."

She was still staring at the zombie, looking like she might reach out and touch it. Her face was so close.

"What is this thing?" I asked, not expecting an answer but getting one from Amy the Mad Scientist.

"This person seems to be infected with the same virus as the others. Black veins, no or very low pulse. But with the eyes and the, er, enhanced abilities? It appears to be a variation in the sickness."

Toby made a sound. "Just like the ones down south."

"These are what your friend was talking about?" I asked. "These, what, Variant zombies?"

"Yeah," said Jax. "But it wasn't something I expected to have to worry about this far north."

"It makes some sense," answered Tanya. "Doesn't it? Because the world wasn't shitty enough, it had to throw in some smart zombies."

"Shh, listen," said Jax. "There are more close by."

We all waited.

Soon, I heard it too, not far off: *shh!*

"Zombies don't shush one another," said Tanya.

"Maybe smart zombies do," said Toby.

"Great," mumbled Jax.

I flexed my fingers around my axe handle. Toby pulled out his wrench. We locked eyes, and I motioned to go closer, at the same time waving my hand for the others to stay where they were. We stepped toward the sounds, which sounded less and less like zombies.

There were people behind the trees. How long had they been there? Had they been following us?

Duchess glided like a wolf past us, toward the sound. She wasn't growling, but her hackles were up. She crept inch by inch, keeping her head and tail low.

There was commotion in the trees.

A figure ran out from behind the biggest trunk, accompanied by a voice calling, "Nick!"

The kid was barely as tall as the dog, and he went running right at her. She barked once, a high, happy bark, and her tail went wild.

"Nick!" A woman ran around an adjacent tree. "I told you to stay put. Come here!"

She stood straight up when she noticed us, clasped the boy's little hand. "Please," she said, backing away and pulling the kid behind her.

I lowered my weapon, and Toby did the same.

"It's okay," I said.

Another little figure with blonde pigtails and jeans with sparkly purple flowers on them darted into the clearing. "Mommy!" This one couldn't have been more than nine or ten, and she was older than the boy.

"Adrienne!" called a distinctly older, deeper voice. A man walked out to where the rest of his family was standing. In his arms, clinging to his long neck, was a small, frail child with the same face as the first boy.

Damn, a family in the apocalypse.

"We're unarmed. Would you please put away your weapons, so you don't scare the kids?" asked the man, handing the little boy to the woman.

Unarmed? How had they survived so long? I didn't ask as Toby and I put our weapons away, mine in my belt loop and Toby's in his utility belt. The mom and dad's faces relaxed as we did. One little boy, the one who had been on his way to give Duchess the scratching of a lifetime, offered us a few semi-interested glances but didn't seem particularly worried, before or after our weapons were put away. He was all about the dog.

The girl was warming up to the idea of Duchess, but she glanced at her mom, presumably for permission. The lady regarded the dog, who was clearly harmless.

Duchess watched us, the new people, and us again. She sniffed around the kids' feet, the mom's hands.

"Nice dog," she said. "Whose is it?"

"Nobody's," I said at the same time as Tanya's, "Everybody's."

The boy, Nick, reached out a hand to pet her.

"Nick, don't!" chided the little girl. "Don't pet strange dogs."

"She's nice, though, Adrienne, see?" he said, putting his hand closer to the dog, who licked his mitten.

"She's friendly," I said.

The kids took my words as full permission. They ripped off their gloves and mittens and descended on the dog with their tiny fingers wiggling. Duchess flopped over into the thin layer of snow, exposing her full belly, relishing the scratches she was receiving. Snow started to fall, swirling around on conflicting air currents.

The little kid in the lady's arms murmured something. The lady put him down but kept a firm hold on one of his hands. They walked, slowly, toward Duchess. The boy ran a hand along the smooth black fur on her side. For whatever reason, Duchess noticed his single soft pet over the rest, and she sat up and stared right at him. He stared at her, mouth hanging partway open, and reached out to touch her cheek. The dog closed her eyes and pushed her head into his palm. His pale little face moved as slowly as the rest of him, forming a big smile.

"Nate, she likes you," his mom said encouragingly. She reached out to touch Duchess before gathering the boy, Nate, up into her arms and standing. The dog watched the little boy go all the way up and then watched him a little longer.

"I'm Sylvia," said the mom. "This is my husband, Henry, and our children, Nate, Adrienne, and Nick."

"Marco," I said, lifting my hand.

"Tanya, my wife, Amy."

"Jax."

"Toby."

"Where are you all headed?" asked Henry. "Looked like you were moving with some purpose before those, um, before you got stopped."

I couldn't understand the aversion to saying the word "zombie." Undead, rotting, eating people, not talking— what the hell else could they be? I rolled my eyes at my group, exasperated. People's ability to avoid the truth was astounding.

But Amy was looking back at me with pursed lips as if she knew what I was thinking and did not agree. *Or maybe they're afraid, Marco*, I could practically hear her saying in her sweet, unassuming way. She would also, probably, tell me that saying something usually meant admitting it was real, and for most people, admitting the existence of actual zombies was too much to deal with. She would be right.

"We're going south," I said. "You?"

"We don't have a clue where we're going," the mom— Sylvia— blurted. She made a choked, laugh-like sound in the back of her throat and dropped her gaze so low her eyelashes rested on her cheeks. Her husband put his arm around her, and she leaned on his shoulder.

"It's been hard." Henry said. "We're from around here, but we've been going in circles. We figure there's somewhere we should be getting to, but—" He ran his fingers through his hair and smiled the same stressed-out dad smile I'd seen on Andrew and Bill a hundred million times. "We have no idea where we're supposed to go."

"Are we lost?" asked Adrienne, the little girl. She lifted her face up to her dad, who kneeled between her and her brother Nick.

"We're not lost, we know exactly where we are. But we need to find a new place with more people. Being with more people will make us safer."

"Daddy." Adrienne pointed up at my face. "We found people."

Henry, Sylvia, Nick, and Nate joined Adrienne in staring at us.

All my muscles tensed up at once. I knew I should say something, but what? We had no reason not to bring them along, except the obvious liability of three kids. Even so, or maybe because of their vulnerability, I felt an unexplainable urge to suggest we join up.

"We're going to Alcatraz Island," said Tanya, glancing at me.

"It's safe," Jax said. "Prison, you know. And it's a national park, so—"

"Yes!" cried Sylvia. "Are you asking? Because, yes, can we come with you?" Her eyes lit up and then filled with tears.

Henry didn't seem convinced, or maybe he thought Sylvia was jumping the gun on the invite. Which, she was, kind of. But again, no legitimate reason to say no. I liked this family. I wasn't sure why, but they awoke a sense of empathy I wasn't used to. It was both disarming and pleasant.

"You can come with us," I said, casting a quick glance around at the others. My people. No one seemed against it. Or to have any immediate issues. I turned back to Sylvia and Henry's family and gave a final nod-shrug thing. "Offer's open."

"It'll be hard to get on that island," said Henry. "I've been there. Treacherous sometimes, especially with a lot of..."

"Zombies?"

Henry didn't even flinch. He just looked at me like, *finally, someone said it*, and nodded. "Yeah, especially with a lot of zombies to worry about."

"Safer, though, once we clear it," I said. "Sustainable. Fortifiable."

Henry smiled. "Could be a real future, at least until all this gets figured out."

"Figured out? There's no fucking way this is going back to normal."

"Marco," Amy chastised me, casting a pointed glance at the kids.

"Well, not normal," Henry agreed as we all started walking south together. "But this can't be how humanity goes out."

"We have to go out sometime," I said.

Henry snorted. "I guess we've worn out our welcome."

Tanya peered sidelong at him, arching an eyebrow.

Bill would have liked this guy. I wondered how Bill was doing. Was he walking, biking, somewhere alive and well at that moment? I never imagined him as dead or undead when I thought about him. Bill's wife Tess probably would have said that was a good sign. Maybe it was.

I knew we were off the original path. But we'd get to our destination eventually, and maybe Cate would be there waiting. Maybe they all would. Either way, I was starting to feel like we had a shot.

Tanya jogged to catch up with me at the front of the group. "Surprised to see you so open with the invite back there, Marco," she murmured so no one else would hear.

"Yeah?"

"Made me proud."

I didn't know how to respond. Luckily, Tanya spoke first.

"I think our chances are pretty good, don't you?"

"I do," I answered. And I meant it. As Tanya had said before, there was safety in numbers. And we had the numbers.

Thirteen: Assumptions

The first few days, I feel antsy. Gardening is, admittedly, a lot easier in the morning than training. Mel and the kids hardly acknowledge us when we join them, which means Sam and I exist in our own little bubble on those days. Chaz and Duchess wander the rows of vegetables and wildflowers lazily, each stopping to sniff the pea plant that no one can figure out how to revive. It appears even the dogs can perceive something isn't right with it.

One by one, each of my usual training teammates asks what's up with my disappearing act. I tell each of them variations of the truth. I want to find other ways to contribute, I tell Calvin, because I know it will keep him off my back. I'm sick of getting up so early every day, I tell Jax and Toby. I still train on my own, I tell Marco. That's not true. I hardly do so much as a push-up on the days I don't train with the group. And on the days I do, it's a lot harder than I recall. Only Ana doesn't ask me. It seems like she knows this is part of my compromise with Sam. When she sees us together, she always smiles, and there's always a hint of sadness underneath it.

Sam keeps to her word, with only a little complaint, to train once in a while. By her second time training, she's good enough that I hardly have to help her at all. She glides through the form, only stumbling once or twice coming out of her roll.

"Looking good," I tell her as she executes a near-perfect swing kick.

"Back at you, babe," she says with an overdone comedic wink.

Across the yard, Marco is honestly killing it. I'm impressed that after so long, he can just jump right back into things. He's doing better than me. Though, to be fair, he has been at it every day since he came back to training.

When I turn back to Sam, she's stopped her forms and is watching me.

"Seriously?" she asks, crossing her arms.

"Pair off!" Calvin shouts.

"What do you think? You ready to try sparring?" I ask Sam.

She shrugs. "Why not? What's the worst that could happen?"

"Sam," Calvin calls as he jogs toward us with Mel in tow. "Since Melody is with us this morning, and since you and she are probably at similar levels, why don't you two try sparring together? Baby, what do you think?"

"Similar levels?" Mel scoffs, giving Sam the up-down. "I'm sure. She's trained, what, twice? Three times?"

"So, go easy on her."

Mel squares off. "Sure, okay. That'll prep her for a horde of Abnormals."

"Cate," Calvin says. "Pair with Marco, would you?"

"Yeah, of course." I try not to make it too obvious that I'm dying to spar with him again.

Behind Calvin, Sam looks supremely annoyed, but is it because I'm not with her, or that I'm with Marco?

Calvin grins. "Great. He's getting better, but he could use a challenge, and I know you'll deliver."

"You know it." I give Sam a quick peck on the cheek and go to Marco. He's drenched in sweat, guzzling water.

"Hey, slacker," I call.

He gives me the finger, drinks some more, and wipes sweat off his face with the hem of his shirt. "You ready for all this?" he asks.

"Please. I'm going to kick your ass back to Washington."

He chuckles. "We'll see."

We start slow, half-speed punches and blocks, a kick here and there. He starts to speed it up once we're both more into the groove. It seems like he's showing off. He's almost as good as me. For a minute, I consider letting him beat me, but that won't do either of us any good, so I get in a few good blocks and one quick swing of my leg as he's coming at me. He topples over, knees to dirt. He's smiling.

"Shit, Cate, I thought I had you."

"Try again in a few weeks," I say, helping him up. He takes my hand. While he's dusting himself off, I take a peek at Sam and Mel to see how they're doing. Sam is holding her own, with Calvin's coaching, while Mel is clearly getting frustrated. Is she frustrated that Calvin is paying so much attention to Sam, or that her own abilities are lacking?

Calvin nods in approval and steps away, back to the rest of the group.

"Your girlfriend is going down," Marco says, tapping my arm. "Melody's not about to be one-upped by an unskilled newbie."

"Says the black belt who got knocked down in two minutes."

"Well played. I'm pretty sure I wouldn't qualify anymore."

"That's what happens when you sit on your ass for months."

"I know, Cate. I'm here, aren't I?"

"Yeah, you are. And I'm really glad you're back."

"Me too." He rubs his shoulder and cranks his neck to the side. "But it'll take some getting used to. I feel a hundred years old."

Behind me, the sounds of Mel and Sam's sparring change. Mel grunts and Sam yelps.

"Hey!" says Sam. "Ease up, Mel! I'm not as good as you!"

I turn around, and it looks like my sister is really going after Sam. Sam doesn't have time to block all of Mel's hits, which she's delivering full speed, with no restraint. She lands a punch on Sam's arm that makes her stumble. Sam jumps back and shouts again, swinging her wooden spoon, hitting air. Mel shoves her with one hand.

"What the hell?" I shout, running over and jumping between them. "Mel, knock it off!"

Mel backs off only when Sam is behind me. Calvin is on his way over, too, his expression flummoxed. "What's happening, ladies?"

"She went all Chuck Norris on me!" cries Sam.

"Maybe you just suck!" says Mel.

"It's my second day!"

Calvin steps up next to me, putting another body between them. "Okay, take a walk, Mel. Sam, pair up with Marco."

Mel glares at Sam, me, and then Calvin, before stomping out of the rec yard. I go after her, but she's moving fast. I don't catch up until after we're out the back door and down the steep stairs.

"Okay what's your problem?" I ask.

"We were sparring, Cate. How will she get better if everyone babies her?"

"Baby her? She's brand new. And you've been weird since she got here. I don't get it; you used to like her."

"You mean when I thought she was just your friend? Before I found out you've basically been lying to me since, since...I don't even know when?"

That's absurd. "I haven't been lying to you! I'm not obligated to tell you everything about me!"

"Why not? I told you about the prank I pulled that put Mike Miller in the hospital. I told you about the time I almost got arrested. How long have you been keeping this from me—years?" Her expression is hurt, resentful. "I've told you every dark, shameful thing about me, and you've been hiding this huge thing for so long."

"This isn't some dark or shameful thing, though, Mel. This is who I am."

"Since when?"

Rude. So blatantly, unapologetically rude. I bite my lip. My nostrils flare. I have a sudden, strong urge to shove her. I take a deep breath and press my hands together behind me.

"Since—I don't know—always? I learned there was a word for it when I was, like, thirteen, fourteen? My first kiss was with a girl."

Mel looks like she's solving a complex math problem in her head. "But what about Joaquin?" She shouts it as if she found the right answer. "I've seen you two flirting since we met him. What about that?"

So she *has* noticed. My ears burn. "Yeah, I mean, it's a small island. He's cute, hormones exist, and him and Marco are the only living humans who are close to my age."

"So, what, you just switch?"

"It's not 'switching,' Mel!"

I feel the anger bubbling up again. I don't know where it's coming from. Indignation, maybe, or pent-up stress. Whatever it is, I want her to know.

"I don't go from straight to gay and back again—that's my goddamn point! Bisexual means whatever the hell I want it to mean. I might have crushes on, or relationships with, any number of people in my life, regardless of what's in their pants! At least I didn't jump on the first guy who came along after the apocalypse!"

I don't know why I said that. It was mean, and Calvin is amazing. I think I said it just to hurt her. And judging by the way her face falls, it worked. Mel chews her cheek, and I can see her eyes doing the wobbly thing eyes do just before someone cries. In an instant, I'm not angry anymore.

"Mel, I'm sorry," I say, putting my hands out in surrender. "That was a mean thing to say. You know I love Calvin. And I know it's a lot to take in. But it doesn't change anything about me, you know. I'm still your sister. I'm still me."

Mel waits a good long minute before saying anything else to me. "But you could have told me anytime, any of those nights we used to stay up talking at home, before the end and after. The winter we spent in the brick house and drank all that wine, we told each other a lot of stuff. And *this*, you hid?"

"It never seemed like the right time. I wasn't intentionally keeping it from you, but it felt like too big a thing to just drop."

"Yeah, and it was."

She's deliberately avoiding eye contact, and the realization comes crashing over me that Mel found out about me—about Sam and me—the day the plane landed. She saw us kiss, and that was how she found out. Damn it.

"I know you think I was keeping it from you. But I was keeping it from everybody. I didn't know how to say it out loud. I was scared."

"Scared of what? Of me? Your mom? My dad? Seriously, Cate?"

"Well, your dad found out by accident a few years ago," I admit. "But he kept my secret. He told me there would be a day when I would be ready to come out to you and my mom. He said it had to be my choice, and whenever it was, he would be there."

"And your choice was *never*?"

"Do you remember the times you said something was 'so gay' when you meant it was bad or wrong or ridiculous? Or the times my mom would wrinkle her nose at a gay couple kissing on TV or in the street?"

Mel looks at me again, right into my eyes, as though she's not sure what I'm getting at.

I go on. "Do you remember that time at the mall, about three years ago, when the person behind the register at Macy's was wearing makeup and a flowered top, and they had short hair and a beard? Do you remember what you said?"

"No, why would I?"

"You wouldn't because it wouldn't have been significant to you. But I do because it was to me. You said they were dressing like a woman for attention, and that they could be gay without being in your face about it. You made all kinds of assumptions about someone you didn't even know."

She shakes her head, backs away a step or two as if she can physically remove herself from the memory. "I did not."

"You did."

"But you know I'm not against people being gay, Cate. I have gay friends."

"Having gay friends doesn't mean you understand. You might not be an outright bigot—I know you're not—but you've got some internalized biases."

"Like you don't?"

"Of course I do. Everybody does. But imagine hearing it from all over, from basically everyone you love, and then tell me how you could ever feel okay telling your family that you're one of the people they've made fun of or cringed at. I didn't even want to admit it to myself until I met a bunch of other people like me in high school. And even then, I called myself a straight ally because one of my gay friends said bisexual wasn't a real thing, which felt like he was saying I wasn't real. It comes from all sides, and it's exhausting."

Her face softens. "I'm sorry, Cate. I shouldn't have jumped on you about it. It caught me off guard. You're right; I don't understand. But you have to know that I love you. I'll try my best to do better, okay?"

I smile. "Okay. I love you too."

"Can I hug you?" she asks, taking a step toward me, lifting her arms a few inches.

"Yeah."

She sweeps me up into a deep hug, and at that moment, I can't remember the last time we hugged.

"I'm sorry I didn't tell you. I should have trusted you." I say this into her hair, where she smells of the sweat from training, the mist that hangs over the island most days, and faintly of her babies. I didn't realize how much I missed my sister.

"You're right," says Mel, breaking the hug slowly and watching me with a crooked little smile on her face. She takes her glasses off, cleans them with her breath and the bottom of her shirt. "But, Cate, I have to say something else. And I think you'll be angry, which is okay, but I need to say it."

I'm sure the smile I try for comes off weird and nervous. "You sound like such a mom."

"I think Sam is wrong for you," she says so fast all her words run together. "I heard you two fighting before, I think we all did, and it sounded bad."

"You and Calvin never fight?"

"We fight. But we make up the same day. And when I have a problem, even if he doesn't get it, he doesn't judge me or try to make me feel bad."

"What's that supposed to mean?"

"I was up with the babies a few nights ago, too, and I heard you in your cell. It sounded like you had a panic attack, and then I heard Sam cursing you out. That's not okay."

"She just doesn't understand, is all. I feel like you're putting me in a position where I need to defend my girlfriend to you."

"You shouldn't feel that way; that's sort of my point. I love you, and I don't want someone treating you badly."

"This isn't about Sam," I snap. It surprises me as much as it seems to surprise her. "You're still upset about before, and you're making it into something it's not. I already made up with Sam. She apologized. We're good now."

"Are you? Because I see the way she pouts whenever you talk to Marco. She's possessive. And I know you'd be training every day if it wasn't for her. You love training. And what's more, she isn't making any effort to understand how you've changed these last two years. And you have changed, Cate. You're way more sure of yourself, or you were. But the minute Sam came around, you went back to the old, self-conscious Cate."

"And Calvin has never said something hurtful or misunderstood you? Please. I've known him as long as you have. You're mad because I'm with a girl, or because I don't depend on you anymore. How do you think I felt when you and Cal got together? I had no one, *no one*, for months and months, while you fell in love and made a family. I was alone until now."

"You had us," Mel argues. "And Nana Mae. And Calvin has always loved you. He trained you, made you a better fighter, and took the time to—"

"So I wouldn't be a burden!" I shout. "Which, by the way, is how I feel all the time anyway. Except with Sam. She needs me. Even when we finally found Marco again, I was the only one without a person. Everyone had someone, and Marco had everyone. I finally have somebody of my own, who is only mine and I'm only hers, and you think there's something wrong with that?"

"Cate, that's not what I'm saying. She's treating you like crap, making you feel less than—"

"The only person making me feel less than," I say, putting my hand up, "is you."

I walk off, not toward the rec yard or anywhere in particular. I don't look back, and Mel doesn't come after me. I don't think I want her to. She had no right, no damn right, telling me Sam isn't good for me, not even ten seconds after she was such an asshole about my being with a girl in the first place. Nope. I reject her assumptions and her armchair assessments of my relationship. Sam and I have bumps in the road, but we're rediscovering each other, like Ana said. Mel doesn't know what the hell she's talking about. Sam and I are fine.

Fourteen: Family

1 year, 4 and a half months ago

I wasn't sleeping. My mind was wandering back to before, to the sisters, Bill, the church. My brain was doing what it wanted because the rest of me was too tired to do anything at all. That was most likely why I heard Sylvia singing to Nick in a voice barely above a whisper.

We were camped out in another abandoned house, one of the few zombie-free places we'd come across in recent days. It was around two weeks after we found Sylvia, Henry, and their kids. Our progress slowed measurably with the presence of the kids. Their family seemed to keep to themselves mostly, and I didn't know about Tanya, Amy, and the guys, but I was fine with that. This was a group of convenience and mutual protection.

Sylvia's voice was pretty in the still, dark house. Soothing. Her old-time starlet resemblance didn't stop at the face. She alternated between humming and singing, rocking Nate's skinny body in her arms. There was clearly something wrong with the kid; he was pale and always had dark circles under his eyes, and his parents were constantly carrying him. But none of us— none of my people— had tried to find out what it was. It really wasn't our business.

Nate started to make noises in his sleep, or I thought he was sleeping. But when I glanced over at him and Sylvia, he was sitting up and panting.

"Mommy," he moaned, clutching at his chest.

Sylvia hugged him close. She hummed some more, sang about animals in the forest. She encouraged Nate to sing along. When he stopped crying, Sylvia stopped singing.

"Nate, baby?"

He didn't answer. She loosened her hold on him, and he fell from her chest to her lap, limp.

"Nathan? Henry!"

Henry woke up, crawled straight to Sylvia, and cupped Nate's head while she moved out from under him. Henry laid his son flat and massaged his chest. "Hey, buddy, can you hear me?"

No answer.

"Maybe we should ask Amy; she's a doctor," Sylvia whispered, moving to crawl toward Amy and Tanya, who were sound asleep.

"I doubt she would know what to do, Syl. Look, he's coming out of it."

Nate's eyes fluttered open and then shut again. His head lolled to the side.

"Henry?"

Henry stroked her back with the hand not touching Nate. "Shh, Syl. The doctors said he could live a relatively normal life with this condition."

"That was with medication, Henry!"

"Mommy?" Nick climbed out of his and Adrienne's sleeping bag and sat next to his parents. He put his small hand on Nate's chest and the other on his own. After a moment of concentration, he said, "Is it gonna be like last time?"

"I don't know," said Sylvia, stroking Nick's and Nate's heads simultaneously.

"We can take him to the hospital again," Nick suggested.

Sylvia's face contorted, but only for a moment. "Well, there aren't, I mean..."

"Nate can't go to the hospital, son," said Henry. "The hospital is closed."

"Nate, Nate, wake up, baby," Sylvia whispered, bending to kiss Nate's forehead. "Please."

I hadn't intended to involve myself, in fact until the moment I sat up, I'd been doing my damndest to feign sleep. But there I was, walking toward them. "Are you guys okay?"

Henry looked at Nate and then at me. "He has a birth defect. His heart doesn't work quite right. We were in the middle of figuring out treatment before."

"Want me to get Amy?"

"I don't know what she could do," Henry answered.

He didn't say no, so I crouched next to Tanya and tapped her arm lightly until she woke up. I knew not to wake Amy. The only time I had tried, I scared her so badly she'd cried in Tanya's arms for almost an hour.

"Tanya?" I whispered as she opened her eyes. "Can you wake up Amy? Something's going on with Nate's heart."

Tanya nodded, still half asleep, and rolled over to brush her fingertips along Amy's shoulder and back.

"Amy, honey. Amy. Wake up. The little boy—they need you."

Amy woke up surprisingly quickly. All those years of medical training, having to be alert at a moment's notice, had apparently paid off. "I'm up," she said.

She stood and tiptoed around Jax and Toby to where Nate's family was still sitting. Duchess followed silently, and when Amy stopped, she lay on the ground next to her.

Henry, still massaging Nate's chest, nodded a hello and kept his eyes on her as she sat down. "It's his heart," Henry explained. "Congenital defect. It seems like it's getting worse."

Amy put her hand on Henry's. "May I?" He moved his hand.

First, she felt the pulse in Nate's neck, then she bent down and put her ear to his chest. "Remind me to find a stethoscope," she whispered to me before going totally still and silent to listen to the boy's malfunctioning heart.

After a moment, she sat back up and sighed. "Without the right kind of equipment, there's no way for me to know exactly what's happening in there. But I think blood thinners might be a good first step. Has he ever taken them?"

"He was about to start warfarin, right before." Sylvia's face wrinkled like she was about to cry. "We never got to pick up the prescription. Would that have made him better?"

"I can't say for sure," Amy said, putting a hand on Sylvia's forearm to calm her. "But the good news is, aspirin can be substituted for warfarin sometimes. It's not quite the same, but for our purposes, it may be sufficient. I even happen to have some.

She walked off and riffled through her bag. When she returned, she was holding a small baggie with pills of various sizes, shapes, and colors. She took out one and broke it in half. One half, she put back in the bag, the other, she gave to Sylvia. "Give this to him when he wakes up, with a little food. He's okay right now, these episodes aren't fatal, just terribly frightening. We'll all keep an eye on him, okay?"

Henry and Sylvia nodded.

"It's good that you're carrying him; don't stop. He can't exercise too much, and even less so while he's on blood thinners. The risks that come from a fall are worse for Nate than other children."

At the sound of his name, Nate's face moved, and his eyes opened.

"Daddy," he murmured when he saw his father's face above his. He sat up weakly.

"Hey, kiddo," whispered Henry, smoothing Nate's hair and letting his hand linger on his son's cheek. "We were worried about you."

"I'm sorry, daddy." Nate crawled from the hard linoleum floor into his dad's lap.

"Don't be sorry," Henry whispered into his son's hair, taking a long inhale. "No need to be sorry."

"Nate, how do you feel?" asked Amy.

"My chest hurts."

"Do you feel dizzy? Can you breathe okay?"

Nate thought about it for a second. "I couldn't breathe good before. But I can now. And I'm not dizzy." He rubbed his eyes. "I'm tired."

"And you can go to sleep soon, my darling," whispered Sylvia. "Right after you eat this." She held out half a granola bar.

When he finished eating, his mom held out the half aspirin. "Now, take this little pill."

"I don't want to." Nate tucked his lips between his teeth to emphasize exactly how much he was not down with taking a pill.

"It will make you feel better, baby, please."

"No! It'll be like last time. Doctors and hospitals and yucky stuff."

"Hey, Nate?" I said, crawling closer to him, "I hate pills too. When I was little, I got sick, and I had to take the yuckiest pill ever, for weeks."

Nate's gaze shifted from the evil half aspirin to me. "You did?"

"Yep. My mom let me take it with juice, and it still tasted awful. But this one doesn't taste half as bad. This is aspirin. I've taken this one, too, and know what? It'll be done in a second, and it's probably going to make you feel a lot better."

Nate deliberated in that little-kid way, solemn and appraising, mouth closed tight. "Okay. But can you take one too?"

"Sure," I said with a big, convincing smile. "Doctor Amy will give me one too. Doctor?" I held my hand out. Amy placed the other half of the aspirin into my palm. "Ready?" I held it to my mouth.

Nate nodded, taking his pill out of his mom's hand and putting it to his lips. "Count to three?"

"Okay. One, two...three." I clapped my hand over my open mouth and made a show of swallowing.

Nate took his pill, too, like a little champ. "That wasn't so bad," he concluded.

"You're a brave kid," I answered, ruffling his hair. "Ready for bed?"

Nate yawned right as I was asking. He curled up into his dad's chest and closed his eyes.

Henry moved as slowly as he could, scooping up his son and laying him in the shared sleeping bag with his siblings. "Thank you," he mouthed to Amy and me.

We shook our heads. No problem. I passed the half aspirin back to Amy, who stashed it with her other pills.

"We'll need to find more aspirin if it turns out to help him," I whispered as we made our way back to our respective spots.

"I'm afraid it might not be easy to find, but we'll keep trying. Thank you for your help, Marco. You were pretty brilliant with him."

I shrugged. "I was around a lot of little kids in some of my foster homes. I guess I learned how to talk to them."

Amy offered a tired smile. "Well, now that our family is three kids bigger, it's a talent I can see you using a lot."

She slid into her sleeping bag with Tanya, who rolled over in her sleep to put an arm around Amy.

I lay on my bed roll made of two blankets folded together. (Jax, Toby, and I were still in search of our own sleeping bags.) The floor or ground where we camped never ended up being comfortable, but that wasn't what was keeping me up. Amy had called us a family. Was I the only one who'd been avoiding getting to know these new people? Before I could delve deeper into that rabbit hole of self-reflection, my exhausted body finally outsmarted my wired brain.

The light, rhythmic drumming of rain on the roof woke me, but as I sat, I realized I was the last one up. Everyone else was packing, stretching, prepping to leave.

"Hey, good morning." Sylvia saw me getting up off the floor. She walked over and stood next to me until I was fully upright, and then she pulled me into a big squishy mom-hug. "Thank you for your help last night, Marco," she said quietly. "You made such a difference."

"It wasn't anything, Sylvia," I said, gently breaking the hug. "We're a family now, right?" The words and the sentiment didn't feel one hundred percent authentic, but I had to admit, especially after the night before, I was starting to feel a vaguely familial bond with these people.

"So," said Toby as he shouldered his big bag and slipped his wrench into his utility belt. "Onward."

Henry, who was nearest the door, pushed it open. Outside, it was raining hard and heavy. "Oh good," he said. "A torrent."

"There are probably some garbage bags in the kitchen," suggested Amy. "We can use them as ponchos."

Tanya grinned and kissed her cheek. "My genius wife."

"What's a torrent?" asked Adrienne from behind me.

"That'll be your word of the day," Sylvia answered.

"Word of the season, more like," mumbled Jax in front of me.

Sylvia didn't hear him. She continued with her explanation. "It means a lot of water, like a fast river or heavy rainfall."

"How do you spell it?" asked Nick.

"T-O-R-R-E-N-T."

"Here we are," Amy called from the kitchen. She breezed in with a roll of heavy-duty black trash bags and began tearing them off and handing them out.

"Thanks, Amy," I said as she handed me one. I cut a decent head-hole and slipped it over my body and my pack.

When we were all bagged up, including the dog, we stepped out into the downpour.

"I would kill for a hot plate of biscuits and gravy right now," Toby grumbled when he crossed the threshold.

"With a steaming, creamy coffee," added Amy, closing her eyes and almost smiling.

"Some scrambled eggs and cheese," Tanya said.

"You guys," I grumbled, "you're making my stomach hurt. Knock it off."

"Honey toast, hash browns..."

"Tanya, come on."

"Pancakes!" cried Nate, who had just a shade more color in his face.

"Oh yeah?" I asked. "Do you want to know what my favorite thing is to put on pancakes?"

"What?" Nate asked, slipping his arms into his coat.

"Peanut butter."

"Ew!" cried Nate and Adrienne in unison.

Nick licked his lips. "And jelly?"

"Never tried PB&J pancakes before," I admitted. "Have you?"

Nick shook his head.

"Maybe one day we will," I said. I didn't know if I believed it; I mostly didn't. But you never knew.

"At Alcatraz?" asked Nate.

"Nate?" called Sylvia as we all exited the house into the cold. "Do you want mommy to carry you?"

"No." He peered up at me. "Can you carry me, Marco?"

I felt my face stretch into a wide smile. "Sure." I crouched low. "You want a piggyback ride?"

"Yeah!"

We walked for hours, talking mainly about food, which sucked. Gave up trying not to listen and instead let myself fantasize about one of my favorite dishes. Macaroni and cheese, a simple but exquisite meal, mixed with peas. My mom called it mac n' peas. She started to make it more and more after my dad lost his job. Back then, I'd been ecstatic to eat boxed noodles and canned peas in front of the TV. I hadn't heard my parents arguing about money, about the drugs they started to deal. I had just been so damn happy to eat my favorite food.

Late into the afternoon, after I had carried Nate for a while, his mom took over. But after the long night she'd had staying up with him, and with the rain pounding ceaselessly, she got tired fast. Before Henry reached out to take him, Toby offered.

Henry's relief was clear. "Thanks, Toby."

"Takes a village, right? Come on, kiddo."

Nate was thrilled to be so high up. Toby towered over all of us by a good head and a half. Nate put his little hands out to tap the wet signs we walked by, and as the city gave way to more forest, he brushed the highest branches he could with his fingertips. Toby, whether consciously or unconsciously, stepped off the road so Nate could touch more trees. Nate picked a leaf off the very end of a branch, one of the last few brittle hangers-on from fall, and crunched it in his hands, sprinkling the powder like fairy dust as Toby walked on.

At the front of the group, Amy came to an abrupt stop. "Did you hear that?"

We all stood still and listened. Over the rain, I thought I heard something, but it sounded far away.

"I hear something," said Tanya. "A person?"

I listened harder, or imagined myself listening harder. There was a noise, and it definitely didn't sound like an animal. As we walked toward it, it got clearer.

"Help!"

Fifteen: Sick

It's pretty easy to avoid Mel for the next few days; our schedules usually don't line up anyway. On the third day, since Sam and I agreed to skip training, we busy ourselves with checking chores off David's master list. It's sunny and warm, so we stick with outdoor errands as much as we can.

We start the morning repairing a broken railing with Toby. I would never have guessed his other hand was his dominant one, the way he swings his hammer with such confidence. He doesn't seem upset with me either. He jokes with us as we hold the wood steady for him. And even though Marco was right, that it isn't about me or my feelings, I am grateful things feel easy with Toby again.

After the railing, we help Murray clean the boat. It's tedious work, but since we're all taking care of different parts, it gives me time to think about what Mel said and what Ana and I talked about. I should have told Mel what Ana said, about fighting for love, not about the way they'd effectively sentenced a guy to die. I still can't believe Marco allowed that to happen. Ana clearly doesn't blame him, but how can she not? If you're in charge and you let the group decide to exile a guy, isn't it sort of on you? Maybe I'm missing something. I only have one account of the way it went down. Perhaps I should ask Marco.

By the time we're done with the ferry, it's the hottest part of the day and Sam and I are both sweaty, so we pick an easy chore next. Mel and the kids usually start with meal prep by late afternoon, so the garden is empty, and we can weed it in peace until dinner.

I catch Mel watching me with a worried face every so often, and even though Sam says not to let it bug me, it does. I have a suspicion Mel's worry about Sam and me is more about her than it is about us.

As Tanya and I wash the dishes after dinner, Mel walks up acting all casual and starts to dry the cups, which it isn't her turn to do, and we don't need any help. I suppress a groan, but the eyeroll cannot be contained.

Tanya glances sideways at me, and then at Mel, and cocks an eyebrow. "What's happening here?"

"Nothing," I say.

"Don't know what you mean," says Mel at the same time.

"You're both very convincing." Tanya puts another cup on the clean pile. "Am I going to have to ask again?"

Mel picks up the cup and dries it way too thoroughly, spinning it around in her towel-covered hand about thirty times. "Cate and I had a hard conversation, that's all."

Spin, spin, spin.

"Melody, that one's dry," says Tanya.

"Hard conversation?" I snort. "There's a whole new way of saying you're a homophobic ass."

"Oh, name calling? I told you, Cate, it's nothing to do with that!" Mel slams the aluminum cup down so hard into the other dry ones it sounds like she may have dented some. "I know how to compartmentalize."

"You sure?" It comes off like I'm taunting her. Maybe I am. Hell with it.

"I didn't anticipate dinner and a show." Tanya regards both of us in turn, a hint of a smile playing around her eyes. "Continue."

"Mel didn't know, about me and Sam. About me."

"I think that was a surprise to us all," says Tanya.

Mel dries the next cup in silence, except for some really dramatic sighs.

"Well, fine, maybe. But that gives her no right to tell me my relationship isn't good." Now it feels like I'm telling on Mel, the way I used to when we were kids. But she messed up, and Tanya asked, and you shouldn't be an asshole if you don't want people talking about it later.

"You said what?" Tanya swivels her head around to look at Mel.

"I didn't say that," Mel protests.

"You said exactly that! You said Sam isn't good for me."

"Well, fine. I stand by it. You two have been arguing, and I've seen her pulling you farther away from Marco and everybody else, and I told you, I heard the way she reacted when you panicked the other night. That's not normal; that's not good!"

"It was fine. Nobody appreciates being woken up in the middle of the night!"

Tanya puts herself between us. "While I don't know all of the details...and I don't want to," she adds when I open my mouth. "It sounds to me like there are two separate arguments happening here. One—Melody, check your homophobia."

"I'm not a homophobe!" Mel shouts.

"If Cate, who is...bisexual...?"

I stare at the cup in my hands. "Yeah."

"If Cate, who is bisexual, regards any of your behaviors as homophobic, then you absolutely need to look within and figure out why. You may not mean to come across that way, but if you are, then you are. Your privilege just makes it hard for you to see."

"Privilege?" Mel repeats.

"I really miss being able to tell people to Google shit. Marco!" Tanya waves Marco over. "Will you please talk to Melody about her privilege?"

"Seriously?" asks Mel.

Tanya shushes her. Marco starts talking, even though Mel refuses to make eye contact with him.

"Okay, bear with me. I'm still learning. But, like, some people will experience life with a certain amount of privilege. Not that we have no problems, but there's some stuff we'll never have to deal with. You know? Like, I never got catcalled before the end. Never really even thought about it until I saw it happen to my foster mom. But I hear it can be really violating and scary for a feminine person. Right?"

Mel huffs as loudly as she can but gives one stiff nod.

"Or you—nobody would get on your case for loving a man, right? Because hetero relationships are considered the norm by most people. But some people might give you grief for loving Calvin because you're white and he's Black. Not in this group, I mean, but you know. The potential exists. Same with Cate and Sam, or Amy and Tanya. Out there, and before, they probably got some epic shit for being a two-girl couple."

"Fact," Tanya interjects. "Amy lost a job once when they found out she was married to a woman."

"I've been called a lot of names," Marco continues, "but none of them ever had to do with my gender or my skin color. And you've probably dealt with harassment because you're a woman, but I bet you've never been bullied for being straight or white."

"Privilege," Tanya reiterates.

Mel keeps drying the same cup. "Makes sense," she mumbles.

"Good. Okay. Thank you for your help, Marco. Go away now. Cate, I don't know what's up with you and Sam, nor do I want to. It's not my business. But your sister loves you, misguided though she may be, and I doubt very much whatever issues she has would skew her opinions that much. I may be wrong. But judging by the strength of her relationship with Calvin, I'd say she has a good eye for what's healthy love and what isn't."

"You didn't meet her other boyfriends," I mumble.

"Shh!" Tanya snaps. "But if that's the case, then she has an even better perspective. I'm not saying your sister is right. But she has known and loved you longer than anyone here, except maybe Bill. Hey, Bill."

As she says Bill's name, he and Adrienne walk up, each holding a baby.

"Hello, family," Bill says, smiling wide, clearly with no idea what he's walked into. "How are we?" The look he gives Mel says maybe he did know something.

"I tried to apologize," Mel says, throwing the towel over her shoulder with a huff.

"The words 'I'm sorry' literally never left your mouth," I say.

Bill eyes both of us and then Tanya.

"I tried with these two, Bill." Tanya glares at us. "Before the end, I would have charged good money for that kind of mediation. In fact, you know what? Melody, take over my dish duty."

Mel stares aghast at the pile of dirty dishes still to be done. "What? Why? I cooked."

Tanya shoves the washcloth into Mel's hands and steps back. "Because, emotional labor is still labor, and it's never free. And Cate, you're collecting eggs for me tomorrow. My wife and I are sleeping in. Now, you two are fighting about nothing. You love each other. Make up already. It's a small island, and no one is interested in taking sides." With that, Tanya saunters off and joins Amy on the grass. She puts her arm around Amy's waist, and they kiss.

Behind them, Sam and Marco wave at me, neither noticing the other. I wave back to both at once.

"So we're still arguing, huh?" Bill asks. When neither of us answers or looks at the other, he kneels in front of Adrienne. "Adrienne, honey, how about you let Mel hold Maebelle and you go find the boys?"

Adrienne glances around as if she knows she's being dismissed from something potentially entertaining. But she obliges. She gives the baby, and then Bill, each a kiss on the cheek before she runs in the other direction.

"She thinks you hung the moon, Bill," says Mel, cuddling up close to Baby Maebelle. "Even Francis is warming up to you."

"These kids have been through more than any child should. And look at them. They run, play; they have this hunger to learn and grow. They're finding a way to thrive." He hands me Baby Andrew, petting his tiny head as I settle him into my arms. "Can't be too angry when you're holding a baby, am I right?" he asks with his signature eye-crinkling Bill smile.

"That beard's getting out of control," I say. I know I'm deflecting. I don't want to talk about this anymore.

"I rather like the beard," says Bill, stroking it into more of a shape. "Listen, I know you two aren't getting on right now. And that's okay, okay? Fights happen. But remember we love each other, and sometimes love means—oh!" Bill doubles over suddenly, clutching at his midriff.

"Bill?" Mel and I both say in unison.

Bill is panting. His face is pale. Sweat starts to show on his forehead. "I don't...know," he says.

"Do we need to get Amy?" I ask.

"Obviously, Cate," cries Mel. "Amy!"

I shout too, moving as fast as I dare with little Andrew still in my arms. "Amy!"

"What's going on, girls?" she asks, already tying up her hair as she jogs out to meet us.

"Bill—I don't know," Mel says.

"He's over here. Something's happening to him," I finish for her.

"I'll take Andrew," says Tanya. "Calvin! Come take your daughter. There's something wrong."

Calvin comes to us and takes Maebelle. "Can I help?"

"Actually, you might want to give her back to Melody. We may need your help lifting Bill," answers Amy.

By the time we get back to Bill, he's sitting on the ground, knees drawn partway up to his chest, eyes squeezed shut. Marco is suddenly at our side, coming from I don't know where. Sam is there too, then Ana, Murray, David, the brothers, the kids. Everyone crowds around while Amy tries to assess Bill's condition. Even the dogs seem to know something is wrong.

"Back up!" cries Mel.

Marco spreads his arms out and ushers everyone back several feet.

"Bill?" Adrienne slips under Marco's arms and kneels beside Bill and Amy. "What's wrong with Bill, is he dying too?" She starts to cry and grab at Bill's arms.

"Hey, kiddo, no, no," Bill whispers to Adrienne. He strokes her hair. "I'm okay. Promise." His face betrays the lie.

"Come here, Adrienne," says Mel, holding out her free hand, "Amy will take care of Bill."

"Amy, what do we do?" asks Marco.

"Bill, can you walk?" Amy asks.

Bill slowly gets his legs under him and nods as Calvin pulls him up and uses his shoulder to stabilize Bill's hunched frame. "Thanks, Calvin," he whispers.

The group parts as Calvin, Bill, and Amy inch toward the cell house where he can lie down. Mel, Marco, Sam, and I follow, and Tanya instructs everyone else to hang back. "We don't need any extra bodies getting in the way."

Once Bill is situated on a first-floor bed, lying flat on his back, Amy starts poking and feeling his abdomen. "Does it hurt when I do this?"

He cries out and swats her hand away. I'm pretty sure it's instinct rather than Bill being difficult.

"I'm sorry, Bill," Amy says, putting her hand on the back of his. "I need to palpate your abdomen."

"Sorry," says Bill. "I know."

"Where, exactly, does it hurt?"

Bill gestures toward his side and lifts one hip a little bit. "My back, mostly, and my...ah...my side."

"Have you felt it for long?"

"No. Oh! Just hit me."

"Pain radiating outward, maybe? Downward?"

"Yes," he pants.

"What's going on?" Marco demands.

"Is he okay?" Mel asks.

"Of course he isn't! Look at him!" I snap, throwing a hand out toward Bill. "He practically collapsed outside!"

"That's not what I mean, Cate!"

"Enough!" Amy shocks us into silence. "Everyone, come out here." She ushers all of us out of Bill's temporary cell and continues in hushed tones, "Bill should be fine. I think I know what it is, and it's not life-threatening. Just very painful. Unfortunately, to diagnose him for sure, and possibly to treat him, we'll need to get him to a hospital."

"How?" asks Sam.

"No way," says Mel. "They'll all be overrun. Especially in a big city."

"Well, not necessarily," Calvin replies. "Unless someone left a door open or something, the undead inside should be long gone by now. They rot pretty fast."

Mel makes a face.

"Except for Abnormals," I counter.

"And living people," Mel adds.

Amy shrugs one shoulder, looks at Marco. "We know of a place, I think."

"We ducked in there last year," says Marco. "The people we found had a good setup. They traded with us. They're friendly." He says the last part to Calvin, who obviously needs convincing.

"If they're still there, you mean," Calvin says, crossing his arms.

Marco tucks his chin. "Yeah."

"We don't have many options," Amy whispers. "Bill is in a lot of pain, and if we have a chance to alleviate it, we absolutely should."

Calvin doesn't hesitate long. "Of course we should."

"So, tomorrow, then," Marco says. "Early."

"I think Bill could use some sleep now," says Amy. "Or at the very least, some quiet rest. His vitals are stable from what I can tell. I'll stay down here with him. So will Tanya. We'll call for you if anything changes, promise. Tomorrow will be a long day. We all need to rest."

"Try to sleep, Uncle Bill," I say and give him a kiss on the forehead. He's so warm, my God. I smile to try to hide my deep worry, but my eyes are already prickly. We can't lose someone else, not Bill. I squeeze Sam's hand as we exit the cell.

"We'll figure this out," says Mel, placing a hand on his face.

She comes out right after me. We don't acknowledge each other, but Calvin gives me a look, with his eyebrows up in his hairline, as though he's asking if we're serious with this argument. And I'm starting to wonder myself. I already miss my sister. But not enough to be the first to say something. I don't have anything to apologize for.

"Okay," says Calvin as soon as we're outside where everyone has been waiting. "According to Amy, Bill is probably going to be okay. But we have to get him to a hospital to diagnose him."

"So the city, then," says Joaquin.

"Correct. Amy and Marco mentioned a hospital that they came across, with friendly people inside."

"Yeah, that could work," says Jax.

"They were cool," says Toby.

"Where are David and Tanya?" I ask.

"With the kids," says Ana. "I figured they didn't need to be out here for all this."

"Thank you," says Mel. She looks tired.

"We'll need a few extra people on this trip," says Calvin. "Murray and Toby, can you handle carrying Bill? I'm not sure he's in any condition to walk on his own, so it'll be about a buck fifty, dead weight."

Toby and Murray both nod. I wish Calvin had chosen a different phrase. Maybe it's superstition, but I don't like hearing Bill being called dead anything.

"Toby? Are you sure?" Mel asks Calvin. "He hasn't been back to the mainland since we left."

"He and Murray are the strongest people we've got."

"I've got him, Melody," says Toby, giving her a reassuring smile.

"And Ana, Marco, and I can take up defense," says Joaquin.

"I'm not staying behind," I object. "You have to be kidding."

"No, of course not," says Calvin. "You and me are with Amy."

"What about me?" asks Sam.

"You're not ready." I turn to Calvin. "How about Tanya?"

"Cate, I can do this," says Sam. "You survived the whole way down with fewer people and less training. I'm coming."

I wave it off. "You've trained a total of three times, Sam. Tanya trains three times a week."

"Which is why Tanya and Jax should both stay behind," says Marco. He watches me, his face apologetic. "We need capable defense here in case we're gone for too long."

"I'm going!" Sam reiterates, scowling at Calvin and me. "Bill is just as much my family as he is yours, and in fact, he's basically the only family I have left. How am I ever supposed to get better if I never try?"

Calvin crosses his arms and sort of appraises all of us. "So it'll be Sam, Cate, and I protecting Amy. Amy can basically handle herself, but she's going to have her medical stuff, and she'll be keeping an eye on Bill, so she'll need us on her six."

"Six?" asks Sam.

"He means, Amy will need us to watch her back," I clarify.

"Jax, David, Tanya, and Melody will stay behind with the kids."

"You don't know how long you'll be gone, do you?" asks Mel.

"No, but it shouldn't be more than a day." Calvin takes Mel into his arms, and they just stand there while the discussion comes to a close.

"Ana, you still got your bow?" Joaquin asks.

Ana shakes her head. "Left it in the apartments the night we came here."

"Well, I have my gun. I'll keep to the front. We'll make it work."

"So, meet here, sunrise?" asks Marco.

"Sunrise," says Calvin over Mel's head, which is buried in his chest. "Let's get some rest. Tomorrow will be tough."

With a quick, quiet goodnight, we all wander into our respective cells.

But two hours later, after checking my watch every fifteen minutes or so, I'm still completely awake. I'm worried about Bill, of course. But for some reason, I keep thinking about what Ana told me, about Matt and the way the group threw him out. How could Marco let something like that happen under his leadership? I have to ask him. I hope he's sleeping as poorly as I am tonight.

Sixteen: Fear

1 year, 4 and a half months ago

It was a human voice. They didn't sound far. They sounded frightened though.

"Stay here," I said, starting to jog toward the sound.

"Sure," muttered Tanya, coming after me.

The one voice turned into two, both of them way too loud. I ripped through the trees, trying to find the people they belonged to. I didn't call to them; no reason to attract even more problems.

Then I saw them, their arms full of twigs and branches, and three zombies closing in on them. They both dropped the bulk of their bundles at once and started swinging sticks wildly at the approaching corpses. Thankfully, none of the zombies seemed to be moving faster than usual.

"Help!" the woman shrieked when she saw me.

She was tiny, maybe five feet tall, and he wasn't a whole lot bigger. The way they were brandishing their sticks made me wonder if they had any idea to go for the head. It wouldn't have surprised me if not, even if it had been more than six months since the initial outbreak. Some people were so far up their own asses in denial, it was unreal.

Tanya and I ran up behind the two zombies that weren't facing us. They were on the ground before the other one had time to turn around. All three had milky eyes. No Variant zombies, at least.

The people were still holding their sticks when I finished with the last zombie, and while I wouldn't call their postures defensive, they were keeping their distance.

"Are you okay?" I asked. "Did any of them bite you?"

At this, the woman dropped her stick-holding arm. Her silver-blonde hair was plastered to the side of her face, nearly covering her eyepatch.

"Bite us? Are you joking?"

"I—no?"

"Of course they didn't bite us." She adjusted her hair and her eye patch, and they both started picking up the discarded kindling.

I bent to help her. "It won't burn wet."

"I got it," she said, snatching the one I held out to her. "Thanks."

"It didn't look like you had it a second ago," said Tanya.

"I forgot my knife at camp," the woman mumbled.

"You have a camp?" I heard from behind me. Henry was there, holding Nick's hand. Everyone else was right behind them. The dog was sitting on Amy's feet as though they'd been there a minute. Duchess shook the rainwater off her fur and trotted over to me.

"I, uh..." The woman stood there like a rabbit caught in a trap, staring at us, ready to flee. But when her eyes landed on the kids, her face changed. "We do," she said, glancing at the guy next to her.

"It's this way," he said. "We don't have much; we're trying to keep on the move, but you're welcome to sit by our fire, if we can ever get one going."

"Thank you," said Sylvia.

The guy dipped his head. "I'm Matt. This is Ana."

We took turns introducing ourselves as we followed them.

"Good to meet you all," said Ana.

"Don't think we've encountered a group as big as yours yet," said Matt. "You all know one another?"

"No, we—"

"Shh," said Ana, coming to a stop. "What's that? Does anyone hear that?"

We all stopped moving. Even the kids were silent.

A stick cracked in the distance.

Footsteps echoed from a different direction.

There was a low gurgle somewhere behind us.

"Shit. Are we surrounded?" asked Jax.

"Might be," whispered Tanya, taking out her knife.

We all did the same as several zombies emerged from the trees around us.

"Keep it quiet if we can," I said.

"Kids," whispered Henry, "I want you three to get in the middle of us grown-ups, okay? And don't move."

The three children shuffled between us and held on to one another.

We were in more trouble than we thought, though: there were at least ten of them coming at us from all sides.

I took one out easily, since it was about to topple off its rotten legs anyway. The noise of fighting surrounded me, but I was already busy with a new zombie of my own, another one of those Variant zombies with "people eyes" and cognitive function. I was beginning to hate those. They were way harder to kill, and the fact that they could stare you in the eye as you killed them didn't help. We were fucking grappling, me and the Variant, which incensed me because the only thing we had on zombies was our brains, and now—what—they were starting to learn too? I cocked my weapon hand back, ready to stab one of its unnervingly lively eyes. It deliberately knocked my knife out of my hand as it closed in, so I grabbed for my axe. My hand slipped on the wet handle.

Matt, the new guy, yelped. In my peripheral, I saw him leap to one side.

Then one of the kids screamed bloody murder.

"Nate!" shouted another.

The smart zombie looked toward the sound, which turned out to be its fatal mistake: I axed it in the fucking face and felt a satisfaction a little deeper than the normal zombie-killing feeling. After it went down, I realized there was only one more, apparently a normal one, which Tanya took out easily.

"What's with the screaming?" I asked.

"It got Nate!" Sylvia moaned, her eyes already watery.

"Let me see," said Amy. "Nate, I'm going to roll up your sleeve now. It will probably hurt. Ready?"

Nate squeezed his eyes shut.

Amy pulled off his torn trash bag and rolled up his sleeve as gently and as quickly as she could. When she found the wound, she made a face that she quickly tried to conceal. The veins around the scratch on his arm were already turning. The whole area around the wound was covered in a web of black spreading so fast we could see it moving. The rain, lighter under the canopy of trees, washed away the blood dripping from the wound.

Amy sighed. "It seems like his heart condition is making this thing spread more quickly than it ought to, and the blood thinners are probably exacerbating it. Who has a scarf?"

"I do," said Henry, handing his over with a pained expression.

"Thank you. Someone, please bring me the thickest stick from the pile. We're going to have to amputate, and we need to make a tourniquet."

"Amputate? No!" cried Sylvia, snatching at their hands.

Tanya caught Sylvia's wrist, gently but firmly enough to stop her. "You know what will happen, Sylvia. It's his arm or his life."

Sylvia hesitated, nodded, and Tanya let go.

Amy wrapped the scarf around Nate's arm, and then knotted it around the stick, using the stick as a lever to make the tourniquet as tight as possible.

Nate winced and squirmed.

Amy put a hand on his shoulder. "Nate, you have to be very, very brave for me now, okay? You can cry, but you can't move. Lie down here, please, sweetheart. Good, thank you. I am going to have to take your arm off so you don't get sick. Do you understand?"

Nate's eyes were wide and fearful, but his mouth was flat. He nodded.

"Good, okay. We'll be right here for you, all right? Tanya, get her out of here."

Tanya lifted a sobbing Sylvia to her feet and walked her away.

"Henry, I need you to hold this tight for me. Hands on either end of the stick, don't let it unwind. Hurry, now."

She handed Henry the ends of the stick. His face was a mask of stone as he took it.

"It's gonna be okay, buddy," he told his son.

"Marco," Amy continued, "is your axe sharp?"

"I think so," I answered, taking it out. "But I just used it. How do we clean it?"

"Pour the hand sanitizer on it. That will have to do. Rub it all over, quick. Yes, like that. Good. Now hand it to me."

I handed Amy the clean axe. She positioned Nate's arm and touched the edge of the blade. Her hands were perfectly still.

"Cutting through bone is no easy task," she said, taking a deep breath and scooting closer to Nate and his dad. "But luckily his bones are still small, and the axe is sharp. Nate, close your eyes, I'm going to count to three. One..."

She gripped the handle. Nate buried his face in his dad's lap.

"Two..."

She raised the axe.

In that instant, Nate started to convulse.

Henry looked around helplessly. "Amy?"

Amy waited. When Nate was still, she checked his upper arm, as far as the sleeve would allow. She pulled the collar of his shirt aside. The veins had crawled past the tourniquet and reached his neck. Amy shook her head. "It's moving too fast; I'm sorry."

"What do you mean, you're sorry?" shouted Sylvia, rushing back over. "You said taking his arm off would save him. That's what you said!"

Amy set down the axe. "Henry, Sylvia, I'm sorry. I'm so sorry. There's nothing I can do."

"No," said Henry, clutching his son to his chest, "NO! Amputate, just do it, you have to try!" His hands, still holding the stick, shook violently.

"That won't do any good now. The infection spread so fast. It's too late."

"What do you mean? What do we do now?" asked Henry, tears spilling down his stubbly cheeks.

Amy touched Henry's arm, and with her other hand, she stroked Nate's feverish face. "Now you hold him. Hold your boy." She stood and let Sylvia sit in her place. "It's time to tell him how much you love him, how special he is. Tell him it's okay. Tell him."

"Is Nate gonna die?" asked Nick. His lower lip trembled. Adrienne clutched his hand.

"Hey, kids," said Toby, sounding like he was trying to keep down a lump in his throat. "Let's go over here for a minute, okay?" He wiped his eyes with his knuckles and took Adrienne's little fingers in his. She kept Nick's hand, and Toby led them away.

"What's going to happen to Nate?" asked Nick.

"He's dying," said Adrienne, wiping water from her eyes. "Just like Grandpa. The monsters killed Nate too."

Nate asked for water, sipped what was given to him, and then his head lolled to the side as if even the effort to drink had drained him. He reached up and took his mom's hand with his black-webbed fingers.

"I'm dying, mommy," he said, "right?"

Sylvia stroked his soaking wet face and gripped his hand tighter. "Yes, baby," was all she managed to say. To hide her tears, I supposed, she bent down to kiss his forehead and let her own forehead rest there.

When his mom sat back up, Nate looked at his dad. "Will I...go to heaven?" His voice weakened with each word. His breathing shallow; the veins creeping up his neck and his chin.

Henry nodded once, slowly. Rainwater and tears mingled on his face. "Of course you will, Nathaniel. You are the most amazing boy."

I felt like an intruder watching this all go down. Their family being ripped apart. So I turned and watched the treetops. In the distance, the dark-gray clouds broke abruptly, revealing a huge swath of blue sky. It was unbearably still in the clearing. I could hear Nate's short little breaths, Sylvia's words of comfort.

"We love you so, so much. You're our sweet, beautiful boy. We love you always."

"I love you, son," Henry said.

"Will you...sing me...a song?"

Sylvia started to sing.

Nate was dead before she finished. His breathing slowed and then stopped, and the only sounds left were Sylvia's voice and the rain. She sang the whole song, I assumed, because it went on another minute or so.

After she was done, Henry said he was gone, and Sylvia moaned low and loud and long. Part of me hurt for them, hurt for Nate and the siblings he left behind. A small but significant part of me worried that her cries would bring even more death.

Toby and Jax and the little ones came back. I turned around. Nate's face was peaceful.

For the time being.

"Sylvia," I said, touching her shoulder. She startled. "Sylvia, we have to, um..."

"Go away, Marco."

"Sylvia, honey," said Tanya, "he's right. It's not your little boy anymore. You don't want to be here for the next part."

"I said GO!" shouted Sylvia.

I flinched. If the sobbing hadn't already attracted whatever zombies were nearby, that definitely would.

"The kid is gonna come back, isn't he?" said someone behind me.

"Shut the fuck up, Matt," snapped Tanya, a ferocity in her voice I had never heard before. "You do not speak."

"Unfortunately," murmured Amy to Tanya, not quite loud enough for Sylvia or Henry to hear. "He is right."

"I know, baby. Give them a minute."

"What if we don't have a minute?" I asked.

"I know." Tanya cleared her throat. It sounded like she was trying to keep her voice steady. She put a hand on Henry's shoulder. He didn't react. "Sylvia, Henry. Adrienne and Nick will be needing you now."

"You don't have to be here for this," Amy said, trying to reassure them. "It has to happen, but there's no reason for you to watch."

"I am not leaving my son," said Sylvia.

"I'll do it," said Henry. "Has to be the brain, right? Do we have to wait for him...for him to..."

"Come back?" I guessed. When Henry cringed in lieu of a verbal answer, I shook my head. "No, you don't have to wait."

"Henry," said Amy, crouching next to him. Her hand was already on her knife. "You don't need to be the one to do this. It's nothing a parent should ever have to do."

"It's the only thing I have left!" Henry's face was pure anguish. "It's the only thing I can do for him anymore. I couldn't save him! But I can make sure he doesn't turn into a monster. I can save him from that."

Amy nodded, stood, and left them alone.

Nate's body was still.

Sylvia rocked back and forth.

"Syl," said Henry, "you should check on Nick and Adrienne. I don't want you here for this."

Sylvia's expression changed a couple of times. She shook her head.

"You sure?" Henry tried to make eye contact with his wife.

Sylvia glanced at him, back to Nate. "Yes," she whispered so quietly I almost couldn't hear her from where I stood.

Henry moved some hair away from Nate's face. "My boy..."

All of us turned away. Toby and Jax steered Adrienne and Nick around. Tanya and Amy held hands, so did Nick and Adrienne. Ana and Matt sat on the ground, where they'd been, both crying.

The sound of the blade was barely audible. Sylvia began to moan again, softer than before. Henry appeared out of the corner of my eye. He went to their children, took them into his arms, and none of them moved for a while.

Sylvia cried over her son's body for a long, long time. The rest of us found things to do, to give her privacy in her grief. Or, as much privacy as could be afforded. I brought water to Henry and his surviving kids. Tanya and Amy checked everyone else for wounds. Ana and Matt stayed quiet, letting Amy examine them but otherwise keeping out of the way. Thankfully, no other zombies came around.

When Sylvia finally stood up and left Nate's body where it lay, she strode over to where Ana and Matt were sitting.

"You." She stared into Matt's eyes. "You killed my son."

Seventeen: Choices

I walk half a lap around the island before I find Marco. Chaz is with him. He waves, starts toward me, and changes direction to walk with me.

"Fancy seeing you here," he says with a smile.

"Yeah," I say, unsure of how exactly to bring up the questions I need to ask him. I scratch the dog's ears, trying to calm the sudden rush of nerves.

"Amy said Bill's gonna be okay, Cate. I trust her."

He's misinterpreting my silence for worry. I am worried, but I trust Amy.

"I know. Marco? Can I ask you something? It's not about Bill."

He glances at me. "Of course."

"I was talking to Ana the other day, and she told me something about your time on the road."

"What was it?"

"She told me about Matt."

I can almost feel the emotion rolling off him. "Oh."

"She said you exiled him, basically? Voted to make him leave because he got scared and Nate got scratched?"

I don't mean to sound accusatory. But as I'm saying it, I'm wondering all over again how Marco could allow something so awful to happen.

"It wasn't exactly like that."

I wait for him to continue. We walk a good fifty feet, and I open my mouth to encourage him a few times, but I don't know what to say. When we circle past the door to the rec yard, the dog heads back inside.

"We'd just met them, Matt and Ana." Marco speaks slowly, as though he's considering every word before he releases it. "And we'd only recently decided to go to Alcatraz."

"Wait. What do you mean you'd recently decided?"

He glances sidelong at me, takes a second more before answering.

"I gave up on Alcatraz for a long time. That day at the church, when I saw you and Melody driving away in the truck, I decided there was no way I could make it on my own."

I stop walking. "You saw us driving away?"

He looks at me all the way, and I guess what I'm seeing on his face is what he must have felt when he watched the truck pull away: Pain. Hopelessness. Possibly resentment too, But I may be imagining that part. I hope I am.

"Marco..." I almost apologize, almost reach out to hug him, almost ask why he didn't run after us. Of course, he probably did. That old junker was so loud, we never would have heard him.

"I tried calling you," he says, as if he saw the question flit across my face. "I was out of breath. And then a zombie knocked me over. By the time I got up, there was no way I could have caught up to you."

I try to think back to that day. Did I even check the rearview mirror as we drove off? Or was I too exhausted and consumed with my own grief and fear to bother? Would I have seen him anyway?

"What did you do then, if you didn't go south?"

"I did go south. I wasn't sure I'd ever see you again, but I had no roots holding me in Connell. In fact, I had pretty good reasons to want to get the hell out of there. Besides, winter was on its way."

"I'm so sorry."

"Why? No way you could have known I was that close. You obviously waited hours for someone to show up. It's not your fault I got held up for as long as I did."

"No, but if we'd have waited, like, two seconds longer—"

"You couldn't have known, Cate," he repeats. "And anyway, I'm here now, so who cares?"

I can't stop myself from thinking that if he hadn't met the people he had, or if circumstances hadn't led him to reconsider Alcatraz, he could be anywhere right now. Dead, maybe. And none of us would be here, because regardless of whether he'd ever admit it, and whether or not he likes it, he's what holds all of us together. Or, at least he's what brought all of us together. Brought us here. A fresh wave of gratitude washes over me, and the urge to hug him comes back. This time, I do.

He makes a small noise of surprise when I wrap my arms around him. He didn't expect to stop walking, and I'm also sort of hugging the side of his body. He rights himself and hugs me back.

"I'm glad you decided to come here."

He breaks the hug, and we keep walking, more slowly than before. "Yeah, I guess I am too. Mostly. So, do you still want to know about Matt, or what?"

"Oh, uh. Yeah, so what happened? It sounded like you were about to tell me Ana wasn't giving me the full story."

"No," he says thoughtfully. "Not that she was lying or anything, but she probably remembers it differently. You know how when something really fucked up happens, it messes with your brain, and ten different people can have ten different memories of the thing, all partially right and all partially wrong?"

"I guess."

"It's true. So, I'm sure neither of our memories are perfect. But no one voted to kick Matt out. It wasn't a formal vote. And Ana had the choice to go with him—you know that, right?"

"Yeah. She mentioned not remembering why she chose to go with you."

"Well, I don't know why either, but she did. So that should tell you nobody was voted out or whatever."

"Okay, so all memories are slightly different. I know. Will you tell me yours?"

"I was dealing with a Variant when it happened. I didn't see exactly what happened. We were going to amputate because we thought we could save him. But then Nate started to seize or something. Like, scary shaking and twitching in his dad's arms. It was horrific. He had a heart condition too."

"Yeah, Ana told me about his heart."

"So I guess it made the infection spread way faster than normal somehow, or his medication did it. I don't know. But he died really quick."

"She told me that too. Skip to the exile."

"It wasn't an exile, Cate."

"Okay, whatever. Skip to Matt not coming with you."

"Well, after Nate died, Henry did the thing. That was probably the saddest thing I have ever witnessed. And after a while, Sylvia came up on Matt and said to him point-blank that he had killed her son."

"Oh, shit."

"Yeah. Henry didn't say much. I don't know if he agreed or if he was just in shock. I mean, stabbing your little boy in the brain—I can't even imagine. Tanya was on Sylvia's side; she was pissed. She didn't outright say she agreed, but it was pretty clear in how she dealt with Matt."

"And Amy?"

"Amy tried to reason with Sylvia, said anyone could panic in the moment, whatever. Eventually, Henry did speak up, but all he said was that we needed to get moving. That's where the trouble sort of bloomed because Sylvia said she wasn't going anywhere with the man who killed her son. She wouldn't let up with the 'killed.' Like he murdered Nate with his own hands. I agreed with Amy, and I thought Jax did too, but Toby seemed pretty angry, even though he didn't really talk except to say that panic was no excuse."

"Oh my God. So you'd already invited them to come with—Matt and Ana—and Sylvia basically changed her mind?"

"No. None of us had even discussed Alcatraz with them yet. We'd literally met them a few minutes before the attack. There wasn't time."

"So what was Sylvia on about?"

"I think she probably knew we'd ask them to join us, since we'd just done the same thing with her and her family."

"So you told them they were welcome, and Sylvia wouldn't go, or what?"

Marco breathes one of his hundred-pound sighs.

"No," he says quietly. "That's the thing. I didn't really say anything. I know when we found you again, I was sort of in a leading position, but that came after. I was scared, and I had learned the hard way, a few times, that I wasn't as persuasive or as much of a leader as I thought I was back in Washington. I was arrogant as hell, Cate. I knew some stuff, so I stomped around like I was hot shit. But in the woods that day, I knew it wasn't my choice. I stayed quiet when the others talked about what to do, and when they sent him off. And after, right after, I realized how wrong I was. We basically killed that guy. Everyone who made him stay behind, everyone who was complicit, me included, we were wrong."

He takes a long, shaking breath. "My old foster mom Cindy, the one who died right before I got placed with your aunt and uncle, she told me one time you're not supposed to make big decisions when emotions are high. And we did. He died because we fucked up in a moment of grief."

"But you didn't," I say, trying to comfort him because he looks like he's about to cry.

"Yes, I did. I decided not to speak up. I felt the wrongness of it in my gut, at least I think I did. But I was just a kid, a know-nothing kid, or that's how it felt at the time. Hell, I still feel like that a lot. I'm only nineteen for Christ's sake, and a year and a half ago, I was still trying to figure out when to speak up and when to shut my mouth. Mostly, back then, it was the latter. So I kept my mouth shut, and he died."

"He might not have died, Marco."

"I know he died. I ran into him, days later, and he wasn't himself anymore."

"Oh."

"Yeah."

"It's not your fault though. You didn't vote him out or make him go, like you said. If anything, it's Sylvia's fault. But it isn't yours."

"Yes, it is. It's all our faults, except maybe Amy's and Ana's, because they tried."

"And Ana came with you anyway, even when it was obvious Matt wasn't welcome?"

"She did. I didn't know exactly why, but I assumed it was because she knew she'd be safer in a group than on her own, especially after we'd basically rescued her and Matt twice. She told him she was sorry, and he left."

We walk quietly for a while, down toward the water.

"Well, you're right," I say as we turn onto the agave trail. "Your stories are a little different. But the result was the same. I wonder why Ana didn't tell me about running into zombie Matt."

"I didn't tell her," mutters Marco. "It was only me and Jax, and we didn't tell anyone."

"Why the hell not?"

He peers at me without turning his head. "What good would that have done? It only would have made Ana feel worse than she already did."

So, instead, he'd kept the guilt to himself. It must have been awful.

"Why'd she tell you all of this anyway?" asks Marco.

"Oh, she was trying to tell me to stop being such a brat about Sam. She basically said, with the world the way it is, I should be grateful just to have someone who loves me."

"You weren't happy to have Sam back?"

"It wasn't that, exactly. We had kind of a rough patch, is all. Getting used to each other again. We're good now."

"You seem good. Was it the other night when I saw you eating alone? When you didn't come out to walk?"

"Yeah. That was right in the middle of it."

"What happened?"

"I don't know."

"Sure you do."

I do, but I don't want to rehash it, and especially not with Marco. Sam and I are fine now, but I know she still has a weird jealousy when it comes to him. "It was just a fight, and at the time, it seemed worse than it was."

"What did you fight about?"

"The first time, well, it wasn't really a fight. I told her about my being immune, and she reacted funny."

"Funny, how?"

"She seemed, I don't know, put off or grossed out or something. She said the scars ruined me."

"She what?" His change in demeanor is instant. He stops walking and stares at me with his mouth hanging open. "What, exactly, did she say?"

"That was it. She said the zombies ruined my skin."

"Ruined, she said ruined?" Marco asks, taking hold of my arm with surprising tenderness considering how angry he sounds. He pulls up my sleeve and touches the lowest scars, the ones from the Abnormal on the roof. "These badass survival scars, the ones that mean you don't ever have to worry about turning, the ones you could have died from? These somehow ruined your skin? Even if you ignore how wrong she is, that's still extremely shallow."

"Yeah," I say quietly, pulling my arm back. "It hurt my feelings. I think I took it too personally. Anyway, it sort of snowballed. I had a panic attack another night, maybe the next night, and that was weird too."

"What's that mean—it was weird?"

"She tried to hold on to me. I think to comfort me, but it felt like I was suffocating, and I pushed her away. I was probably being pretty rude—I don't remember—and she got mad. That was the night I talked to you about it." I'm talking fast, trying to get past the subject.

His forehead wrinkles. "So she got mad when you needed space?"

"Well, no. I mean, I think she was probably mad that I was being so rude about it."

"That's bullshit. You don't have to be nice when you're asking for space. She has no claim to you, Cate."

"Jesus, it's not like that, Marco!" I shout. "She was tired, and I woke up sobbing, which probably scared her to begin with. She wasn't trying to lay claim or whatever, she wanted to hold me and make me feel better. It's not her fault I'm so messed up!"

"Okay, one, shush, and no you're not. Or, way more accurately, we all are. I mean—" He gestures to the world as a whole. "—how can anyone not be a little messed up? But I think you're surprisingly well-adjusted for someone who has been through what you have. And, two, I'm not blaming anyone, I'm just saying if someone says they need space, it's no one's right to get shitty about it."

"You sound like Mel," I snap. "You and her, it's like a we-hate-Sam club."

"I don't hate anyone, but apparently, I'm not the only one who has noticed some untoward shit going on between you. Isn't that kind of a red flag? Would your sister ever do or say anything that wasn't for your absolute best interests? Would I?"

I open my mouth to say that he wouldn't have known any of it had I not just told him, that he's been so up in his head lately he hasn't noticed anything around him. But I don't want to talk anymore. I don't even want to look at him right now. I focus on my shoes, planted on the ground. I tighten my jaw until my head hurts. My whole body shakes, probably a mixture of the nighttime chill and the anger coursing through me. I feel betrayed—by my best friend and my sister. How can Ana, who barely knows Sam or me, see what they can't? That Sam is my person and I'm hers, that love is something to make sacrifices for and hold on to, even if it's hard sometimes?

"I'm going to bed," I say finally. "You should too."

Marco stares at me as if there's stuff he wants to say. But he just shakes his head, the tiniest movement, and rakes a hand through his hair the way he does when he's stressed. Good, he deserves it for sticking his nose in my relationship.

"Goodnight, Cate. See you in the morning."

"We'll be there." I place extra emphasis on the *we* and practically jog back inside.

I stop as I pass Sam's cell on the way to my own, and I watch the rise and fall of her deep-sleep breathing. She would feel so heartbroken if she knew what my family was saying about her. How dare they? They have no idea. They don't understand the rightness of Sam and me, the connection. The reason we found each other again at all.

When I get to my own cell and lie down, I squeeze my prickling eyes shut and resent the few tears that roll down my face sideways into my pillow. Marco and Mel don't deserve my tears. They don't know how wrong they are. But they don't have to. I know, and Sam knows, and that's all that matters.

Eighteen: Lead

1 year, 4 and a half months ago

Three days after we let Matt go— made him go was closer to the truth— I saw him again.

We hadn't made it very far, having spent the better part of the first day burying Nate, and the second day sitting vigil by his grave. Nobody could make Sylvia move. Nobody tried. We all knew the likelihood we'd ever go back, would ever be able to find that spot again, despite the marker we made, was slim enough to be inconsequential. So, on the third day, we finally left the place where Nate died.

We walked for hours, hardly speaking. Ana, the newest addition to our group, didn't talk at all. I knew her decision must have been hard, to stay with us when the others had forced out her boyfriend, or whatever Matt was to her. The continuous glares from Sylvia didn't help. So, I checked in on her when we stopped to eat.

"Are you all right?" I asked.

"Do you have any water? I ran out yesterday morning."

"Of course," I said, fumbling with my backpack zipper. "You could have asked before."

Ana took the bottle I handed her and quietly regarded everyone else. She seemed guilty to have taken it at all. She probably felt out of place, she probably wondered why she'd come with us at all.

"I'm sorry about Matt," I said as she sipped the water.

"Lot of good that will do him," Ana muttered into the bottle.

I almost asked her why she'd come along, then, if that was how she felt. But I figured I knew why, and somehow, the more I censored my harsh words, the easier it was to be kind. "You are safer with us though," I told her.

"Yeah," she said, studying her fingernails. "I know."

I started to get up but stopped when Ana kept talking.

"I was going to break up with him. Before."

"Oh," I said, crouching awkwardly between a sit and a stand.

"We weren't compatible. He was nice, but you know. No spark. I knew it before I took this road trip with him too. I live in Idaho. Lived. Anyway. While we were gone, this bullshit, and suddenly we were stuck together."

For some reason, I found myself telling her I had lived in Idaho, too, for a minute. Ana didn't say any more though. Just nursed her water bottle and stared at the rest of the group.

Someone tapped me on the shoulder. Jax. "Want to come collect some more wood with me? I think it'll be another slow day. You know."

He nodded toward Sylvia, who was leaning against a tree with her knees drawn up to her chest and her head resting on top of them. Toby and Henry were playing a half-hearted clapping game with Nick and Adrienne, doing their best to keep the kids distracted from their mom, from the loss of their brother, from all of it.

"Okay," I said. I told Ana we'd be back soon, trying to sound reassuring. "Keep drinking. Last thing we want is for you to pass out from dehydration."

Ana put the bottle to her lips in answer.

"Dehydration?" asked Jax when we were out of earshot. "I thought we had plenty of water?"

"She ran out a while ago. She didn't want to ask us for any, I think."

"Makes sense. Doesn't want to feel like a burden after we kicked her friend out and whatnot."

"I guess. Did we do the right thing?" I wasn't sure which answer I wanted. I'd started to feel really uneasy with the way things had gone down that day.

Jax stopped walking and shook his head. "I don't know, man. I just don't know. Doesn't feel right, though, does it?"

Through the trees, we spotted a mess of red. We took out our weapons and ventured closer, glancing at each other every so often to make sure we were on the same page. At least with Jax, I knew I wouldn't have to worry about an unexpected bout of fear getting me killed.

When we passed between the last couple of trees, we both lowered our weapons. The whole area reeked, the tangy scent of fresh blood. There was only one zombie, its abdomen completely hollowed out, parts of it spread across the forest floor. It reached for us, but it couldn't do anything more: Its legs were bones, as was one of its arms. Black veins stood out across its face.

I stepped closer. "Is that who I think it is?"

"Oh my God," said Jax. "It's Matt."

We stared at Matt's undead body, his vacant white eyes and one reaching arm. Though his backpack looked full, neither of us went for it. We had done this to him, all of us. We were responsible for Matt's death, for making him a monster. In that moment, I knew the answer to the question I'd asked Jax before. We had not done the right thing. There was no way sending a man to his death was ever right. After way too long, I took a few more deliberate steps in his direction and raised my axe.

"Want me to do it, Marco?" asked Jax behind me.

"No," I said. In a way, it felt like what I was about to do, putting Matt down, was the only thing I could do for him. *I should have spoken up for you. I'm sorry, and I promise I won't ever let something like this happen to anyone again.* I brought my axe down on zombie Matt's forehead. He went limp.

"Damn," said Jax as I wiped my axe on the backpack.

"Let's get some firewood and get back. It'll be dark soon."

Before we had gathered much wood at all, we heard noises coming from camp. We exchanged a quick glance and immediately dropped the firewood. We sprinted back; thankfully, we weren't far. When we skidded into the clearing, nine zombies were crowding around our people. Sylvia was alone, cowering against the tree. It wasn't clear if she noticed the zombies or not, or they her. Ana and Tanya were ready, and Duchess was growling at the ones in front of them.

"Marco, Jax!" called Toby, his wrench poised to inflict some damage.

Behind him, Henry held his kids close, unable to do much else.

Ana had a knife, but she was shaking and pale, clearly terrified.

"We got this," I said, though the ratio of able fighters to zombies was *worrisome.*

"Keep it tight," Toby said, and then to Ana, "Aim for the head."

Jax and I took down a few within seconds by sneaking up behind them. I had to rock my axe to pull it free, though, and in the time it took, two zombies noticed me, and one charged, full speed. A Variant.

"Perfect," I said as I staggered my stance and bent my knees. The thing was bigger than me. It would have taken me down if I hadn't prepared myself. When it hit me, I did stumble, but I recovered quickly enough to get my axe handle in its mouth before it bit down on my arm.

"Damn it!" I yelled, clutching the axe in one hand and its wrist with the other. As it swung at me with its free hand, I had no choice but to abandon my axe and duck. In a moment of adrenaline-fueled clarity, I rushed its legs, my shoulder connecting at the knees, and I took it down. It brought my axe with it, but I wrenched it free and swung, crying out in triumph at the sound of the blade splitting the thing's skull. I stood, wiped my forehead, and turned to take on the next one.

But there were none in my immediate vicinity. My people had done a decent job without me, and there were only three left: one apparently very smart zombie, fighting with both Toby and Jax; one old rotten thing stumbling toward Henry and the kids while the brothers were occupied; and one heading straight for Sylvia, who was still on the ground. She stood on wobbly legs. She had no weapon.

"Mommy!" cried Adrienne. She struggled, broke free of her father's grip, and ran at her mother.

The whole world seemed to slow down then. The zombie turned, attracted to the new sound. It outstretched its arms to intercept Adrienne. Adrienne kept running, but by the time she realized the zombie was coming for her, it was too late. The corpse closed in, its fingers an inch from her ponytail. Just as it closed its grip, someone tackled Adrienne off her feet, and the zombie grabbed air.

Ana lay on the ground, cradling a sobbing Adrienne. "It's okay," she said, "I've got you." Adrienne buried her face in Ana's neck, letting herself go into a full meltdown. Poor kid had almost died, and she absolutely knew it.

Toby and Jax dropped the Variant zombie, and camp was finally quiet again.

Sylvia, no longer crying or cowering, stomped over the fallen zombies and snatched Adrienne away from Ana, glowering. "Don't touch my kid."

"I was just trying to help," Ana said, standing up and brushing the dirt off her jeans.

"We don't need your help," Sylvia shrieked. "Your boyfriend killed my son!"

Adrienne's crying got louder, more frantic.

"Syl, honey," Henry said, "Ana saved Adrienne's life."

"She wouldn't need saving if we weren't here! If we had kept on our original path, not detoured into the woods, I would still have all of my babies! That bastard coward stole my child from me, and then we took on his tramp companion for no damn good reason! We should have left them both to rot!"

"Sylvia, enough!" I heard myself saying. I didn't know what would come out next, but I had to speak up, finally.

"It's not Matt's fault Nate died. It's not, and even if it was, it certainly isn't Ana's. You lost someone. A child, and I can't even imagine, Sylvia. I am so sorry that happened. But you don't get to take out your grief on other people. Ana just saved Adrienne's life! I saw it, and so did you. You don't have to be friendly; I know things take time to heal and stuff. But you don't get to treat a member of our group—our family—that way. It's not okay."

Sylvia didn't meet my gaze or Ana's. But when Adrienne hugged Ana around the middle, Sylvia didn't stop her.

"Thank you, Ana," Adrienne said.

Ana petted Adrienne's hair, but her gaze was still on Sylvia, as though she was afraid the mother bear instinct would come out again.

"I'm so sorry, about your son," Ana finally said. "I didn't say it before because I figured you wouldn't want to hear it from me."

"You were right," said Sylvia.

"Sylvia," Tanya said, "she's trying."

By then, the rest of our group had gathered around us.

Adrienne ran to her dad. Henry got down on one knee and wrapped his arms around his kids. He kissed the top of Adrienne's head a few times.

"Thank you, Ana," he said over her little blonde ponytail. His eyes were bright with unshed tears.

That night, I set my bed roll toward the outer edge of the group, close to Ana. As everyone else was settling in, she reached out of her sleeping bag and took my hand.

"Thank you, Marco," she said. "What you did, how you defended me, it meant a lot."

"No problem." I wasn't sure why I was trying to be nonchalant about it. I meant everything I'd said. We were as close to a family as I would ever have, probably. So, for the first time in months, since before I had lost Cate, I opened up a little. "I, um, haven't really had a family in a long time."

"No?"

"I was in foster care for years, and when all this happened, I lost my foster family too. But then I found Tanya and Amy, and the rest of them, and at first, I was hesitant. I didn't want to be responsible for anyone else, not when I'd basically failed with the last people I tried to help."

Ana's eyebrows drew together. "What do you mean, 'be responsible for'?"

"You know, protect. I tried to protect my foster family, but now I don't even know where they are, if they're alive or not."

"Those are the people we're meeting at Alcatraz?"

"If they make it, yeah."

"Marco, how old are you?" asked Ana, narrowing her eye.

"Eighteen."

"You're the same age as my little brother. He was like you, always trying to protect me and our mom. Provide. But Marco, you're still a kid. If anything, we should be protecting you."

It reminded me of something Tess had said once, when all of this first started.

"I knew it was the wrong call to send Matt away," I blurted, and felt like an ass.

Ana's face got sad. "It wasn't on you, Marco."

"I just meant I knew it was wrong, and I should have spoken up. He would still be here if I'd tried harder. But I didn't because I figured I wasn't the person to make that call."

"Well, I understand. I guess you're right; you should speak up. Especially to help others. But that doesn't make it your fault."

I thought about his mangled corpse that afternoon, the sound my axe made when it ended his suffering. "I'm sorry I didn't try harder with Matt," I said, swallowing the huge lump in my throat.

Ana smiled. It was sad, but it was something else too. "No more apologizing. Everyone feels guilt in situations like these. I understand, and I can't take that away. But you can use it. Now you know your own strength. The way you stood up for me today, you can keep doing that for other people. There's no reason not to. You have a strong sense of compassion; I can tell. So, follow that, and I guarantee others will too."

I stared at her, not quite sure what to say.

She squeezed my hand, which I realized she was still holding, closed her eye, and let it go. "Get some sleep," she whispered. "I have a feeling we'll finally start to move forward tomorrow."

I closed my eyes, shifted around on my blanket, pulled the one on top of me up under my chin.

"Ana?" I whispered after a few minutes.

She didn't say anything, her breathing was deep and slow.

"Thank you," I whispered into the darkness.

Nineteen: Mend

I'm awake long before I need to be. I sit in the corner of my cell—it feels more like a cell than it has since day one—stroking the dog's ears and watching through the little window as the gray gives way to blue, waiting until I hear movement in some of the other cells. Joaquin walks past my doorway first. He glances in as he does and looks surprised to see me on the floor. He stops.

"What're you doing down there?"

"Couldn't sleep."

"Worried about your uncle?"

"Yeah, among other things."

Joaquin steps tentatively into my cell. "What things?"

"Just, this plan. We haven't had so many of us to watch out for since the night we came here."

"Watch out for, yeah," he says, sitting down next to me. "That's how it feels, though, right? I mean, they're all trained, some more than others—" He glances toward Sam's cell. "But the four of us, the normal Frisco supply team—you, me, Calvin, Murray—we're so good at what we do. We get in, we get out."

"Nobody gets hurt."

"And today, adding so many unknown factors, it's..."

"Intense," I finish for him. "Scary."

"Still, thinking that way will only make things harder. Maybe even invite danger." He stares out the cell door, and his fingers move to the cross around his neck. "We just gotta have faith. In ourselves, in our people. Nobody wants to die, right?"

"Mmm." I nod, but I'm not totally on the same page as he is. Nobody wants to die, but that in itself can cause problems. If you're too scared, you can mess up. All it takes is a second of distraction, of indecisiveness. It must be nice for Joaquin, to have faith the way he does.

He pushes himself up and holds out a hand, which I take. "So, go wake up your girlfriend, and I'll see you on the dock." The smile he gives me as he leaves isn't sad, but it isn't just a smile either. He's trying, though, and I'm thankful for that. I don't need any more tension.

I get my shoes on, go into Sam's cell, and tap her awake. It takes a few tries, and finally, I pull the covers off her feet. She stirs.

"Sam? You ready for your first run?"

She makes tired noises.

I bend down and kiss her cheek as she sits up. "It's fine if you don't want to go. It's better for everyone if you're honest about it."

"I know. I am being honest. I want to go."

"It's just that these runs involve a certain level of danger anyway, and this one has a lot of moving parts, a lot we've never done."

"I know, Cate. I can do this. I'm not being stubborn, and I'm not too proud to say that I'm afraid. I am, of course I am. But that doesn't mean I'm not capable."

I stare at her while she puts on her shoes. Her face is stony and determined. "You're right," I tell her. "Come on, let's get going."

She starts to follow me out.

"Hey," I say, putting a hand out to stop her. "Weapons?"

"Oh. Right." She picks up her new hammer and her old knife. "Guess I'll really need these today." She makes a noise, not quite a laugh.

"This way is easiest," I say, pointing to my own axe, the handle of which is snug in my front belt loop. She does her own the same way.

We hold hands as we walk the length of the cell block. Sam rests her head on my shoulder, and a secret, petty part of me hopes Marco and Mel both see how happy we are as we walk outside. But Mel isn't out in the rec yard to see Calvin off like she usually does. No Marco either. They're probably back inside, with Bill.

"I want to go check on my uncle," I tell Sam. "You coming?"

Sam hesitates. "No, you and Marco and your sister need time alone with him." She doesn't even flinch when she says Marco's name. That's something, at least.

The last thing I want right now is to be in close proximity with either my sister or Marco. I know they'll be there when I get to the cell Bill stayed in last night. Sure enough, there they are. Mel is sitting at the foot of Bill's bed, and Marco is standing next to her. Bill's face is still pale, and judging by the dark circles under his eyes, he didn't get a lot of sleep. When he sees me, he says good morning and the others look up. Mel's face clouds instantly. Marco seems worried, like I'm a snake that might strike out and bite him. I hold his gaze like a game of chicken until he backs down, choosing instead to stare at the floor.

"I'm going to check on preparations," Marco says, skirting around me as I enter the cell.

Mel bends down to kiss Bill's forehead. "I should see how Calvin is doing."

"Melody," Bill stops her, taking her hand as she turns to leave. "Wait. I want to talk to you girls."

Mel glances at me. I glare back. She sits back on the bed. Her back is stiff and straight and she's trying hard to look impassive. I crouch next to the other end of the bed, holding Uncle Bill's free hand.

"Listen, girls," Bill says. "I don't expect you to just kiss and make up. That's not how it works, ever. Not with siblings, spouses, friends. Letting go of anger is hard, and the angrier you are, the longer you hold on to it, the harder it is. But sooner or later, this thing will fizzle out. You can't stay mad forever, at least I hope not. And you both know you love each other."

I wish people would stop saying that, as though loving someone excuses shitty behavior, or mends huge differences in character. You can love someone more than anything and they can still be wrong, they can still hurt you. And then, like a snap of the fingers, I understand what Mel has been trying to say about Sam and me. I still think she's wrong, but her intentions aren't. From her perspective, there's a side of my relationship with Sam that isn't functioning right. I watch Mel, but she's looking down at Bill. Her cheeks are red.

"I'll see you soon, Uncle Bill." She backs away from the bed, throwing me barely a glance before she leaves the cell.

Bill seems to know what's in my head. He nods once in her direction, squeezes my hand, and smiles. "See you on the boat, kiddo."

"Thanks, Uncle Bill." I hug him, but not too tight.

"Mel!" I call, running after her.

She stops immediately and turns. She doesn't look angry. Her expression reminds me of the time I was really sick and slept for three days straight. I didn't eat, hardly spoke. The face she made when I finally came downstairs for the first time is the face she's making now.

"I..." I'm not going to say I'm sorry, not when I don't know what to apologize for. My mom would say it's not a real apology. So I say the first thing I can think of. "I understand. You're worried, right?"

"Well that's what I said, isn't it?" she answers, putting her hand on her hip. "What I've been saying." But her face softens again; her mouth turns down at the edges. She fiddles with her glasses. "I know it seemed like I was butting in."

"Yeah, it did." Damn it, with that tone. I need to try harder. I'm still mad, and I'm allowed to be, but I can also be nice. "But I probably could have handled it better."

We start down the main path toward the dock. We're both quiet until we reach the second switchback, not even a hundred feet from the boat. The silence doesn't feel heavy though. The horrible tension between us is finally lifting.

"So you really like her, don't you?" asks Mel.

"I love her. We've been dating for three and a half years."

"Are you including the last two?" Her mouth twitches, a miniature smile.

"Okay, yeah. But really, Mel."

"I know. I can see it."

"Cate!" Calvin calls from the bottom of the path. "Coming?"

We're the last people here, aside from Murray and Toby, who are still carrying Bill down, and Amy, who's probably supervising.

I wave so he knows I heard him.

"Stay safe out there, okay?" Mel says, opening her arms.

I hug her tight. "I'll see you soon."

Twenty: Silence

Focus.

Breathe in, out.

Nothing is going to happen.

I know I'm wrong as soon as we're within sight of the dock. There are a bunch of them milling around.

"That's a lot of zombies," calls Murray from his post. No use talking quietly, not with the rumble of the boat's engine.

"Okay, but they're normal zombies at least, based on the aimless wandering," says Marco to whoever is listening. He's tapping his foot. "So there's that."

Calvin is pacing.

We all know this won't be near as easy as we hoped.

"The hospital is only a few blocks away," Amy says as we get closer.

"So there's that too," I add. "Those people better still be there."

"Don't get your hopes up." Calvin uncrosses his arms to touch the handles of his knives. "We don't ever see survivors on our trips in."

"We also don't usually see so many dead right off the boat," Joaquin says behind me.

"We'll do what we have to," I mutter, looking at Joaquin and then, pointedly, at Bill. "We'll be back on the island tonight."

"Maybe not all of us," says Ana.

Murray kills the engine.

"All right," says Calvin. "Ana, Marco, and Joaquin have got Bill and the guys. Cate, Sam, and I will assist Amy."

Amy takes her stiletto knife out and flips the blade open. Suddenly, I wish I hadn't missed so much training recently. *Duck, roll, crouch, swing. One, two, three, four.* I recite the form silently, visualize it in my head.

As if that will make up for the many missed sessions.

Sam stares at me. She's clearly afraid but trying not to show it. I feel like I've done us both a disservice by not making sure we trained more. No. I can't go into something this important feeling that way. One, two, three, four. Joaquin was right, attitude makes a difference. Maybe we'll all be okay.

I look back at Sam and try to come across as confident as I can. "Duck, roll, crouch, swing," I tell her. "Stay close to me."

"Ready?" Joaquin asks as we pull closer to the dock.

Nobody answers. Toby and Murray pick up the makeshift stretcher Bill is lying on and shift their weight as the boat stops.

The zombies are reaching for Ana and Marco as soon as they walk off the ferry. They take the nearest ones down easily, but more are coming. So many more. Marco and Ana keep them at bay while Joaquin escorts Murray, Toby, and Bill onto the dock. The rest of us jog down after them. Amy isn't too bad with her knife, considering how often she has to use it. She falters a bit from time to time, but it seems like she can basically handle herself. Which is helpful, because although I can too, Sam is doing more dodging than anything else. We're making fair time. This is okay. We're okay. There are only a few left by the time we reach the street.

And then, a few blocks inland, it's more than a few. Marco seems less afraid somehow than when we were on the ferry coming in. He's mouthing words, counting the zombies. It's a good idea. Three right in front of us, six or so coming out the doorway to the left, four behind us, and to the right, a narrow alley. My immediate thought is to make a break for the alley, but when I step to the right, Calvin says my name, shakes his head.

Two gunshots, two bodies drop.

"Joaquin, put the gun away!" someone says.

Up front, Marco takes one down with ease. It's as though he never stopped training. I hope it comes as easily for me. As though the zombie behind me can hear what I'm thinking, it grabs for my arm, and with barely a thought, I shove into the thing's grip, knock it back with my elbow, and kick it in the gut. It doesn't go down though. Barely stumbles. Calvin hacks at its spinal cord with one of his huge knives to finish it off. Not as easy as I'd hoped, but not as bad as I'd feared. All right. I can do this.

"Cate!" Sam screams from my left. She's grappling with a zombie that's small by adult standards, but she's having a hell of a time with it. I run toward her, but Amy stabs the thing in the back of the head before I get there.

"Thanks, Amy," I say. But I don't back off. It's clear that although I can pretty well handle myself, Sam is floundering. For all her confidence back on the island, she is nowhere near ready for something like this. I have to keep an eye on her.

Calvin takes out one, then another, and three more come around the corner ahead of us, surrounding the people in front. Calvin sprints over to help them. Between him and Ana, Marco and Joaquin hardly get any action themselves. Ana is a machine. It has been a good while since I've seen her with any actual zombies, but damn, she's on fire. Amy, Sam, and I are alone in the rear now, but it's all right. There are far fewer back here. We're okay.

But the thought barely forms in my head before Sam is yelling again. I make my way toward her. She sees me, yelps, and shoves herself behind me just as a zombie reaches out toward us. It catches my hand, leaving deep, dark scratches in the flesh. I cry out, a mixture of anger and pain, and Sam lets go of me and runs a few steps away.

"Cate!" Amy calls, and a zombie standing right where I was a second ago takes her down. Thankfully, Calvin is on it. He rips the thing off Amy, throws it down, and lets it chew on his metal prosthetic leg as he stabs it in the temple. Amy nods her thanks as Calvin helps her up.

As he turns to go back toward the thicker concentration of zombies up front, Calvin gives me a look. "You good?" he asks, eyeing my bloody hand. He knows, for me, it's just a wound.

"I'm good."

He glances at me, Sam, and Amy, then nods, quick and curt. "I'll stick back here for now."

It reminds me of Ana's callous demeanor. He thinks I messed up going to Sam instead of covering Amy as I was meant to. But what was I supposed to do, let her die? I'm immune. I can take it. I flex my hand—the scratches aren't as deep as they felt—and move on. There are only two more back here. Ana is handling one, and the other, in its bright red hoodie, is so far back, and so slow, it might not even be a problem if we keep moving at this pace.

At the front of the group, Ana, Marco, and Joaquin are surrounded still. Are there more? I can't even remember how many there were before. So much for counting. It doesn't matter. They're in deep shit up there. But I know I need to stay where I am. Marco stabs two in rapid succession. But while he and Joaquin are both distracted, I watch as one creeps in behind Murray. It's like slow motion. I'm way back here, I can't stop it. It grabs for Murray's jacket with blood-crusted, claw-like hands. I yell Murray's name. He can't do much of anything, not while he's carrying Bill. At the very last second, in one unbroken movement, Ana turns and brings down her axe on the zombie's hands. They come off clean. But it must have been recently reanimated, because the stuff that comes out is semiliquid and splashes all over Ana, Murray, and Joaquin.

Joaquin shouts, slapping at his face and spitting. "It's in my mouth!" he cries. He makes some more sounds, scraping desperately at his face and tongue with his hands, backing away from the fray.

Ana turns and reaches for him. "Joaquin, get— AH!"

"Ana!" shouts Murray.

The zombie in the red hoodie, standing right where Joaquin was a second ago, clamps its jaws onto Ana's shoulder. The exact same spot Rob was bitten. She screams again, kills the offending zombie, and spins around in a fury, clearing three more zombies before she slows down and touches the spot where she was bitten.

In the temporary absence of zombies, we all turn to watch her. Her face changes: anger, recognition, horror, and finally, understanding. The face of a woman who knows she's dead.

"Ana..." Joaquin approaches her, hands out, palms up. Contrite. There's still blood all over his face, but his own potential infection is dwarfed by her actual, certain infection.

"We keep going," she says, only glancing at him. "We're close."

She's right. We arrive at the hospital doors within a minute or two and get inside without any further incident. The people Marco and Amy mentioned don't seem to be around, but there's one closed room full of very old corpses in blue scrubs. On the door there's a note written in black marker:

THEY GOT US, WE GOT THEM.

WE WON'T BE MONSTERS. LEAVE US HERE.

"So what, they got bit and locked themselves in there to turn and rot?" asks Sam, though it's obvious what happened. "Why not end it before the turning?"

"It's not as easy as you'd think," says Calvin quietly. "But they did the right thing, keeping themselves from hurting anyone else."

We find a wheelchair for Bill and follow the signs to the room Amy needs for him.

Before she takes him away to examine him, she instructs Calvin to check Ana's shoulder. "Joaquin, Toby, would you come with me, please? Just in case."

Calvin sits in front of Ana and reaches for her hand to lift it off the bite, which is dribbling blood between her pale fingers.

"Don't," Ana says, jerking away. "You know what this means for me. Deal with Cate's wound first."

"Ana, you know I can't turn," I remind her.

"You can still die of any number of infections. I'm dead—" Her jaw flexes and her voice shakes. "—no matter what."

"Let me at least stop the bleeding." Calvin doesn't wait for an answer; he pulls her hand away and pushes a clean piece of gauze against her shoulder. They lock eyes for a second, an exchange of thanks and sorrow and love, and she puts her hand over his to hold the gauze in place as he moves away to see about my scratches.

I watch Ana while Calvin cleans my wound with a stinging liquid and dresses it. The guilt I feel, however baseless, is deep and painful. Every time I get a zombie wound, every time someone else gets one, I remember I am alone in my immunity. What's only a scratch for me is death for everyone I love. And I do love them, all of them. I want to tell Ana I'm sorry, but she'd ask why, and I don't have a way to answer that doesn't smack of self-pity.

"I was right," Amy says, pushing Bill into the room in the wheelchair. "Bill is going to be fine. I've got him on what seems to be this hospital's very last IV drip. And by the way it looks, we are indeed alone here."

"Not one zombie or human as far as we could tell," says Toby.

"Good to know," whispers Ana. "At least I can die in peace." She chuckles, sort of, and closes her eye. Her face is losing color so fast. Her skin almost matches her hair now.

"Ana," Amy murmurs, moving to her side. "I'm so sorry this happened to you. Can we get you anything?"

Ana shakes her head and tries to smile. "Not unless someone has a bottle of wine."

Murray steps forward and takes a flask out of his pocket. "How's whiskey?"

"When did you get whiskey?" asks Marco.

"Had it since before," answers Murray. "Flask was a gift. Don't drink much myself, but, you know, end of the world and all... I figured there'd come a time when I might need it. It's all yours, Ana, if you want it."

Ana takes a long sip, sputtering as she finishes. Murray tenderly wipes a drop of whiskey from her chin with his thumb. She thanks him. "I forgot how harsh this stuff is. But it's much appreciated. Where's Joaquin?"

"He's patrolling the halls," says Murray. "I suspect he didn't want to see what he did to you."

A few of us glance around at one another. I don't know if I blame Joaquin, but I don't know if he's totally free of guilt either. And it seems, for the most part, that's how we all feel. It isn't the time to judge, however, and even though Murray let his anger speak for him just then, I think he knows that too.

Ana doesn't say anything. She looks down for a minute, and then all of a sudden, she claws at her jacket, unzips it, and tries to shrug out of it. The pain of the movement makes her cry out. Calvin helps her get it off, and Sam and Murray gasp when they see what's underneath. Stemming from all sides of her wound are a network of black veins, big and small. Even the tiny capillaries are black. I've never seen it get so thick before killing someone. In the zombies I've come across, some have a lot of black, but nothing this advanced. Mrs. Minkin, the first woman I saw go through the change, had only a few large veins turn black before she died. My uncle Frank died pretty much instantly. I knew Ana was strong, but, Jesus, this is unreal.

For the first time ever, Ana looks self-conscious. Of course she is, with all of us standing around staring at her. I nudge Sam and Calvin, who are standing on either side of me, and we all turn away. Ana stands on shaking legs and asks Murray to help her to a nearby table so she might lie down. Once she's on her back, she closes her eyes. Her expression isn't peaceful though. Her face is scrunched up in pain.

"You'll bury me next to Jacob?" she asks. "Don't leave me here."

"We would never," croons Murray, stroking her silvery-blonde hair. "But you don't need to think about that."

"I do." She pushes herself up again, all the way to a sitting position, and hugs her knees to keep herself there. Murray scoots onto the table behind her so she can rest against him.

"It won't be long now," she mutters. "I feel it, taking over my body. It hurts, Murray." She takes a shaking breath, lets it out as a few tears drip down her face. "It hurts so deep. My bones, my skin. I'm on fire. And my brain, I swear I can feel it shutting down." She lets out a low moan and before our eyes, the blackness stretches farther up her neck.

"Do you want to lie back down now?" asks Marco.

"No—" Ana shakes her head. "No. I'm restless. My body is fighting it. And I feel Rob here with me. I'm going to see him again, I think." She chuckles, but it turns into a wet cough. "I never believed in anything after death. Always assumed death was it, but now, I don't know if I'm hallucinating or what, but I see him, as clear as if he's standing right behind you, Amy." She stares at the space behind Amy, and her face takes on a new tranquility.

Amy glances over her shoulder. Though there's no one, she nods. "You'll be together again soon, my friend."

"Joaquin?" Ana asks again. I don't know if she forgot or if she's asking for someone to find him. Marco volunteers, taking a long look at Ana before he runs out the open door into the hall.

"They'll be back any minute," says Calvin. "Rest now, Ana."

She smiles, lays back, blinks slowly, so slowly I'm not sure her eye will open again. I feel everything go completely still as she lets out a ragged breath and doesn't inhale again.

"Found him!" Marco is panting as he and Joaquin come running back into the room.

"Is she..." asks Joaquin, going to Ana. He's wiped the blood off his face.

A spiteful little part of me thinks, *How dare you look at her, how dare you speak.* So I guess I do blame him at least a bit, but I keep my gaze focused on Ana. She doesn't look like she's sleeping, the way you hear dead people are supposed to. Her eyebrows are still knitted together, and her mouth is twisted. The most tenacious black vein has reached her chin.

"Ana..." Joaquin whispers, stroking her unbitten arm.

"Joaquin." Ana opens her eye and smiles a little. "You're back. Are we still safe?"

Joaquin nods. "Ana, I'm sorry, I'm so sorry, I didn't—" His voice catches, and he retreats to the far corner of the room.

Ana makes a few little noises, and then she's quiet again. Murray strokes her hair, starts to hum a song I don't know. Her face relaxes the smallest bit. But then her whole body stiffens, her face points skyward, and she yells, "Please! Somebody has to end it because it hurts. It hurts so bad, and I can't go on like this. Please. Marco. Help me."

Marco's face is strained and red, his eyes shining wet like the rest of ours, and his mouth is pulled back in a grimace. "Ana, I can't."

She grabs his hand. "Yes, you can, Marco. You're my friend. I need you. Please, please do this. I don't want to hurt anymore; I don't want to be one of them. Please." She begins to sob. Ana's strength, the strength I always took for granted from the moment I first met her in the woods, finally leaves her.

Marco is frozen in place. His hand rests on his knife. He's crying. "Oh, Ana."

I want to reach out and touch him, give him comfort, support. But nothing can make this easier, and Marco is steeling himself for what will undoubtedly be the hardest thing he has ever had to do.

"I'll do it, son," says Murray, putting one hand on Marco's shoulder and drawing his knife with the other. He cranes his neck so he can gaze at Ana's face, and holds the weapon ready. "You're sure this is how you want to go out, Ana?"

"I'm sure," says Ana. "I'm dying already. I want to do it my way."

Marco takes Ana's hand. Amy takes Toby's hand. Sam takes my hand.

"I want you to know," says Ana, "that in your own ways, you have each made my life beautiful. Even after the whole world went to hell, we made a family. I love you all."

"We love you, Ana," says Marco.

"I love you dearly, Ana," says Amy. "And so does Tanya."

"You're one hell of a human being," says Calvin. "And I'm proud to have known you."

"I love you, Ana," I manage before I'm choked out by sobs.

"I hardly got to know you, Ana," says Bill, "but the person I've come to know is fierce and brilliant. You will be dearly missed."

"Gonna miss you like hell, Ana," Toby says. "Jax will too. You kicked our asses into shape. You helped me get back to a normal routine after I lost my hand. Thank you."

"I..." Murray starts to say. He takes a breath, tries again. "I, you..."

"I know," Ana says, reaching up with her good arm to touch Murray's bearded, tear-soaked cheek.

"I will never forget you, Ana," he finally says. "Thank you, for all of it."

Joaquin doesn't say anything. I turn to see him watching from the corner. He's wringing his hands, and his expression is blank, like he's feeling too much and his face doesn't know what to do.

After almost a whole minute of silence, Ana speaks up, her voice a low whisper. "Murray, it's time."

Murray kisses the top of her head. His final words to Ana are soft and slow. "It has been an honor to know you."

I can't watch. I turn and bury my face in Calvin's chest. He wraps his arms around me. Sam clutches my hand tighter.

The knife makes that sick slick-squishing sound, and something hits the floor. When I hear movement, I turn around. Murray is covering Ana's face with her bloody jacket. His knife, still wet with her blood, is by his feet. He walks into the hallway without a word, his shoulders shaking. Marco and Toby follow him out.

There's silence in the hospital.

Twenty-One: Escape

1 year ago

We traveled the last leg of our journey at a staggeringly slow pace. At first, whole days went by where Sylvia wouldn't get out of her sleeping bag.

"I thought she was ready to move on," I whispered to Tanya on one of those mornings.

Tanya's expression was one of mild disgust. "Are you joking? She lost a child, Marco. You don't move on from that."

"No! I didn't mean *move on*, I meant—you know—move along, as in, get on the road."

Her face softened into an expression of sad resignation as she watched Sylvia. "She's doing everything she can. We'll get there. All we can do is travel as much as possible, whenever possible, and try to keep one another alive."

And that was what we did. After seven weeks—many days of no progress at all—we finally made it to San Francisco just as summer was coming to a close.

The city was no more or less zombie-infested than I had expected. But the old woman from Jax and Toby's old group had been right: there were far more Variant zombies there.

There was one that attacked as we crossed a toll bridge laden with abandoned cars. Although it didn't so much attack as check us out. It sprang out from behind a car, and before anyone could kill it, it jumped on a van and vaulted over the tops of cars until it was out of sight.

Another, one that had to have been around ninety when it was alive, watched us intently as we passed by the car it sat in. We only knew it was a zombie because of the tiny black vein peeking out from under its sweater collar. Toby had wanted to smash a window and kill it, but I persuaded him not to. It was closed up in a vehicle, after all, and wasn't posing a threat. So, mumbling expletives, he'd left it alone, and we continued into the city. It didn't follow.

We'd planned to go straight to the pier to see what could be done about getting to the island as soon as possible, but Henry pointed out (rightly so) that we should gather as many supplies as possible before going over, because nobody knew what we'd find or when we'd be able to come back. So the group began a slow sweep of San Francisco, searching for anything useful. We did all right on everything but food, finding five cans in total. Our packs got heavier.

"Hang on," I panted, slowing my run to a walk. Even months after my last cigarette, I still couldn't run very far without getting winded. I sucked in air, ignoring the burn in my lungs, and tried hard not to stop altogether.

"Why can't you run?" asked Adrienne.

The kid never stopped asking questions, but somehow it didn't get old.

"I used to smoke cigarettes," I said between breaths.

"That's what happens when you smoke," added Ana. "You can't run without losing your breath."

"And you're reduced to a cautionary tale, apparently," I mumbled.

Ana shrugged.

I stared at the building behind her, trying not to say anything I'd regret. Something caught my attention in a dumpster. A pair of eyes. I waved everyone down and pointed toward the dumpster. The eyes watching us weren't white, which meant either a person was somehow surviving in a dumpster, or we had one of those Variants spying on us. I took out my axe and stalked toward the probably-zombie.

The eyes disappeared. Not so fast! I threw open the lid with a yell and raised my axe to kill the sucker before it had a chance to jump out and bite me.

But what was sitting inside the metal bin made the axe fall out of my hand. A child cowered in the refuse. He stank terribly, and his red hair was matted and greasy.

"Please," he said and reached his arms up to me.

I lifted him out because what else was I going to do? I could hardly stand the smell coming off the poor kid as I carried him down the alley toward the rest of the group.

"Is that a little boy?" asked Jax, even though it obviously was. Would I cradle a zombie?

"What's your name, sweetie?" asked Tanya, reaching out to touch his face.

He pulled away and buried his head in my neck. If he wasn't so emaciated, I'd have had a hard time carrying him. He was tall enough to be four or five, but he weighed as much as a toddler.

"It's okay," I said. We all started walking again. "My name is Marco."

The boy said nothing.

"What's your name?"

"Um...Francis."

"Do you know where your parents are?" I asked.

Francis didn't answer.

"We'll take care of you, Francis," said Amy behind me.

Francis's hold around my neck tightened. We kept going.

We got to the pier late that afternoon. It wasn't absolutely crawling with the undead, but it wasn't a cakewalk either. We stayed hidden, watching them move around in the twilight. Beyond that, the island. Alcatraz. We'd almost made it.

"Oh my God," whispered Tanya.

"There it is, brother!" said Jax, shaking Toby's giant shoulder.

The island was a distant silhouette against the sunset sky. Maybe I was getting a little choked up because it was almost over, but it was goddamn beautiful. The island itself, though, looked lifeless from where we stood. No lights, which I guessed probably meant the others hadn't made it there yet. If they had, it would be obvious, wouldn't it? *Or*, whispered the cynical part of my brain, *maybe they did get there, and they're dead*. But there was no way for us to know until we got there.

If they hadn't made it, if we somehow found Cate and Melody and Bill, even Gary, and we all went to Alcatraz together, we had a real chance of dealing with whatever we found. Hell, maybe they had found one another, and then some more people.

So, it was probably good there were no lights on the island yet.

"Well, what do you think?" asked Henry. "How do we get over there?"

"Best bet is the ferry." I pointed to the big boat sitting at the dock. "But there are no lights on, which means my people haven't made it yet."

"Marco," Henry touched my shoulder. "Wouldn't it be better if we went now, waited there for them where it's safe?"

"Then how would *they* get there?" asked Ana. "There's one ferry. Anyway, can any of us drive that beast?"

Nobody answered.

"Well, there are these zombies to think about too, right?" I tilted my head toward the pier. The last thing I wanted to do was finally bring the plan to fruition without half the people who belonged there with us. "I think when it's time to go, we'll just sort of know. You know? May as well find a place to stay nearby in case they come through here."

Tanya and Amy smiled as if they understood.

"Fair enough," said Henry.

Sylvia looked displeased; Jax and Toby seemed unconvinced.

"But I'm open to suggestions. This should be a consensus. What do you all think we should do?"

"I think we should find a place to sleep," said Henry. "Syl, you and the kids are beat. And I could use a few hours' rest before whatever's waiting for us on the island. We're here. Let's take it slow, see if Marco's family shows up."

Sylvia deliberated. Adrienne yawned and stared up at her mother. Sylvia dipped her head in assent.

"Can't hurt to have more people when the time comes, I guess," said Jax with a shrug.

We backtracked up the street we'd come down, searching buildings and parking garages. Occasionally, someone would point to a suitable-looking building and someone else would find a reason to turn it down. The running theme seemed to be that we had unlimited choices, so we may as well choose a secure spot, and comfort was also a well-liked idea.

But being that choosy meant we were still out in the open when darkness fell, and several relatively fresh zombies wandered into our path. Several more joined them, and twenty-five more after that.

"Holy shit," whispered Jax as we slipped down an alley. We jogged as quietly as we could, but the kids were crying. Of course they were. A zombie had killed their brother.

Francis was quiet, but his iron grip on me hadn't let up since I'd pulled him out of the dumpster.

"How many?" asked Amy without daring to look back.

I tried to count, but I couldn't. "A hundred? More? We gotta get out of here." I put Francis down. "You have to run now, okay? Hold my hand. Don't let go."

Francis, his gaze darting between me and the oncoming zombies, nodded.

A little farther down, even more zombies lumbered up the street toward us, blocking us from the front as well as the back. But there were three turn-off points between us and them.

"What do we do?" wailed Sylvia.

"Up ahead," I cried, taking out my knife and securing my grip on Francis's hand. "Turn down the first clear alley, go!"

We ran.

Halfway down the alley, a zombie staggered out from behind a dumpster. It lunged at the first person it could— Amy. Another came behind it, and two more around the nearest corner. Duchess attacked the first one, sinking her teeth into its pant leg and yanking it away from Amy. It stumbled backward and fell flat. As soon as it was down, I knifed it in the eye, careful not to jam the blade. The one behind it had Tanya by the backpack and was pulling her in.

"No!" shouted Amy, and she grabbed Tanya's hammer and beat the thing down.

The other two came for me and Toby. Mine was close to rotting off its legs anyway, so the kill was easy. Toby was having trouble with his, and of course he was. Even in the darkness, the thing's brown eyes were obvious. I took hold of the Variant in a full nelson while Toby delivered the death blow.

"Close one," panted Toby, then, "Shit—Ana!"

When we turned the corner, two more zombies moved toward Ana, claws out and mouths agape. Ana turned too late, and one of them grabbed on to her zipped-up Carhartt coat. She flailed, which succeeded in shaking off one just in time for the other to get hold of her. Jax shoved one away and wrenched Ana's sleeve from the other zombie's hands. He stabbed it in the eye when it reached for him instead. Its fingertips barely brushed his cheek as it crumpled to the ground. Toby's hammer met with the face of the zombie Jax had shoved away.

"Thank you," Ana said to both of them as we ran.

We ended up back on a regular street. We tried the first door we found, a cafe with giant windows. It would be a terrible place to try to fortify, but it was better than the middle of the street. It was locked, though, as was the next door. And the next.

The horde found us again. And they weren't alone: Above us, several Variants sat on fire escapes and hung out of windows to watch us. The whole area was crawling with them.

Francis followed my gaze and started to cry.

"No more doors; we gotta move!" I shouted.

We ran. My lungs started to burn right away. We must be making some good distance, but when I turned around, I could still see their white eyes in the dark. Overhead, most of the smart ones were still watching us. But some of them were following, jumping from rooftop to rooftop. Gaining.

Sylvia called out to us. I glanced back. They were falling behind. The kids were too slow.

"Toby!" I called. "Kids!"

Toby turned to Sylvia's family. "Right! Come on!"

He slowed to let them catch up and dipped to his knees just long enough to situate Francis, Nick, and Adrienne on his shoulders and back.

"Hold on!" he shouted. The kids grabbed on, their eyes wide and terrified. Toby sprinted, pulling ahead to the front of the group. Sylvia and Henry were right behind him.

I coughed, stumbled, but caught myself. We zigzagged through streets and alleys, trying to lose them. The Variants kept closing in.

"What are we, gonna, do?" asked Toby between breaths.

"Keep running." My lungs! I wasn't sure I could go much farther.

As we rounded one more corner, I stopped dead. I had to. I couldn't breathe. The group stopped, too, but with a barrage of "Why'd we stop?" and "We have to keep going!" between the noise of a hundred zombies chasing us down, and it was all I could do to stay standing.

"This door's locked too," said Amy as if she thought that was why I had stopped.

"They're all locked!" snapped Sylvia. "Every door is locked, which is why we're going to die out here. We never should have come!"

"They're coming!" cried Adrienne.

"Hey!" called an unfamiliar voice.

We looked around. A little light blinked on and off in a doorway. A flashlight. Above it, a bespectacled face. "Come on, hurry!" He waved a hand to emphasize.

We crossed the road, tentatively.

"Come inside, quickly!" He waved us all into what turned out to be an apartment building. As he shut the door, the horde of zombies shuffled around the corner and continued by us.

There were sounds of relief all around. Tanya and Amy embraced each other; Ana sank to the floor and started crying.

"Thank you," I said, turning to the man and woman who had let us in. "You saved our lives."

"We're glad we got your attention," said the woman. "Saw those things coming round the other side of the building, and all of you, running. We didn't know if we would make it down the stairs in time!"

The man nodded.

"Well, uh, I'm Marco. These are my people."

The man smiled graciously, offering a wide, genuine smile to everyone, even the kids. Francis was the only one who didn't meet his eyes. He hid behind my legs as soon as Toby put him down.

"Welcome, all of you. It is beyond words to see more living people. My name is David, and this is my wife Eunice."

Twenty-Two: Return

The walk back to the ferry is slower, and mercifully, it's easier than it was on the way in. A few zombies wander through, but we get rid of them with ease and barely have to stop at all. Amy wheels Bill right next to Toby and Murray, who are carrying Ana's body on the stretcher. Nobody speaks. I glance at Joaquin. He's in the back of the group. He looks at me, but I can't read his expression. A few hours ago, he and I were sitting in my cell, and he was telling me that if we just had faith and kept our heads, Bill would be okay, and we would all make it back. I wonder if he's thinking the same thing.

When we're within sight of the pier, Marco jogs to the head of the group. He runs around in the spaces between nearby buildings, back and forth, scouting for zombies. There aren't any. It's just as quiet outside as it was in the hospital. A single seagull flies over us, toward the island.

"Hey," calls Marco, poking his head around the corner of the closest building. "Come see this."

"Marco, we should go," says Calvin.

"Down this way," says Marco. "I found boats."

"Boats? Multiple?" I ask.

Marco nods. "They're big enough for all of us."

"All right, wait here," says Calvin. "We'll be back."

He and I follow Marco. When Sam starts to come with, I put out a hand. "Stay here. We'll be right back."

"Can't I come?"

"You need to stay here and help in case something happens." I don't mean for it to come out sounding as harsh as it does. I'm not mad at Sam.

With a sheepish expression, she backs up and stands next to Bill, who holds her hand.

"Would you look at that," says Calvin as we get to the end of a short alley. With one knuckle, he raps on the side of one of the five rowboats hanging on the wall. "Solid."

"Could these actually work? Could they replace the ferry for good?" I ask.

"I think they could," says Marco. "They're more sustainable, and quieter."

"They'll do just fine," agrees Calvin. He cracks his neck and hoists one off the wall by himself. "Let's go, children! Grab a boat. We'll come back for the other three."

The boat Marco and I pick up is a lot heavier than I anticipated. My grip on it feels precarious. I wobble underneath my end of it as we make our way back.

Though no one smiles when we bring back the boats, everyone is relieved. A little less beaten down than before. *Almost everyone.* I try not to look at Ana's still form. As soon as Calvin sets the first boat down, explaining that there are two more, Murray and Toby place her body carefully inside. Once they are both unencumbered, Murray stands and lets his head hang low for a second. Behind him, Joaquin is watching.

"Right," says Calvin after a moment. "Joaquin, stay here. Keep them safe. I'll help out with the other boats."

When we get back to the island, Mel is waiting for us at the dock as she always is. I rush over and hug her as soon as I step off the rowboat.

"Hey," she hugs me back with the arm that isn't holding baby Andrew. "You found boats. How's Bill?"

"He's fine, but, Mel..."

I watch her face change as she scans the boats one by one, and finally sees what's happening in the one farthest back. The body under the coat. Her relief is obvious when she sees Calvin's face, but then she studies every person coming in, trying to figure out who is under the coat.

"Ana?" she whispers, walking to the end of the dock as the last boat comes in.

"She was bit." My voice is thin, weak. I feel dizzy when I look at the coat-covered body that, this morning, was my friend. My family.

"How?" asks Mel.

"It was nobody's fault," answers Bill. But behind him, there's some uncomfortable shifting. Calvin and Marco both glare at Joaquin.

We bring Ana into the old Officers Clubhouse where Jacob is already buried. The building is gutted, has been for decades, according to Marco. The facade—great gray columns and walls—is all that's left of the original structure. There are no windows and no doors; the place where the roof should be is open to the sky and the elements. Inside, during the daylight hours, it is bright and beautiful, and you can see the ocean through the window openings. There's an informational sign that describes what the building used to be. A place to unwind, to relax. To rest.

Inside, there are several tall cement pillars that probably used to help hold up the roof. Now they stand free, without real purpose. When we buried Jacob, we wrote his name on the side of the pillar closest to his grave. Marco writes Ana's name on the same one while Murray and Jax dig her grave. Their grunts and huffs are the only sound aside from the occasional sea breeze or bird call.

Everyone is here, even the kids, just as they were when we buried Jacob. Mel had originally thought to keep them away from the bodies and the mechanics of it all, saying she would bring them to visit the grave once it was done. But Calvin had spoken up, telling her Jacob would not be the last loss of life and trying to shield them from it was futile.

When the grave is dug, Murray and Calvin lower Ana's body into the ground. We each take a handful of dirt, even the kids, exactly like we did with Jacob. No one voiced a desire for this ritual; I think we all want closure in any small way we can have it, and since they're our people, and they touched each of our lives, it seems appropriate for us to all have a hand in releasing them to their final rest.

Jax swallows hard as he lets his handful of dirt fall over Ana's legs. "She was so many things. A hell of a woman."

"She went down fighting," says Toby, releasing his dirt. "Protecting her people. Best death any of us can hope for."

Murray stands over the grave, his face tilted upward, his lips drawn back from his teeth. "Ana, Ana." he whispers. "Goodbye, Ana. I'll think of you always."

A few people simply say goodbye as they let their dirt go.

"She loved us all," Calvin says, stepping closer to her graveside. He stares right at her, her face, the bloody spot on her shoulder. He sprinkles his dirt, tears slipping down his face. "She was my best friend."

At the edge of the group, Joaquin shrinks back farther from all of us.

I step up to the grave and open my hand. I don't see where the dirt falls. I'm watching Ana's face. She does look peaceful, as much as a person can. "Thank you, Ana," I whisper. "I'm sorry. I'll miss you."

"I, uh—" Marco sniffs, wipes his nose on his arm. "I never had a sibling. I used to think how cool it would be to have a big sister."

He bows his head, clenching the fist that holds his dirt. "Ana was what I imagine a sister ought to be. She gave me strength, courage. She made me believe I could do and be what our people needed. What I needed. I don't even think she knew she was doing it, not at the time, maybe not ever. I should have told her." He drops the dirt at her feet, picks up a shovel, and starts to bury her.

The crowd thins out until only a few of us remain. Mel kisses Calvin's cheek and takes the kids away. Calvin touches the pillar where Ana's name is, and I guess he leaves. A long time or maybe no time passes. Sam gives my hand a squeeze and starts trying to lead me out. I hesitate, but when she pulls more insistently, and Marco doesn't look up at us, I follow her out and back toward the cell house.

Dinner is bland, and nobody talks much. I eat slowly and very little. Marco sits close enough that we could talk, but we don't. Sam keeps her eyes on me, affectionately petting my hand or my arm or my knee. I know she's trying to help.

Joaquin isn't at dinner.

By the time everyone is done, the kids are yawning and so are Mel, Amy, and Bill. We all walk inside together and part ways without speaking. As soon as I enter my cell, even though every muscle in my body aches and my head feels like it weighs about fifty pounds, I know I won't sleep. I try, sort of, lying on my bed without so much as taking off my jacket or boots. When it sounds like everybody is asleep, I get up and go back outside.

Clouds are gathering overhead. Rain starts to sprinkle, little more than a mist. Down by Ana's grave, there's a figure. Joaquin. I don't know if he ever left, come to think of it. He doesn't see me as I pass by, or he doesn't react to my presence, so I keep going.

I'm not sure whether I was hoping to see Marco or not, but there he is anyway, following the same route we always do around the island. He keeps coming toward me, not slowing or stopping when he gets to me. I turn around to join him. At first, neither of us says anything. When I glance up at him, he's staring at the ground ahead of us. There's a footprint in the cement path I never noticed. It's filled with water. I wonder how long it has been there, if it was made by one of the thousands of tourists who used to visit this place, or if it was there even before them.

"Couldn't sleep?" Marco asks, barely above a whisper. It's a question he's asked me countless times.

"No," I reply, same as always. I wish like hell things didn't feel so weird and fractured between us.

Probably because death is so fresh on my mind today, my mom's face, Andrew's, Mae's, and everyone else's run through my brain, unchecked, unasked for, one after the other. Blood and screams and my family being taken away one by one. After all the usual faces, there's Ana. The memory is so clear and even though it's not as bloody or horrible as everyone else's deaths, the pain it elicits is visceral. I have to stop for a second and catch my breath. I count it out, silently begging myself not to collapse into a full-blown mess and at the same time knowing I will.

In four, out eight.

I sit on the cold cement. The moisture soaks through my jeans. I don't care.

Marco crouches next to me on one knee. He reaches out a hand but pulls it back. "You need space, or what?"

I shrug and keep counting. I'm not falling apart as I expected, not really. Just crumbling.

"What can I do?" he asks.

"I'm okay. I can't believe she's gone," I whisper. I finally start to cry, and I don't try to stop myself. First, it's for Ana, then, everyone.

I don't know how long I sit there on the wet ground. Marco stays next to me; at some point he sits and scoots closer so I can lean on him. The rain picks up. We're both sopping wet by the time I pull myself together, and we stand up. I gather my jacket tighter, even though it's just as wet and cold as the rest of me.

"Sorry. Thank you."

"Why are you apologizing? It's okay not to be okay, Cate." Marco's voice sounds hoarse, and when I peer up at him, I can see he's been crying as well. "I miss her too. A lot."

I don't think about it much before I pull him toward me. I wrap my arms around his waist and he reciprocates. We stand still, my face buried in his sweatshirt and his in my hair. His breath catches a bunch of times, and I know he's letting himself go, same as me.

"Why is this so hard?" I ask. "I don't remember it being this way, even after my mom..." A new wave of sobs takes my voice away.

"It was, a little," he says, stepping back. "But—" He pushes a lock of wet hair out of my face, tucks his own behind his ears with the other hand. "I think this feels different because we're allowed to feel it. Every other time—at your house, at the church, on the docks—we had no time to mourn in the moment, to come to terms with what we saw or who we lost. We had to keep moving, keep fighting. Even when you finally got a minute at the church, with your family, to mourn your mom and your stepdad, I think we were still in shock. I know we were. It was so much pain and fear in such a short time. This is how it feels to grieve. This is the way it's supposed to be."

"Well it sucks," I say, pressing my knuckles into my eyes.

"It really does. But it's better than the alternative."

"I guess."

We don't say anything else. There's nothing to say. We start to move, slowly, letting our feet drag even though we're both soaked and shivering. We pass the stairs to the rear entrance of rec yard; Marco takes his hoodie off but doesn't make a move to go in. I don't think he wants to be back inside any more than I do. The rain slows until it's more of a heavy fog.

As we get farther from the rec yard, he moves closer to me. I reach out and take his hand, an automatic gesture. He opens his fingers to allow mine to lace through. For a brief second, I'm worried about what Sam would think of this, but it's gone instantly. People can be friends and hold hands. People can be friends and hug, and talk, and touch, and be alone together. Just because Sam is insecure doesn't mean I have to change my relationship with Marco. And for the second time in two days, the things Mel said, the same things Marco repeated, make more sense.

We pass by the wrecked plane, still sitting where it crash-landed. Weeds are starting to grow around it. Soon, the island will claim it the way we've claimed its passengers.

"I think there's something wrong with Sam and me."

Marco doesn't reply right away. He seems to be thinking about what he's going to say good and hard before saying anything. Probably trying to be diplomatic and not come at me with an *I told you so*.

"Why do you say that?" he finally asks, not letting go of my hand or looking at me.

"Because..." It's a good question. Because it's true, I guess. And even though I only just acknowledged it for real, I think it has been true for a while. "I guess because I can see it now. What you and Mel were talking about. I'm not saying you were right," I add in a hurry.

"Even though you kind of are."

When I glare at him, his mouth twitches.

"I think I changed a lot while we were apart, and I think maybe Sam..."

"Didn't?"

"No, yes she did, because we all did, like you said before. But I think she changed less, or in a different direction? I used to be more social, more open, and now, I don't know. I'd rather train than tend the garden, and I'd rather fight zombies than hang out on the island. And I'm kind of mean now."

"Oh dear God, no you aren't."

"You know what I mean. Remember how chatty I was the first time we met?"

"I remember a Bowie shirt and a lot of eyeliner. You talked, but you weren't exactly bubbly. I think you joked about murdering your cousin." He starts to smile, but he probably remembers the same thing I do—my cousin Gary's actual murder months later at the hands of that disgusting predator Alex and his gang.

Every time I think of Alex, even though he paid for Gary's death in kind, I feel an onslaught of emotions: fear, rage, helplessness. My insides go cold. I clench my fists and concentrate on each step we take.

Marco turns to me as if he can maybe sense my shift in headspace and wants to help me past it. "All I'm saying is, Sam had a pretty stable setup the whole time she was with Bill. She lost her mom, but after that, she didn't lose anyone else. And she didn't have to fight for her life. You changed, because how could you not? And she may have hardened a little, but if she got all the way here and still doesn't see the benefit of training daily, she must have had it relatively easy."

"She and Bill both said their main issue was finding food and water."

"There you go. But just because things aren't perfect with her now, I'm not saying you should give up. I'm sure that wasn't what Melody meant either."

"It's not only that, though," I blurt out. "Something happened. Before Sam and Bill got here."

"What?"

"I don't know, but last time we went to the city, Joaquin and me..." Joaquin and me, what? What exactly happened? I cringe when I think of it now. It feels more wrong than it did that day. I also thought Sam was dead at the time.

Marco stares expectantly. "What?"

"It's silly. I was messing around in one of the closets in this fancy apartment we were scavenging. I had this sparkly red dress. He came up behind me—"

"Yikes."

I glare at Marco. "—*Anyway*, it felt like we maybe had a moment. Or something." I shuffle my feet. "I haven't told Sam about it. I wanted to, at first, and then I really didn't. I don't know what to say, or if it's even necessary. Things were so good with her, and I didn't want to spoil them."

Marco nods slowly, absorbing the new information. "Well, I'm pretty sure you know I think Joaquin is a bit of a weenie and you can do a hell of a lot better."

I chuckle. "Population is pretty limited these days, Marco."

Marco smirks. "Being single beats dating a weenie, Cate."

I shove him playfully.

"But all of this aside, in my experience, if being honest is going to spoil something, it probably isn't great to begin with."

"So you think I should tell her?"

He shrugs. "It's not my call. But it sounds like you need to have an honest conversation to see if you fit together anymore, whether you tell her that part or not."

I think of what Ana said a few days ago. At the time, it seemed to be exactly what I needed to hear. *Fight for it*, she said. Fight for Sam and for love in general because the odds that we would even find each other were astronomical, and didn't that mean something?

Or did Sam's love for me serve its purpose by getting her here, to safety?

"But hey," Marco says, interrupting the mess in my brain. "Think you'll be back to training soon?"

"Sam and I haven't been much lately, have we?"

"Not much. I miss my sparring buddy. It's way too easy to kick Joaquin's ass, Calvin is always busy, and I swear Murray goes easy on purpose."

I feel a flutter of amusement at the idea of musclebound Murray holding back while skinny Marco tries to harass him into fighting harder. "I'll come back soon."

"There's some role reversal for you," muses Marco. "Weren't you pressuring me to come back pretty recently?"

"I was. Thanks for not being as big a jerk about it as me."

He squeezes my hand, lets go, and rests his elbow on my shoulder. "Not my style. You know you should come back. You will when you're ready."

"You're right."

"I know; we've covered this. I'm always right."

"Shut up." I giggle, ducking out from under his arm.

"Soon though, right?"

"Soon. Promise."

When we come up close to the doorway again, Marco asks if we're ready to go back inside. I'm not. The last thing I want is to lie down in the dark and the quiet and let my mind flood with memories I can't bear and thoughts I don't feel capable of dissecting. But my body is tired, and my head is still killing me, so I say yes, and we walk in.

Our shoes squeak on the floor, and someone, probably Murray, shushes us loudly. We stop, take them off, and carry them the rest of the way up to our cells.

Marco stops at mine and steps closer to me. I lean my forehead on his chest, and we both whisper goodnight before he turns and makes his way to his own cell.

Chaz is fast asleep on his rag pile. I'm grateful to have his company tonight. I peel my wet clothes off and drape them over the rails of the cell. They won't dry by morning; I'll have to wear my dress tomorrow. It's a bit cold for that, but it's the dry dress or the wet jeans. I lie down on my hard little mattress and try to position my head so my soaking wet hair isn't right under my face. I close my eyes, open them a moment later, close them again. I won't sleep, I'm sure. But at least being horizontal makes my head pound a little less.

*

I open my eyes slowly. I haven't slept at all. I don't even want to check my watch. The sun is about up. When I hear movement in the other cells, I know I can get out of bed without disturbing anybody. I run the risk of having to interact with people, of course, but only if I leave the cell.

It hasn't been dusted in, well, ever. I could do that; I could clean my little space today. Sam will probably come over. She can hang out too. We'll stay inside, away from talking mouths and staring eyes and hugging arms. Why does everybody get so touchy when someone dies? I'm pacing. The dog is watching me. I stoop to one knee, scratch him right behind the ears. The very softest part of him. He wags his tail and sits up awkwardly, the first movements of his day. He's always so happy just to see me, to see anybody. He shuffles out my doorway and turns toward Mel and Calvin and the kids.

I start to pace again, but I stop at my little built-in table. My wooden training spoon is the only thing on it since I tossed all my weapons to the floor and hung my clothes on the bars when I got in last night. I guess I should get dressed, at least, before anyone walks by. But the spoon stops me again. I turn back to it, and there it is again, just for a moment—the thing that caught my eye in the first place.

It's a single shiny thread running from my spoon to the wall behind the table. It's not two inches long, and I only see it in the sunlight where I'm standing. But as I crouch down again, this time to check under the spoon, I see a small funnel-shaped web.

A fat brown spider comes scurrying out toward my face. I yelp and jump up, brushing myself off even though I know it isn't on me. It's there, on the end of the table.

"Sorry, spider," I say as I reach for the spoon. How long has it been? Can't have been that long. It just feels that way. I slip my dress on and leave the cell, taking my spoon with me.

"Cate?" calls Sam as I cross in front of her cell. She catches up with me, slides her hand through my hooked arm. "What's this?" She touches the spoon. She knows what it is, of course. She's asking why I have it.

"I'm going to training."

"We weren't going to train today though."

"I am."

"Why?"

"Because of what happened in the city? Because we should have been training this whole time. It was a bad idea to stop."

Sam leans her head on my shoulder. "What happened to Ana was awful. But we couldn't have stopped it from happening."

"Maybe we could have. We've been into the city a bunch, and we've never had an incident. And I was scared this time, Sam. Not like I usually am—not alert. I was frightened. I know you don't want to train, but I hope you will soon. I'm going though."

Sam lets her arm slip out of mine and stays in place while I continue on. "See you at breakfast?"

She's not coming.

I feel immediately resentful, but I breathe it away and try for compassion. There's a reason she's not coming, and I have no place to be pushy when this is my first day back. "Yeah. See you."

As I leave the cell house, the first person I see is Bill. Sitting on the steps leading down into the rec yard, his eyes closed and face pointed toward the sun, he looks peaceful, if a little pale.

"Uncle Bill!" I call, jogging toward him. "How are you feeling?"

"Hey, kiddo." He gives me a squeeze with one arm as I sit next to him. "I'm okay, thanks. World flips inside out, and I end up with something as common as kidney stones. Old age is a bastard. But Amy says as long as I keep my calcium balanced and stay hydrated, I shouldn't have to worry. Not sure where I'll get calcium in the apocalypse, but hey. Maybe we'll find a cow to bring back." He grins as if he's joking.

"You're not old." I bump him with my shoulder. "And we'll find something on our next trip to the city. Remind David. He'll add it to the list."

"I'll do that." He takes off his glasses and wipes them on the hem of his shirt. Eyeing my wooden spoon, his smile grows. "You'd better get to training, now. Marco will be glad to see you."

"Cate!" calls Marco, jogging away from the group of stretching, yawning people. "You joining us?" He says it all casual, but I can tell he's glad.

"I'm back," I answer, standing. I squeeze Bill's shoulder one last time and set off down the stairs with Marco.

"If I'd known all it would take was one more ask, I would have done it ages ago."

"It was time," I say, unsure of how to relay my spider and spoon experience.

When I peer over Marco's shoulder and see Calvin stiffly pacing back and forth where he used to stand chatting and stretching with Ana, it hits me all over again. My head swims and my chest tightens.

Marco stands so his shoulder is against mine, as if he can feel my heart racing. "Calvin and I talked about not having training today at all, but—"

"That's not what she would have wanted."

Marco's smile is sad and so tired. "Exactly."

"So, shall we?" I tap his arm with my spoon.

"You're pretty eager to get your butt kicked, Cate."

"It hasn't been that long, Marco."

"Felt like it."

It did. I don't say it out loud, because the feeling mingles with a growing resentment for Sam, her having kept me from training just because she didn't enjoy it. And I know it's not her fault. It's mine. Every morning I decided to skip training, it was my own selfishness driving it. I may not have been directly responsible for Ana's death, but I have to wonder: if I had been at the top of my game, if Sam had taken training seriously or stayed behind, would I have noticed that zombie in time, might Ana still be alive?

I push the thought aside for the time being as we start to spar. I finally feel like I'm doing the right thing, training, and I want to savor it. Marco holds back, though, and I am unreasonably irritated by it. I strike out harder, hoping to drive him into defense mode, and it works.

"Okay, slacker. You think you're tough shit? Come on."

He ducks, rolls away from me, and when he comes back up into his crouch, he swings my legs out from under me. I hit the ground hard. That will be a bruise.

"Shit, ow, Marco," I say as he helps me up.

"You're not even mad."

I smile. "Okay, fair." I pull out my spoon and put up my hands. "Now you're the zombie. Don't expect any favors."

"Wouldn't dare after the thorough beatdown I just delivered." He smiles too and drops his spatula. "That was embarrassing for you."

I lean away from his first strike, easy stuff. But the second one, delivered with his other hand, gets me across the jaw.

"Ooh, neck scratch. You're super dead."

"Damn it!"

I was opening my mouth to say something similar, but it seems someone else beat me to it. Marco and I stop our sparring and turn to see what's going on. Across the yard, Murray and Joaquin are at it, and it seems like Murray is almost chasing Joaquin. He swings his faux weapon faster and faster, his arm is a blur, and a few times, he gets Joaquin in the rib area. Joaquin makes sounds each time but otherwise doesn't fight back. His tool is several feet from him on the ground. Joaquin tries to block the hits, but Murray is putting some real aggression into it. Suddenly, Murray abandons his weapon hand and uses the other to hit Joaquin full across the face. Joaquin spits, and from where I'm standing, it looks like blood. Murray continues to stalk Joaquin, who is, for whatever reason, still not fighting back.

Marco and I exchange a look, but he doesn't seem to be concerned. Where the hell is Calvin? He never lets it get out of hand this way. When Mel—his own wife—went too hard on Sam, he was right there. So why is he standing by with his hands on his hips, watching this go down?

I jog toward the pair and jump between them. Murray lets up the second it's me in his face instead of Joaquin. But he doesn't seem happy about it.

"Cate. Move."

I cross my arms and plant my feet. "Murray. Step away."

Marco follows me but doesn't say anything. Doesn't back me up.

"We're sparring," Joaquin says. "Get out of the way, Cate."

"Sparring?" I make zero effort to mask my incredulity. "This isn't how we spar, and you damn well know it. We use fake weapons, so we don't hurt each other, for God's sake. That—" I point to the spit on the ground. "—is blood. So, what the hell is going on?"

Calvin saunters over, taking his sweet time. "Little rough over here, boys." He glances at Joaquin's bloodied mouth and something passes over his face. Satisfaction?

"A little?" I ask. "When has anyone ever bled during practice?"

"We're training for real life, Cate," Calvin says without looking at me. "Things get intense out there, and some of us clearly need more reminder than others. It's just a little blood in his mouth, right, Joaquin? No reason to stop fighting."

Ah. I understand now. "I think this is dangerous and unnecessary. But you're right. If Joaquin says he's fine, then okay. I've had enough sparring. I'm gonna jog the trail."

Without waiting for replies from anyone, without looking at Murray and Calvin's smug faces or Marco's complacent face or Joaquin's messed-up face, I turn and run out the back exit and down the stairs. I keep running, even though I'm out of breath pretty quickly. In passing, I wonder why we don't add more cardio in with our routine. It seems pertinent to zombie training in that we do end up running from them more often than not.

The image of Murray hitting Joaquin plays in my head a couple of times. I haven't wanted to address the many exhausting feelings swirling around in my brain concerning Ana's death, didn't want to face them head on, but the atmosphere around the training yard felt like the air before a storm. Something is brewing.

So, how do I feel about Joaquin's role in what happened? It was so fast. He'd definitely stopped fighting, that is true. But would he have been able to stop the zombie from biting Ana had he not gotten scared? Would another have taken its place? It feels like I'm wandering into destiny territory, the idea that certain things will occur no matter what. Do I believe it?

I can't. To believe everything happens for a reason means my mom and Andrew were meant to die on my birthday two years ago, and Aunt Tess was supposed to be killed right in front of Uncle Bill, and every other horrible death we've seen was always going to be. So no, I don't believe it.

But it doesn't change the fact that Joaquin might not have been able to stop the zombie. What if, instead of trying to spit out the blood, he'd jumped to another fight, another person to protect? Ana was the one person in the whole group—well, her and Calvin—who I'd have guessed wouldn't need protection. It was happenstance, then, wasn't it? Joaquin truly believed he might have been infected by ingesting the blood, and who can blame him? So, whether he moved away to help someone else or because he was afraid, the result would have been the same.

My last conversation with Ana comes crashing into my brain. Matt. His exile. His fear. A reaction based on instinct. Fight or flight, she said. And without a doubt, I know I can't possibly blame Joaquin, and I know none of us should.

At dinner, it's clear nothing has changed. If anything, it might be worse. After Bill takes the kids inside to get ready for bed, the mood shifts. People are talking, but no one is talking to Joaquin. His face, thankfully, seems to have been tended to.

"Remember the time Ana was trying to teach my brother to shoot an arrow?" Toby says. "I've never seen more patience."

"Even when he slipped, and the arrow gave her a big old welt on her arm," says Murray.

"Although, to be fair, she did stand back a few feet from then on," Marco adds, snickering.

"Wouldn't you? I can't shoot an arrow to save my life," Jax calls over his mouthful of food.

"When I was still recovering," Mel says, "just after we got here, Ana was my savior. She brought me books from the bookstore, came in and told me about what was happening around the island. She made me feel like I was still a part of it."

"I didn't know she did that," Calvin replies. "She took over training for me, too, so I could be up with the babies at night."

"She helped me tick off about half my list of repairs as well," says David. "It's amazing she found the time."

"She was a giver," Toby agrees.

"She talked me down when we were fighting," I whisper to Sam. "She's the reason it didn't last longer."

Sam glances at me, but her face isn't what I expect. She looks confused, or maybe offended. "Oh," is all she says.

"She was one of our best, I think," says Calvin.

"That she was," Murray answers, lifting the flask he gave to Ana in her final moments. "To Ana."

"To Ana," says most everyone else. Even Joaquin.

Calvin and Murray both turn to stare at him when he speaks. Their expressions darken.

"You," growls Murray, advancing toward Joaquin a few steps, "do not speak her name. You're the reason she's dead."

"Murray," Amy chides quietly. "Joaquin didn't kill Ana."

"Oh no? From where I stood, it looked like he got squeamish from a bit of blood and left an opening for one of the dead fuckers to move in and bite Ana. Am I wrong?"

"He was afraid," I say.

"We all get scared, Cate," Calvin says. "That's not an excuse to allow one of our own to get attacked, to get killed."

"So, what are we saying, then?"

There's some uncomfortable movement, people watching Joaquin, Murray, me.

"I wasn't there," says Mel. "But if Joaquin did what they're saying, then something has to happen." Of course she would be on Calvin's side.

"Something? What?" I ask.

"He has to go," says Murray. "He killed her; he can't stay. He doesn't deserve the protection of a group. He forfeited his right when he let that thing get Ana."

"That's absurd," I say. "There's no way in hell we're going to force Joaquin to leave."

"Who's forcing?" Calvin says. "As far as I'm concerned, Joaquin doesn't belong to us anymore. We don't have any obligation to him. He can stay or go, but he's not our problem."

"That's effectively forcing him out, isn't it? If we don't feed him, and we all but shun him, what's the difference? Uncle Bill was right when he said we don't have to understand someone's beliefs to respect—"

"Bill also said you should respect someone's beliefs as long as they're not hurting someone!"

"I wasn't done, Cal. I know he messed up. Joaquin knows it too. Do you think he doesn't feel remorse? Joaquin and Ana were friends too. You don't own grief. We all feel it, and we all feel it differently."

"We also all feel fear, but we don't use it as an excuse to abandon our duties. Before, if one of my team had done something like that, it would be a hell of a lot worse than them having to find their own way. They wouldn't get a chance. And no matter what you say, we all know Joaquin's fear, his actions, directly contributed to Ana's death."

"Are you sure? Are you one hundred percent sure?" I ask. "We're talking about another one of our own. And I'm not saying I have the answers. But I know Ana would agree with me, that one single moment of fear shouldn't dictate a choice this heavy, this final. Do you think Ana would want him gone? Would she say he's not ours anymore because of one horrible mistake? He was scared, you guys. We all get scared. But in Joaquin's mind, it isn't simply the infection. To him, it's a one-way ticket to hell."

Calvin is silent. His arms are crossed tight over his chest, his gaze darting back and forth between Joaquin and me, with the occasional glance at the gravesite.

"Cate's right," Marco says from behind me. "One death can't be undone by another, and sending Joaquin out on his own would be death for him."

"I can handle myself, Marco," says Joaquin.

"Really?" Marco rounds on him, gets right in his face. "Because it seemed a lot like you couldn't when you got blood in your mouth and flipped out. You cannot handle yourself, which is why we're in this situation. So shut up, man, because I know we have our differences, but I'm trying to help you out here."

"He killed Ana," Murray says. "How can you, of all people, say he belongs here? You were closer with her than most of us. You said it yesterday. She was like a sister to you."

Marco sighs and takes a long moment to formulate his answer. "That's why I know Joaquin belongs with us. Because I knew Ana. Better than you did, better than Calvin or Cate. And that's why I know, without any doubt, if she was standing here right now, she would say the same thing. Joaquin is our people. We can be angry with him, fine. But he's not going anywhere."

Toby steps up. "Marco is right. Jury's still out on whether or not I agree with him," he admits, glaring at Joaquin, "but Ana would."

"Just take a second, you two," I say to Calvin and Murray. "Think past your anger to next week, next month. How will you feel if we do make Joaquin go, and on our next run, we find him dead? Will you feel then that justice is served? Will you feel better about Ana when you see Joaquin with white eyes? Because it will be on you."

Neither man speaks.

"So, we put it to a vote," Toby says. "It's the only fair way to decide something that involves us all."

"It isn't something to vote about!" I shout. "This is someone's life—our friend!"

"Cate," Marco murmurs. "He's right. A vote is the right call."

"Fine, then. Who wants to kill Joaquin?" My phrasing is harsh, and maybe a little manipulative. But it's his life. He won't make it alone; no one would. Luckily, after a dozen tense heartbeats, nobody raises their hand.

"And who's for letting him stay?"

Several hands go up. A lot of people don't vote at all.

"I guess that's it, then," Murray says. He spits and walks toward the cell house.

After the hellish dinner is over, the others head inside, and I hang back. Sam does too, staying close to me, and we do little laps around the rec yard.

"That was tense," she whispers. "You were really good though. Did you actually believe everything you said?"

"About Joaquin? Of course. The talk I mentioned, between Ana and me, she shared a part of her trip here and it kind of changed my perspective."

"Ah, yeah. The talk with Ana. The one where you were planning on staying mad at me for a lot longer." Sam's voice is laced with something heavy.

I stop walking. "Well that's not totally fair. You were the one who didn't want to talk to me."

"I needed space, Cate!" Sam shakes her head and continues more calmly, "Anyway, I was talking about the part where you said he'd die for sure if he went off on his own. You think so?"

"Yeah, I'm sure he would."

"Why? He's pretty competent. Didn't he used to be your partner when you guys went into the city for supplies?"

"Well, y-yeah. I mean, he might make it. But I wasn't going to let him get screwed over on a maybe, just because he got scared. I mean, hell, you got scared out there too."

"I'm a lot less competent though," Sam reminds me with some self-awareness I didn't expect. But going to the city was probably a kind of awakening for her.

"So why haven't you been back to training?" I blurt out.

"I don't know. I guess I feel, like, unwelcome? You all have this routine, and I fumble around like a kid."

"We all looked that way at first. Practice is the only way not to."

"God, not this again." Sam scoffs and shakes her head. "We don't all have to be fighters. We're never going to have to live in the city, are we? So why can't I just garden and clean and help out with the kids?"

"Because of what happened when we did go in. Can't you see how your mentality is selfish?" I didn't mean to say that. But I can't say I don't feel it. For some reason, I continue. "You're putting it all on me, and Calvin, and

Marco. Even Mel goes to training more than we have this last week. And she has five kids!"

"Yeah, I remember how Mel trains," Sam says.

"That's not... I mean... Sure, okay! You have no reason to train. You don't need to know how to protect yourself. As long as I'm right here, all the time, you won't ever need to, huh?"

"I can protect myself better than you think, Cate. I might not be an ultimate zombie-fighting champion, but I'm not dead yet."

In an instant, all the fight rushes out of me. "You're right." I just want something, anything, to be okay, to be nice. I take her hand. "You'll be okay. We're safe here, and it's not as if you're the only one who misses training now and then." She misses it a hell of a lot more than anyone else, but there is no reason to poke that bear. "I'm sorry. I think my brain is kind of fried."

Sam smiles a little. "Well, emotions have been running high all over the place. It's okay."

"Want to go inside?"

She slouches and sighs in relief. "Yes, please. I've been hoping you'd say that. I'm exhausted."

"Me too," I lie. Well, half lie. As always, my body is ready to sleep for a year, and my brain is a beehive.

We don't talk as we ascend the steps into the cell house, or when we part ways at Sam's cell. We just kiss, hug briefly, and retreat to our beds.

Twenty-Three: Rescue

3 months ago

After we told David and Eunice about our Alcatraz plan, they pretty much invited themselves. It was fine by me. After they saved our lives, I was planning to ask them anyway. We all decided, though, that our original plan to stick around and wait for Cate and the others was still the best option. The more people we could bring over all at once, the better. We would keep gathering supplies, rest, get our strength back up, and when we found them, we would be ready.

Months flew by in those apartments. At first, we were all Alcatraz, all the time. Or, everyone else was. I kept stalling and watching the island for signs of life. I thought I saw something, the briefest glimmer just once. Never again. But sooner or later, we would find some sign of Cate or Bill or someone on our patrols. I continued my vigil.

I can't remember who first suggested venturing out farther, outside city limits and even to nearby towns. Probably, we were all developing some cabin fever by then. Even with patrols, where teams of two or three would go out, we felt stuck, static. We were so close, but our momentum had dried up. It was mostly down to me. If we were going to Alcatraz, if we were this close and able to go whenever, it was worth it to wait for the rest of my people. And at first, everyone agreed. About eight months in, they started to get restless, saying we could leave, make a base on the island, and do weekly sweeps to find my people. That was when I started to find reasons to change minor parts of the plan, to postpone for one more week, and another, and another. People grumbled, but we all wanted the plan to be perfect, and we were doing so well in that building, considering the state of the world. We were safe, and that was no small thing. We even had a few working vehicles.

Anyway, we went farther out. And farther, farther, until we were an hour's drive away. Being out of the city and back in open air was its own reward, but we also found more people. We found an old man who, after hearing about the Alcatraz plan, told us he could drive the ferry. We also met a ginger dude named Angus ("Angus Murray, call me Murray, nobody calls me Angus"), who saved my ass when I strayed too far from the group. He was as good a fighter as I was, easily, and seemed to be kind of sweet on Ana. Then there was a pair of guys, one stoic gray-haired statue named Rob, and one a year or so older than me named Joaquin. Him, I had trouble warming up to. There wasn't a reason, although I found it irritating as hell the way he refused to use knives to kill zombies, opting instead for guns. Tanya made a point to tell me I should address the masculinity of it all. So I stuffed the feeling away. She was probably right.

Since arriving at the apartment building, I had somehow taken on more of an active leadership role. That meant that, although I still helped Ana train people, she was the officially unofficial commander-type person. At first, it was just her, Jax, and Toby who went out on the road. But it seemed like every other trip for a while, they would come back with one more person. Our group grew faster than I could learn names. Soon, Ana had a core group of five other people, all trained with close-range and long-range weapons. Training them was pretty easy since fighting was basically a prerequisite for surviving that far into the apocalypse.

I went about half the time, just to get out. I trusted Ana and her team. Which was why we almost didn't find Gary in a camp we came across. I pointed out the group of men to Ana. She nodded but kept walking. I watched as we snuck by. They were shouting at one another, one of them threw an empty glass bottle at the other. It shattered, making a third guy jump.

That set off an avalanche of insults and more projectiles from the rest.

The jumpy guy looked up and around. For a millisecond, I thought for sure he was staring right at me because by then, I was staring at him. I knew him.

I put a hand on Ana's shoulder as soon as we were far enough to talk. "Those guys, did you see them?"

"We've seen them around," Ana whispered as we made our way back to the vans. "They have a more fortified camp over by the stream, but that's all of them. They're a dangerous bunch. Not worth trying to engage, for trading or anything else. They're nowhere near us, and we should keep it that way."

"Did you see the one they were taunting?"

"It seems as though he's less a part of the group," said Murray, "than kept by it."

"I know him."

They all stopped and looked at me.

Ana narrowed her eye. "From before?"

"From before. That's Gary."

"Gary, as in your shitty foster brother?"

"The very same." I opened the passenger side of the van I was driving. We loaded our finds and ourselves into it, slammed the doors, and were on our way back to the apartments.

"So, we need to get him out, then."

A rather large part of me wanted to say that he was alive, and hadn't Ana just said those guys weren't worth engaging? But I bit my tongue. Bill, if he made it all the way to the city, would be devastated if I hadn't at least tried to save his son. Even Cate would remind me that he was still family, still a person, and people were always worth saving. Of course they were.

"Yeah. We do."

"Er, Marco," said Murray from the back seat. "Don't get me wrong, lad, but I think you need to sit it out. He's your family?"

"Yeah, and?"

"We've observed those men. We will need to have all our wits and none of the stuff that comes with family when we extract the boy."

"I'll drive," I said. The words left my mouth before the thought took shape. But I knew he was right, and I knew it would be good for Gary to see a familiar face as soon as Ana's team got him out. So, driving was a good spot for me.

We took the night to plan it out. Apparently, the group didn't move around much. Ana's team would hide, wearing all black to camouflage themselves. They would hold the group at point of arrows and blades and get Gary out. I would wait by the vans, all set to go in different directions so we couldn't be followed. I'd drive Gary's van on a looping route back home, and the others would be decoys until they were sure they weren't being followed. Then, they'd head back to the apartments too. The plan was excellent, clean, and it would almost definitely work.

The next morning, we prepared and cleared the alternate routes, but by the afternoon, when we were scheduled to leave, I had a giant pit in my stomach. Fear, and some plain nerves. I was finally going to see a member of what semblance of a family I'd had, but it was Gary. Still, I decided as we closed in on the rendezvous point, he'd find a way to fit in.

I stood waiting by the three vans, gazing around and seeing nothing worth dealing with. A few zombies passed by, but none took notice of me, so I left them alone. Time seemed to slow to a crawl for a while. I kept glancing back toward where Ana and the others had entered the forest. I felt like I was looking every minute or so. At one point, I almost went in after them. It had been too long, hadn't it? What if they needed me? Had I made a mistake, waiting by the vans? Ana was strong, and she could take care of herself, but what if this was the time she couldn't? I paced around the vans in a tiny loop, deliberating. She could do it; she would be fine. Or she wouldn't, and we would lose another person we cared for.

But before I decided to charge into the woods, they came back out. They had a lot more people with them than I had expected. There was even a dog. But no Gary, as far as I could see. Murray came up to me first, holding his fitted cap in his hands.

"Gary died, Marco. I'm sorry. But these women, they knew him." He backed up, and the new people approached.

There were four of them. A guy and an old woman I didn't recognize, and a girl and a woman I did.

"It's them, isn't it?" asked Ana, smiling as if she already knew the answer. "The sisters."

It was. I couldn't believe it; my heart pounded in my throat and my knees were suddenly made of jelly. Cate was sort of looking at me, but her eyes were half-closed, and her head was bleeding. She stumbled and hit the ground hard. I reached down to help her up, taking her dirty hand in mine. "Cate?"

She seemed to finally see me, her dilated pupils focusing on my face.

"Cate." I squeezed her hand, allowing myself to smile. It was real, she was really there.

She smiled and passed out cold.

I greeted Melody and the other newcomers, noting Melody's gigantic baby bump with a "congratulations" that felt strangely plastic. Murray and the new guy loaded Cate into the backseat of my van. Ana started toward her van.

"Ana?"

She turned back to me, and before I could think about it too much, I ran over and hugged her.

"Thank you." My voice was muffled, so she probably couldn't hear it shaking.

"For this? This is what we do."

I let go and shook my head, wiping my cheeks with the back of my hand. "Ana, you brought my people back, at least two of them. And not just that. Thank you, for, for coming back. Thank you for being here."

Ana smiled. "We're a family. I'll be here as long as you'll have me. You ready to go home?"

"I am."

Twenty-Four: Jump

I will never get to sleep. The sun will be up anytime. I swing my feet over the side of the bed and sit slouching on the edge of the thin mattress for a few breaths before I drag myself up and shuffle toward the door to the rec yard. I've been up all night thinking of Sam, Ana, Joaquin. I thought I was sure about a lot of things, but now that I have room to think and digest it all on my own, I find I'm conflicted about at least one.

Even though we're not fighting, I feel farther from Sam than I have since she got to the island. I think I felt closer to her when I didn't know if she was alive or not. But that was more the idea of her, I guess. It's easy to romanticize someone who isn't there. I love Sam, I do. But is it enough? Or, perhaps the more important question, is it even the right kind of love? If everything can change, love can change too. Has mine?

"Cate?"

I squint. It's not Marco coming toward me in the darkness as I expected. "Sam?"

She waves. I let her catch up to me before I start walking again.

"Hey," she says.

"Hey."

"You okay?"

"I'm fine." Why do I feel disappointed?

"You were expecting Marco, right?"

I don't say anything, which I suppose says enough.

"Yeah," says Sam. "Figures."

"Well, you've never shown any interest in nighttime walks, is all."

"And you've invited me so many times?" She makes a noise, shakes her head, and glances at me. "Sorry."

"I haven't invited you, you're right. I guess it's..." It's my thing with Marco, but how do I say that to Sam without upsetting her? And why does it still upset her? How can anyone expect to be the only important person in someone else's life?

"Cate? What's in your head?"

"I don't want to be mean, but in a way, it is a Marco and me thing. It started after my mom and Andrew died, and it became a kind of ritual for us. I'm not saying you can't come out once in a while and walk with us." I add the last part hastily, and it doesn't feel genuine.

"No, just that you don't want me to." Sam stomps a few paces away, and then back to me. "God, what is it with you and Marco? Be honest with me, Cate, because I am really starting to think you're not. Did something happen with Marco while we were apart?"

"No!" I shout. More quietly, I clarify. "Not with Marco."

Sam raises her chin. "But with someone. Who?"

"Joaquin."

Sam stares at me as though she's hurt and betrayed and not so much angry as resigned. "Ah. So, I was wrong about Marco. Why didn't you tell me sooner?"

"I didn't know how. Honestly, it was basically nothing. More of a...moment, I guess?"

"If it was nothing, you wouldn't have said it was."

I twist up my mouth, trying to find the right words. I don't want to hurt her. "We didn't even touch. Nothing actually happened. But I found myself entertaining the idea of—you know—moving on."

"Moving on," Sam repeats. She turns her focus to the middle distance, not looking at me or anything really. "All those times I saw you look at him, or the other day during training when you two partnered, it seemed weirdly uncomfortable for how well you know each other. I should have known." She takes a deep breath. "Was this before I came back, at least?"

"Yes! It was. I missed you so much, and from the minute you came off the plane..." My eyes start to sting; my mouth is bone-dry. "I was so happy to have you back," I choke out.

Sam tilts her head, brows furrowed. "You were? As in, not anymore?"

My insides squeeze and drop. I didn't realize it until she articulated it. The use of past tense. "I guess, I feel different. Like we're different." It's a simplified version of how I feel, but it's something.

"I do too. I feel confused. I think we both changed—I mean, everything changed. And when we finally got back together..."

"We didn't quite fit."

"Can we still?"

She's asking as if my answer will be it. But I guess it will. Whatever I choose affects us both. Could hurt us both, but aren't we hurting already? I thought we had no choice but to embrace each other, even when it hurt. Ana's words struck so deep when she told me to fight for it. I gave up pieces of me to appease Sam, to fit Sam. I thought I had to.

"I think we can," I start to say. "But—"

Sam grabs my hand and leans in. "You think?" Her tone is so hopeful. No trepidation whatsoever, which somehow feels worse. "But?" She backs up as she registers the last word. Her expression is excruciating.

"But, do we want to?"

"I do," Sam answers. "But you don't."

I shake my head even though she's still staring at the ground, but she looks up. Her lip trembles, and her face breaks into a million pieces. Damn it, the last thing I ever want to do is hurt Sam. My Sam. Is she my Sam anymore? More to the point, am I her Cate? Or am I New Cate, incompatible with New Sam to the point of toxicity?

"I think if we keep trying to fit, we'll end up hurting each other."

"You mean hurting each other more."

"Exactly."

"So that's it, then?" She shrugs, shakes her head. "We're finished?"

Why is it so hard to declare the end of something? To say when? It's the same feeling I used to get standing up on those really tall rocks at the lake, the ones we used to leap off of into the water. Anything could happen; it's terrifying and freeing. You give up control once you jump, for better or worse. But if you deliberate too long, you'll scare yourself out of it. You just have to jump.

"Yes," I say before I can think about it much more.

She flinches. "Okay, then. Wow. Okay."

"It's just, we're so different now. We worked well back then, but have you considered we might have grown apart?"

"Of course I've considered it." Sam's voice takes on a defensive quality. Almost venomous. "When you first had issues with me, issues I didn't even know about, you went to Marco, who doesn't know me."

"I tried to talk to you the very next day. Which, by the way, was his advice. You really hurt me with the whole "zombie ruined your beautiful skin" thing, you know. I'm immune to this plague or virus or whatever it is. Immune! And I didn't ask to be, but it's the only reason I'm still here. Anybody else gets bitten on the hip, so far as we know, they fucking die. So what if I have some weird scars? I'm alive! Marco told me it was a superpower when he found out. You made me feel like it was something shameful and ugly. Something to hide."

"Jesus Christ, with Marco again!"

"Damn it!" I scream. "You know we're only friends! Can I not have friends? And are you even listening to me? Don't you hear me when I say you hurt me?"

"I—" Sam's mouth hangs open for a second. She grits her teeth. "I am listening. I didn't realize I hurt you. I'm sorry."

I take a few breaths. Shake my head. "It's whatever. It doesn't matter now."

"Now that we're over, you mean, and I'm alone again. You don't know what it's like."

"Sam, we all dealt with awful stuff on the road. Honestly, I think all of us had it worse than you, from what you and Bill told us."

"First of all, it's not a damn contest. But that's what I'm saying. You have a new family, new people. You all understand one another and coexist, and here come Bill and me, crash-landing into this little community. Do you have any idea how weird it is? No, not weird. That's a ridiculous understatement. I walk on eggshells all the time. I want to fit in so badly, and no matter what I do, it feels like I'm an outsider."

"I met these people a few months ago, Sam. A week before we came here."

"But you knew them; you built this together. Started from scratch, together. And that's not even really my point, because I could handle being a bit of an outsider for a while. I could even handle your sister going Mister Hyde on me as soon as I got here, or the borderline-military training schedule, if I had you."

"You—" I start to say "do," and almost say "did," and settle on "What do you even mean?"

"I never had you, not like before. Before, we were best friends. We were Velcro—and I know you felt it because you just said you did—but we were different once I got here. And after so long and so many miles, and thinking the whole time 'It's okay, I'm going to see Cate again soon,' it was such a letdown. It sort of crushed me. And I tried to make it work, but I think I ended up getting sort of desperate. And that's not how it should be, if it's right."

Tear tracks glisten down her face in the moonlight.

"Sam," I begin, but I don't know what to follow with. I want to reach out my hand, but I clench my fist instead. *I love you*, I want to say. But the more I think about it, the further I get from doing it. "Are you okay?"

Sam isn't looking at me, but out toward the water. "You're my only connection to this place, you know?"

"I'm not. What about Bill?"

"Bill is another connection to you." Sam shrugs. "I felt pretty out of place before. God. I'll really be adrift now. I don't know if I ever should have come."

I have no idea what to say. I feel like Sam is being dramatic, which and I guess is fine; we did just basically break up. But she knows she belongs here. Where else would she go? I look at her, then in the direction she's staring. Eventually, she turns around toward the cell house.

"Okay. Goodnight, Cate."

By the time I turn around, Sam is jogging back toward the building. I walk another full lap to give her a chance to get inside, and maybe to see if Marco will show up. When he doesn't, I go in.

Sam is already in her cell, so I take my time climbing the stairs. It happened so quickly. One minute, we were us. A very short, very honest conversation later, we weren't anymore. I am only mildly surprised I haven't broken down yet, but I figure I'm tapped out for the week after losing Ana, burying her, and fighting to keep Joaquin.

A light is on in a cell down the way. Marco's. His thin, off-white curtain diffuses the light, giving the whole doorway a warm glow. There's a familiar pencil-to-paper scratching sound coming from within. I shuffle to his cell, linger outside for a second, and stick my hand inside, wiggling my fingers. When he doesn't say anything, I poke my head in. At first, he doesn't notice me.

There's a sort of buzzing sound in his cell. I look around for a second before finding its origin: nearly hidden by his tangled hair are a pair of headphones. He bobs his head in time to whatever he's listening to, scratching away on the sketchbook he has propped up on his knees. I creep into his cell and sit at the foot of his bed. He finally sees me. He slides the headphones down around his neck and pushes the pause button on the portable CD player sitting next to him.

"Hey," he whispers, setting the drawing pad aside.

"Hey. You didn't walk tonight." I don't know why that's what comes out of my mouth, but I feel my face change, and Marco looks worried. I kick off my shoes, draw my knees to my chest, and rest my head. "Sam and I broke up."

"Shit, Cate, I'm sorry. What happened?"

"Nothing," I say a little too loudly. "We just sort of...talked, and that was it."

"Are you okay?"

"I'm fine, I guess. I didn't expect this to happen."

"I don't think people usually do. Not that I'd know."

"What do you mean?"

"Dating doesn't appeal to me, I guess. Never really has. Want to cheer up?" He reaches for the headphones.

I settle against the wall next to him. "Yes, please."

"Okay."

He jumps off the bed, landing lightly on his socked feet, crouches down, and pulls his old ratty backpack out from under the bed. He riffles through it, pulls out a CD case, and swaps the CD in the portable player for the one in his hand. "Put these on," he says, handing me the big, over-ear headphones.

I do.

Smiling, he holds his finger over the play button. "Ready?" he mouths, or maybe whispers.

I nod. A familiar sound plays, soft music with a broken beat and ghostly vocals. It's the album I was playing when my aunt and uncle first brought him to our house to meet us, the same album Marco had pulled out of his backpack to show me that he had it too. The first thing we ever had in common.

A shiver runs up my spine, across my shoulders, over my face. "Marco."

He keeps smiling as he picks up his sketch pad and starts drawing again. I can see it now that I'm next to him. It's a sketch of the lighthouse outside, a simple outline, but big enough to fill the page. Marco smudges some of the lines with his thumb to create shading.

I close my eyes and let the music move through me, color my mind like a drop of ink in clear water. I used to take it for granted, the peace music can bring. The feelings it can evoke. I never thought I'd hear familiar music again. I never thought I'd see Sam again either. But while the music is filling me with joy and peace, I feel as though, until now, I've been weighed down with above-average anxiety and feelings of inadequacy. By my relationship with Sam. The thought disappears and is replaced with self-chastisement, but there it was. Was Sam somehow holding me down? I wasn't exactly happy before she came back, but I had a community, shelter, a purpose. Training made me feel good, like I was in control of my body, whereas the last two days, getting back into the routine, have been painful and awkward. It's not her fault I stopped going, but I made the choice because she asked me to. That's not healthy, is it? If you love someone, you don't ask them to give up something that makes them better, makes them feel good. Feel useful.

But she told me why she asked me to stop going, or, she basically did. She has felt out of place here since she arrived. But not for lack of trying. Everyone (okay, everyone but Mel) has been welcoming to both her and Bill. And Bill had no issues finding a thing, a reason to get up in the morning. He took up the dad role with ease, and now he's basically a Godfather to all five kids. Did Sam even try to find a thing, or did she expect me to be her thing? And I know now, sitting here with my best friend, someone who only wants me to be better, that I never wanted someone to depend on me that way.

Was I better off before Sam came back into my life?

When the song is over, I desperately want to listen to more, but I am not about to waste his batteries when he was so generous in the first place. And I am exhausted. So I take them off, slip them back over his ears, mouth "Thank you," and tiptoe out carrying my shoes.

I am surprised and grateful to find Chaz in the corner on his rag pile. As I scratch his ears and head, I vow inwardly to find him and Duchess a more suitable bed next trip into the city.

Right after I make that silent promise, as I crawl into my own bed, I try to push the city and all of my other worries away. Getting Sam out of my head is the hardest. But to my surprise, the feeling that comes first isn't sorrow or hurt, it's relief. It's just enough that I feel myself slipping into the darkness and warmth of deep sleep.

Sam stays clear of me for the next few days. I am surprised to see her at training every morning. At first, I think it might be a ploy to get my attention, but when I chance a smile and wave at her on the second day, she ignores me. After five days, she's good enough to knock Jax on his ass once or twice. She stays away from me as much as she can on such a small rock. And I get it. She has anger to release, and training is the healthiest way to do it. Good for her.

On the eighth day, though, she's not there. She isn't at breakfast either. I even take my time eating, finally starting to get uncomfortable with her absence. I had hoped we could be friends—or, if not, then something similar—but she's clearly still trying to avoid me. When I find Bill and the kids gardening in the mid-morning drizzle, she's not with them either. I didn't even consider that she might have stayed in bed, that maybe she isn't feeling well. But when I check her cell, she isn't there, and neither is any of her stuff. Sam's cell is empty. Only then does it occur to me to be worried.

At about noon, I tell Marco and then Calvin, who are showing Francis and Adrienne the four-count formation, that Sam and her stuff are missing.

"Missing?" asks Marco. "She probably moved cells. Wouldn't you?"

"Yeah, I heard you and Sam broke up last week," says Calvin. "Tough stuff. Sorry, kid."

"Thanks, great, but no, I mean missing. Has either of you seen her all day?"

"Well, no."

"Me neither."

I couldn't tell you why the idea forms at that moment, except that I always jump to the worst possible scenario. Without excusing myself, I run out of the rec yard, through the cell house, out through the other doors, and down the main path. I stop dead as soon as I can see the dock. I count, count again. One, two, three, four. There are only four boats.

I run back to the guys who have taken up their kid training again as though Sam isn't gone.

"She stole a boat," I pant, trying to catch my breath. My lungs can't get full enough. My heart, my gut, my head, all feel as though they're made of lead. "Sam. Stole a boat. She's gone."

"Calm yourself. I'm sure it's fine," Calvin murmurs, eyeballing me and then the kids as if to remind me they're there. "Okay, lesson over!" He fist-bumps Francis and high-fives Adrienne. "Good job today, guys. Let's go find Melody."

"Is Sam coming back?" asks Adrienne as Calvin starts to lead them away.

I force a ridiculous fake smile onto my face. "Of course."

As soon as the kids are out of earshot, I whirl back to Marco. "She's going to be okay, right? We're going to go get her."

"She's going to be fine," Marco says, "we aren't even sure what happened." But his answer sounds as thin as mine. He has no idea.

"She might be dead already," I whisper. What were the last words I said to her? My brain is spinning. They weren't the right ones, that's for sure.

At about two in the afternoon, Amy notices the fifth boat on its way back from the city. The pit that has sat in my gut since I saw Sam's empty cell loosens somewhat. But not for long. The only person in the boat is Murray. How long has he been gone? Did I see him at training?

I rush to the dock and start interrogating him before he's even touched it.

"Murray! Sam?"

Murray puts a hand up. "She's fine. But she isn't coming back."

"What do you mean? What happened?"

He finally reaches the dock and starts to tie up the boat. "She stopped me on my way out to training a few minutes before sunrise. Pulled me into her cell. She told me about you and her, Cate. I was sorry to hear it. And she asked me to get her to the city."

"And you just did it?" I shout. A few floating zombies stir in the water. One reaches out a hand at me, and I stab it in the head with such force I almost tumble in with it. "You didn't think taking her to the city by herself might be a terrible idea, given that she barely trains *at all*?"

Until this week, which now that I think about it, makes me wonder when she decided to leave. How long did she plan this?

"Of course I didn't just do it," Murray snaps back. "I told her that, and I told her food would be scarce unless she went deep into the city. But she said she'd made up her mind and was only asking me so she wouldn't have to steal a boat to get away. And I told her I couldn't let her go, not without talking to the others, and we'd take her in on the next errand. She said, rightly so, that she is an adult, and she isn't a prisoner here. So I loaded her up with supplies, helped her clear out a place to stay, and gave her a torch to signal with in case she needed anything. I told her to keep signaling until she saw a reply, and that I'd keep an eye out for her."

My eyes start to prickle while he talks. She's gone. I saw her again, touched her as recently as yesterday. I don't know what to say to anyone. As soon as someone else starts talking, I turn and walk back up the path.

"Cate, hey! Wait up." Marco jogs after me.

I keep walking, but more slowly. When he catches up to me, he doesn't talk either, which I am thankful for. I don't want to talk. I want to be left to what's in my head, even though I am well aware what's going on in there isn't particularly healthy. The idea that she will probably die alone, and the accompanying images, make my stomach churn. I keep putting my feet down, keep moving away from the docks, the last place Sam touched on the island. The last place she could have been stopped. Could have been saved.

Marco stays silent next to me until I find myself in front of her cell. He looks confused for a moment when I walk in, but I ignore him, and he leaves.

I kick off my shoes and curl up on Sam's bed. The cells are all the same, but it's different in here. The windows are in a slightly different spot than they are from my cell's point of view. They get blurry as my eyes fill with tears again. I don't cry like I did when we lost Ana, even though Sam is likely to suffer a similar fate. I am too tired, tired of losing people, tired of not being able to stop it. So I drift in and out of sleep, peppered with dreams of happy past-Sam and less happy recent-Sam. Sometimes, dark images find their way in, the ones I'm not sure about, that my imagination can go wild with.

At some point, I vaguely register Marco coming into the cell with my blanket and pillow, offering the latter until I lift my head, and sliding it underneath. He says something as he covers me up, but I turn over until he goes away. I know it's rude, but I know he doesn't care.

I wake up hours later. It's dark, which could mean it's about five, or that it's the middle of the night. But as I'm bending my stiff, achy body to pull my shoes on, Marco comes by the cell and stops halfway in.

"Oh. Hey," he says with a smile. "Welcome back."

"What time is it?" I ask, squinting at my watch.

"About seven. Dinner soon. I was coming up to see if you wanted to eat." He catches sight of my boots, untied but on my feet. "I guess you do."

I shrug. Stand up. Walk out of the cell. I don't know if I want to eat; I'm not hungry, but I can't be in there anymore. It was starting to feel like a tomb. Instead of Sam's cell, her room, it's the place she used to be. I want to seal it off and never look at it again. Maybe after dinner, I'll have Marco close it. He's still the only one who knows how to operate the cell door mechanism.

The air is chilly, the kind that causes an instant shiver when you step outside. I pull my sweatshirt tighter, wishing I'd brought my jacket. Oh, well. I won't be outside for long.

"Hey, stranger," Calvin says good-naturedly, patting me on the arm as I get in line to dish up. His expression says he's happy to see me and also quite unsure of what else to say.

"Hi."

"How you doing, sweetie?" asks Mel as she places some cooked vegetables on my plate.

I peer up at her. She's smiling, her cheeks red from sitting by the fire. She looks concerned, maybe relieved. Maybe I'm imagining that part. Even Mel wouldn't revel in this.

"I'm fine."

I sit on the outer edge of the group forming around the little fire. It's definitely getting a little colder at night. Does Sam have blankets? A coat?

Amy sets her plate right by mine and settles herself delicately next to me. "Do you want to talk about it?"

"I don't know what there is to say. Sam left. I broke up with her, and she went away."

"I heard."

"Of course you did. The population of this island is, like, fourteen."

Amy doesn't respond.

"I just—I can't believe she left. In what world is your life worth making a statement?"

"And what statement is that?" asks Tanya, settling on Amy's other side.

"I mean, you know. That I shouldn't have broken up with her, or she's better off without me, or something."

"Do you really think Sam made the decision to leave, knowing all that entails, just to send you a message?" asks Amy.

"Not everything is about you," says Tanya. "In fact, I think you'll find that more isn't about you than is."

"Well, she did it right after we broke up, didn't she?"

Amy inclines her head, regarding me as if I'm someone to pity. I hate it.

"She was unmoored. You were a big part of her life. That is true. But something tells me her decision wasn't totally about you. Some of us never went out of our way to make her feel welcome. But either way, she is gone. And now you both have to move on. Want to know what my mother told me the first time I got my heart broken?"

I stare at her in place of an actual answer. My fingernails dig into the palms of my hands. I don't, actually. That's what I want to tell her. I don't want your advice or your pity. Keep them.

Instead, I keep staring, grinding my teeth together.

"She said, 'You get tonight. Tonight, you cry and you mourn and you shout if you need to. And tomorrow, you wake up, wash your face, and move forward.'"

I chew on my cheeks. I'd think it was stellar advice if it wasn't about my heart, my pain. But it is. "No, I don't think so. I don't need to accept this."

"No?"

"No. I'm going to go get her. Hey!" I stand up, walk toward the center of the group. "We can't just let one of our own go to her death. That's basically what this is. I don't fault Murray, because he was respecting her wishes, I guess, but this is bullshit. We have to go get Sam."

Calvin stands too, and he takes his plate to the stack of dirty ones. "Cate. You're tired and hurt. This situation is nothing like any breakup any of us have experienced." Something about his posture as he walks back toward me reminds me of fighting-Calvin. He's ready for a confrontation. So he definitely disagrees with me.

"Yeah, that's true," I say, crossing my arms. "She could literally die."

"But she made a choice."

There it is.

"It was the wrong choice. She was—what did you say, Amy? Unmoored. People get reckless when they're hurting. And that's my fault."

"She thought about it, clearly," says Mel. "And she's an adult. Not to mention, going into the city, when we have no way to know where she is, is irresponsible and could end up hurting even more people."

"Okay. First, Murray knows where she is. Second, you know that by not going to get her, we're condemning her to die, right?"

"She condemned herself," says Joaquin quietly, staring down at his empty plate.

I round on him. "What did you say?"

"I'm not saying she deserves to die. I liked Sam okay. But she decided to go, knowing she might run into trouble. She knew that last time we went in. And she went anyway."

"You're one to talk!" I shout. "I goddamn defended you when no one else would! It would be you in the city alone right now had I not fought to keep you here!"

"And I am thankful. But if I had gone to the city, I would have made it work, or died. Sam is in the same position. Only difference is, she put herself there."

"I can't believe what I'm hearing! Does anybody else think this is absurd?"

Amy puts her hand on my shoulder. "I know this is hard. But she's in charge of her own life as much as you are. She made a choice, and we need to respect it. Even if you did find her, who says she would want to come back? You can't force her to be here."

"I gave her the means to signal if she needs us," says Murray. "Her place faces the island, and she need only flash the light and I told her I'd be there."

The fight goes out of me, as fast as it came. It's replaced by desperation. They are ready to sit there and let her die.

"Can we at least put it to a vote?" I ask.

"Okay," says Calvin. "Fair enough. Let's do it. Everyone here?"

We all look around at one another. Everyone's gaze lingers on me for a second.

"All right, so. Who agrees with me that Sam is in way more danger than she needs to be, that she's one of us, and our only choice is to go get her?"

I raise my hand, expecting it to at least be a pretty even split. But the only other hand that goes up at first is Bill's.

"I don't want to force her to come back or anything," he says. "But I want to see her, and make sure this is what she wants."

"Fine, but you do think we should go. Anyone else?" I stare directly at Marco. His hands are down. But slowly, he raises one hand halfway in the air.

"All right, three in favor," says Calvin. "And who thinks that Sam is an adult, that she made her choice, set a boundary, and we should respect it until such time as she signals for help?"

Everyone but David and Amy raise their hands. Even the kids do, but I know they're only doing it because Mel is.

I make eye contact with every person whose hand is raised against going to get Sam. I feel betrayed, angry, hopeless. I'm not sure who I am angrier with—Sam, for leaving in the first place, or the people I thought I knew, effectively deciding to wait and see if she dies.

"We're supposed to be a community, a family," I say as all the hands go back down. "We're supposed to watch out for one another."

I turn and run back toward the cell house as several people start to reply at once. I don't care what they have to say. They don't get the satisfaction of justifying their cowardice or selfishness or whatever it is that's preventing them from helping one of our own.

I don't want to see anyone tonight; I don't walk with Marco. I walk past Sam's cell, not looking in. She's not there. It isn't her cell anymore.

I fall onto my bed, letting out a low moan. My head is heavy; the dull ache that has been building behind my eyes since I first found Sam's empty cell has crescendoed into a hammering. I turn over and over on the mattress that somehow feels harder and lumpier than it ever has, adjusting the blanket that feels thinner and less adequate with each degree the temperature drops.

When the dog enters my cell ten minutes or two hours later and settles on his spot, I drag my body out of bed and curl around him. It's warmer with two of us under the blanket, and soon his breathing is deep and even. I try to match the pace with my own breaths, and my heartbeat slows and the pounding in my head subsides the tiniest bit.

I must have fallen asleep because the next thing I know, the dog is gone, and someone's creeping into my cell.

"Cate?" whispers Marco. He tiptoes toward my empty bed, and when he notices the lack of an occupant, he backs up, glances toward the door, the bed, and finally finds me in the corner. He tilts his head. "Hey."

I don't move.

He picks up my shoes and places them next to my feet. "Come outside. I want to show you something."

"I'm not in the mood, Marco."

"I know. But what if I told you I know why the peas are dying?"

I try not to let on that I am a tiny bit interested. Not enough to get up and go outside though. "So just tell me."

"No. I want to talk to you anyway. Come on; I'll meet you in the rec yard."

Twenty-Five: Flicker

The sun is still below the horizon. The air is thick with cold sea mist. Marco leads me out of the rec yard and along the path. We stop above the garden.

"Okay, you got me out here. Congratulations."

Marco puts a finger to his lips and points with the other hand toward the garden where Chaz is trotting around with Duchess. They sniff around, their tails swishing slowly back and forth. Duchess wanders off toward the agave trail. Chaz makes a beeline for the peas and hikes a leg on them.

"I saw him do it yesterday morning. I meant to tell you, but...you know."

"Gross, Chaz," I mutter.

"So, throwing away any that the plant does yield, right?"

"You mean the ones we haven't already eaten?"

Marco narrows his eyes. "Ew."

"So, not that I didn't love the visual, Marco, but you could've just told me."

"I know. I wanted to talk to you."

We start toward the agave trail where Duchess is still meandering. The gravel crunches under our feet. The dog looks up at us, wags her tail, and returns to her investigatory sniffing.

"I think you're right," Marco begins in a halting, tentative tone, "about going to get Sam."

"You sure seemed to agree with me last night. Really confident with your vote." I pump a little extra sarcasm into my voice, combination residual anger and mistrust in his sudden change of heart.

"Hey, I voted, didn't I?" He shuffles his feet. "I've been thinking about it, though, and I agree with you. Or actually, I agree with Bill. We shouldn't go with the intention of bringing her back, if it's not what she wants. But we should go and make sure she knows she's welcome. And if she does want to stay out there, that she's as safe as she can be."

Not quite what I want to hear, but it's a way to get to Sam. "I appreciate it, I guess. But the group voted not to go last night."

"Right, but I think we can change their minds, or at least enough of them."

"How? I presented a pretty damn compelling point. Don't let our own people die. What else is there?"

"Well, you could start by not being so aggressive about it."

"Aggressive? I'm not aggressive. That's bullshit. And I'm right! So even if I was aggressive last night, I have reason to be!"

"Maybe you did. But it's not an effective persuasion tactic, is it?"

We walk up to the steps leading into the rec yard and turn back before we climb them.

"Remember how abrasive I was at first?" Marco asks. "Back when all this started?"

"You were an ass half the time."

"Yeah, and it got me into some trouble. All I'm saying is, I think if we approach this with the littlest bit of diplomacy, we can—"

"Shut up."

"Okay, that's exactly what I'm talking about."

"No, just shut up and look." I grasp his shoulders and steer him toward the city. "Do you see it?"

It's just a flicker, a tiny little twinkle.

"It's the sun reflecting off a window or something."

I shake my head. "Sun rises in the east."

He gazes at the sky, then back to where we saw the light. "What was it, you think?"

It happens again, not one flash, but a series of them. Some sort of pattern. We watch it go two more times.

"Marco, it's a flashlight. It has to be."

"I think you're right."

"I think that's Sam."

"If you're right, we need to get everyone up."

Without another word, we run back to the stairs, through the rec yard, and into the cell house to wake everyone and tell them what we saw.

We gather at the part of the agave trail where we can see the signal most clearly, where Marco and I were standing. The whole city is silhouetted against the rising sun, but not for much longer. In a minute, it might be too bright to see the signal.

It flashes again.

"There! Did you see it?" I ask impatiently.

Calvin pulls his messy hair into a headband. "Yeah, I did. Doesn't seem to be a reflection."

"Of course it's not," I snap.

Marco nudges me. I roll my eyes. Right, diplomacy.

"That's an SOS. No question."

"Joaquin, how do you know?" asks Tanya.

"Scouts."

"He's right," says Calvin after it goes again.

As the sun comes over the top of the buildings, it stops.

"We're going now, right?" I ask. We shouldn't have waited even this long. I hope we're not too late, that she only stopped the signal because the sun came up or the battery died, or...something that isn't horrible and irreversible.

"I think it's obvious we need to go," Marco agrees. "Murray told Sam to use the flashlight, and there is a clear signal for help."

"Only, I didn't tell her to use a specific signal," Murray says behind me.

I whirl around. "Well, who else could that be, shining an SOS at Alcatraz island?" I yell. "Sam probably knows some Morse code. Her mom was super outdoorsy and a wealth of weird information. Who cares which signal she chose? It's a call for help, and we all know it!"

Marco touches my arm. "Cate, chill. No one's disagreeing that we need to go, right?"

"I should go get a torch," Murray says, "to let her know we've seen her."

"So we'll go now," I say more than ask. "Today."

"We need to plan a bit better than 'go now,' don't you think?"

I take a breath in an effort not to rip Marco's head off his body. "Fine. Two hours, and I'm leaving with or without you."

"I'm coming," Mel says.

Calvin and I both turn to stare at her.

"Melody, baby," Calvin starts to say.

"No, Cal!" Mel's eyes are wide, her cheeks red. "I'm not staying behind again, no way! I've been training, and I survived a long-ass time before we met you!"

There's a shocked silence where everyone glances from Mel to Calvin and at one another. A few people back up.

"Melody is a strongest fighter!" shouts Nick, more words than I've heard from him in maybe a week. He scrunches his little face up and puts his balled-up fists on his hips.

"That she is," I agree. "But this is very dangerous, and we love Mel. We just want her to stay safe."

"But more people means more eyes, more weapons," Mel argues. "Cate, I'm doing this, and if you don't support me, then so help me I will lock *you* in a cell and make *you* stay behind for once! I can help, just let me help!"

Calvin speaks soothingly, stepping closer to Mel and putting an arm around her back. "You're right. I think this is a bad idea, and I'll spend half my energy trying to keep an eye on you. I know, you don't need me to, okay. I just love you, that's all. It's hard to want to watch you running directly into harm's way."

"Well, maybe you'll understand how I've felt every time you and Cate go into the city, then."

Calvin kisses Mel's head. "I get it. Let's get your knife sharpened and find you a better jacket. Something they can't bite through."

I've been waiting on the dock twenty minutes by the time the allotted two hours are up. Everyone walks down together. Mel, who has shed her flannel for a sturdier outer layer, stoops to kiss the kids goodbye.

"I'll be back in a flash, sweetheart."

"What if you get lost like my mom?" whimpers Adrienne.

"We'll keep her safe," Calvin says.

"Marco won't let anything happen to her," says Francis.

"That's right," Marco answers, giving Francis a high-five.

"I bet Uncle Bill will let you do whatever you want all day." Mel winks over Adrienne's shoulder at Bill, who nods and takes hold of two little hands. With her other hand, Adrienne grabs Nick's. Mel and Marco step away with one more wave.

Tanya and David, each holding one of Mel and Calvin's babies, bring them forward for Mel to kiss. She sniffs their tiny heads as she leans in, and a tear rolls down her cheek after she pulls away.

"Baby," Calvin says, wiping one away with his thumb.

"No, I'm fine. It's fine, I'm fine. We'll be back before you know it, kids. Be good, please, and I'll see you this afternoon."

They all watch us situate into the boats. I sit next to Mel. She waves at the kids, smiling, until Bill leads them up the path. She looks around once they're out of view, at the island, the water, the zombies floating around us. Most of them aren't even moving anymore, their brains having decomposed into mush. She wipes the back of her hand across her cheek in what I guess she thinks is a discreet way, ducking her head and pretending to peer over the side of the boat.

"Gosh, the stink down here is incredible." A sniffle disguised as a whiff. "Has it always been this bad?"

"As far as I can remember," I answer.

Mel looks around some more, tapping her foot on the bottom of the boat. I exchange a glance with Calvin, whose brows haven't unknitted themselves since Mel decided she was coming.

"Mel, are you sure you want to do this?"

"Of course, why would you say that?"

"It's just—" I am about to tell her that she obviously doesn't want to, that I can tell she's terrified, but a warning expression from Calvin makes me stop short. "The kids. They're so upset and worried."

Mel clasps her hands on her knees. "They'll be fine. I want to help, Cate. It's not about me wanting to prove anything, you know. Amy was right last night. People didn't—I didn't— make Sam feel as welcome as she was. And she really was. And sometimes...oh, God, if I cry it's only because I am so mad at myself."

She takes a gulp of air and continues with a wobbly voice. "She was your age, Cate. Is! Is your age. And instead of trying to help you guys, to guide you, I formed my whole opinion of her around a snap judgement, a bad one, and I acted like a real jerk as if she was some kind of enemy rather than the person you love."

She starts to really cry, but makes no move to get up as Murray and Jax begin to untie the boats. "I can't imagine how I would have felt if Calvin's Nana Mae had treated me that way. I should have been acting like your sister. If I had gotten to know Sam better, maybe, I don't know." She sniffles, takes the last shaky breath that always comes at the end of a crying jag, and continues in a steady voice. "Anyway, that's why I'm going. I am just as responsible as anyone else for her. Maybe more so. She's ours, like you said. She's family, and she's not safe out there." Her gaze falls on the city.

I lean my head on her shoulder. "I appreciate you, Mel. But I worry about you too."

"I'm ready. I need to do this." Mel takes her glasses off and wipes them on her sleeve.

The early-morning sea air cools the exposed skin on my neck and hands and face as we row farther into it. Mel zips up her oversized jacket. There's no SOS anymore, not since Murray flashed Sam back. I content myself with the thought that it was there about two hours ago.

The sounds of the oars are the only thing I can hear aside from the squishy thud of my own pulse. As we cross the water, at around what I imagine is the halfway point between the island and the city, the sky darkens, and it starts to rain. It's like needles on my face. Overhead, it sounds like thunder might be building, a repetitive, far-off sound. Hopefully, it won't pass over us until we're safe on the boat back home.

When we are almost there, Mel grabs my hand the way she used to before we went over the drop on a roller coaster. But instead of anticipation, the grip feels fearful. I know we're doing the right thing, my conviction has not waivered at all. But there's still a small grating voice in the back of my mind, an itch I can't scratch, that asks, *What if?* What if someone dies, what if it's my fault this time?

I clutch Mel's hand tighter. No matter how this ends, it will be over soon. I'll stay by her side; Calvin will too. We'll find Sam, and get the hell back to the island, and Mel will have an adventure story for the kids. Who knows, maybe she'll enjoy it. Maybe Mel will want to start going on supply runs from time to time. That would be nice, to have her in our little company. She used to find stuff I never would have seen when we were on the road together. She would be an asset, for sure.

But first, we have to get through this. We will though. It will be fine, I tell myself over and over, using the feel of Mel's hand in mine to ground myself and ward off what feels like a building panic attack. I breathe, in four, out eight. Even though I am terrified and sick with worry, I'm grateful to have my sister with me.

The boats close in on the pier. The rain pounds, harder and harder. There's no sun anymore, and no flicker. That's okay. I'm sure she's close by. I would hide too. It's the smart thing to do. Soon, I'll see her again. Soon, we will be eating dinner in the rec yard, all of us, together.

"You ready?" I ask Mel.

"I am. Let's bring her back."

Acknowledgements

The more I write, the more I come to love the cooperative nature of publishing a book. To everyone whose efforts resulted in this book, thank you, thank you, thank you.

To the team at NineStar, you are incredible. Raevyn, thank you for everything you do to make this group feel like a family. Elizabetta, I can't thank you enough for helping make this book the best version of itself, and for working so hard to help me correct my extraordinary misuse of commas. To the rest of the editing team, thank you for polishing this thing and making it as shiny as a horror story can be. Natasha, once again you have given me the gift of a stunning cover. Thank you.

Taylor, your publishing advice has been invaluable and much appreciated. Tash, your support and kind words mean the world. Thank you both, so much.

To my people—both bio fam and found fam—you're everything to me. Stephen, I am in awe that you're not sick of talking about zombies, plot twists, and minor details by now. You discuss these things with me more than anyone should have to, and you are always up for more. I don't know how you do it. Thank you for that, and once again for your beautiful chapter artwork. May we create together for eternity. Dad, thank you for encouraging me to write, which sometimes meant a bit of badgering (badger, badger, badger). Thank you for being the kind of dad who tells your kids "go for it," regardless of what "it" is. Mom, thank you for keeping everything I ever wrote, even the weird and creepy stuff, for encouraging me every step, and for talking about my books to probably every person you meet. Paris, your intelligence and sense of possibility are magical. Your ability to simultaneously coach me on current teen stuff and mercilessly roast me when I fail at being cool is incredible. Never let up. Never lose your sharp wit, or close your wide-open eyes. You are the coolest little sister on the planet. Ethan, I am so glad you're back. Welcome home, Man Cub. I've missed you. Megs, Abi, and Jourdan, you're the people of my heart. You're the community I always hoped to find. Thanks for every word, every joke, every moment.

David, thank you for teaching me (and then reminding me until it stuck) that Everything Matters. Thank you for your patience and your time. You are one hell of a mentor.

Bethany and Debara, thank you for the very long discussions about The Joaquin Moment, and for your discerning eyes and helpful critique in general.

Taz, I'm so glad we found each other in the Writing Community. Thank you for being my Beta Buddy.

Chaz, the dog who inspired the one in this series, who would lie at my feet (and sometimes, impossibly, would climb all of his seventy-five pounds into my lap) while I wrote this story. I have nothing specific to thank him for, other than being my bestie, my bear, the first dog I ever called mine. He died before this book was finished, but his spirit will live forever on Alcatraz Island.

And you, reading this now, whoever and wherever you are. Thank you for picking this book. I hope you enjoyed it and maybe found something worth holding on to, somewhere in the pages. If you read book one and decided to give this one a shot, thank you especially for sticking with Cate, Marco, and their funky little family.

About the Author

M. Rose Flores lives in the Pacific Northwest of the United States with her spouse Stephen and their three fluffy beasts, collectively known as Legion (the cats, not the spouse). She is currently working on a degree, two novels, and two collaborative graphic novels. When Rose isn't writing or studying, she works as a professional dog trainer and loves every part of it, even the copious amounts of drool. *The Island* is her second novel, the sequel to *The End*.

Email: writemod7@gmail.com

Facebook: www.facebook.com/writemod

Twitter: @writemod

Other NineStar books by this author

The End (Abnormal/Variant, Book One)

Coming Soon from M. Rose Flores

The Beginning

Abnormal/Variant, Book Three

Everything will be okay.

I repeat the words in my head, over and over, though I don't believe them. The rain bears down on the boats, an unrelenting torrent soaking every strand of hair and fiber of clothing. Not one person seems to notice. Everyone looks ahead to San Francisco. We're almost there.

My jacket hangs heavy and dripping on my body. Is that the reason my shoulders are rounded as if I'm collapsing in on myself? Or is it the fear, inching toward desperation with every stroke of the oars? Their rhythmic splashing is nearly drowned out by the rain, the distant thunder, and my own heartbeat as we close in toward the city. Toward Samantha.

Our boat bumps the end of Pier 33, followed by the other one. I grip my sister's hand. Mel squeezes back and turns up the corner of her mouth for a fraction of a second before letting go to adjust her jacket, her hammer, her glasses. She's fidgety; I get it. I can't imagine how nervous she must be, and she has far more cause than the rest of us.

But it will all be over soon. Because somewhere close by, Sam is waiting for us. All we have to do is find her. Soon, we'll be on our way back to Alcatraz. Safe. Together.

If she wants to come with us. If she has magically forgiven me for breaking up with her. Damn it. Ever since I saw the SOS a few hours ago, I have been so intent on bringing her back—so set on getting to her before something terrible happens—I let myself forget why she left in the first place. Or maybe I never let it sink in. Maybe the idea of Sam choosing to live and die alone in the city rather than spend another second on Alcatraz with me was too painful. Her face appears in my mind, the expression the same as it was when I told her we were done. Hurt, disappointed, angry. Maybe, the face I find will be that one.

Or worse, the face we come upon will be emotionless and vacant, not from shutting herself off, but from something far worse. Something irreversible. The image in my head morphs, turning bloody, black-veined, and white-eyed. Sam, but not Sam. Something one of us will have to deal with. It doesn't have to be me. Does it? Should it? I glance down at my axe. I'm dizzy for a minute even though I'm still sitting. My body sways on the little boat bench. Mel nudges my shoulder, I think.

"Cate?" her mouth stretches a little farther this time, an approximation of a reassuring smile. "Ready?"

I shrug.

"Hey, we're going to be okay." She wraps an arm around me. "No matter what."

I know she means, "whether Sam is alive or not; whether she comes back with us or not." My insides harden and twist. When I lock eyes with her again, and she's still trying to smile, guilt seeps into me. It should be me reassuring her. Mel hasn't left the island since we got there. She hasn't seen a single ambulatory zombie since the day we escaped the city; she's been safe with her babies and her garden for more than three months. She should never have come.

It will be okay.

I try like hell to believe it.

Murray gets out of the first boat to tie it up. He isn't driving us in and out on the ferry anymore, not since we found the rowboats, but he takes his inherited role as boat captain seriously. He moves to help Jax with the second boat. Behind them, silent shadows bustle around on the pier. They're tough to distinguish in the gray morning light, but they look about the size and shape of adult humans.

"Did Sam find people?" asks Mel, taking hold of my hand again as I help her off the boat.

"When's the last time you met anyone alive out here?" asks Joaquin, his hand automatically moving to his gun.

"Never." Mel's voice sounds small in this big space. She surveys the area. The last time she was here it was the dead of night, and we were fighting our way off the mainland.

The area is full of debris. Shattered glass, garbage, pieces of rope and chains. It has always been this way, but it feels more dangerous now for some reason. One single black suitcase sits off to the side. Has it always been there? Surely, one of us would have checked it out. We use Pier 33 as our point of entry every time we go into the city for supplies, and Joaquin and I never miss anything of use. Surely, someone would have noticed such a thing sitting there, so out of place, so conspicuous.

Up ahead, the shadows continue to shift.

Who are these people? If they were with Sam, she would have told them we would be coming. I can count at least ten of them, far outnumbering our six. So why are they hiding?

"Hello," calls Marco as we all inch farther up the pier. He sounds a little bit nervous too, which is disconcerting in itself. In the almost three years I've known him, I can only remember seeing him uneasy a handful of times.

"Sam?" calls Calvin. "We saw your signal." He brushes Mel's knuckles on his way past us, glancing at her, wordlessly checking on the mother of his children. She dips her head.

"We came to bring you home, Sam," I call out. But even as I'm saying the words, a blooming, viscous certainty spreads through me, coating my insides in cold dread: whoever this is, it isn't Sam.

They emerge from all around and gather. One of them holds a flashlight, but their hands are otherwise empty. No bags, no weapons, nothing. Their bodies are varying shades of gray, their eyes clear and unclouded. Black veins peek out from under their clean, untattered clothes.

Mel sucks in a breath and holds my hand tighter. It isn't a reassuring sisterly squeeze anymore; it's fear. These are not people.

Thankfully, as I already guessed, Sam is not with them.

"Shit," mutters Jax behind me. "I've never seen this many together at once."

Why *are* they all together this way, just standing there? We know by now that not all zombies are equal, but I don't think any of us knew they could organize. This many can't possibly be here by chance. It's as if they were waiting for us.

"No," I whisper. That can't be right.

"What is this?" Mel asks, glancing at me, at Cal, at the squad of Abnormal zombies staring us down. "What's happening?"

"It's a goddamned trap," Calvin says, pulling his Bowie knives out of the sheaths on his legs and taking one giant step forward. "Melody, get behind me."

They must have seen Murray bring Sam here yesterday. Maybe the Abnormals followed them and waited for the right moment to call us over, knowing we would come for one of our own. Sam might have been dead this whole time. She might not have survived her first night alone.

Seagulls circle over our heads—at least fifty of them—all screaming, undaunted by the rain. What are they doing? Waiting for corpses to scavenge, probably. Not ours though. Let them feast on zombie flesh after we drop every last rotten one. I grind my teeth and take hold of my axe, fighting the urge to unleash a feral scream, ready to demolish these killers, these soulless monsters. They have taken nearly everything dear to me over the last two years. They are everything wrong with the world.

Mel has to let go of my hand to take up her hammer. Under the skin of her neck, her pulse thumps. She wipes her hands on her jeans, takes a deep, shaky breath, and pushes her glasses up her nose. I want to hold on to her, to protect her. She has never been a fighter. She shouldn't even be here.

Joaquin and Marco square off on either side of us and take up their weapons, making no secret of it. Why would they? These zombie assholes must know we won't go down without a fight. And if they didn't before, they will now.

Also Available from NineStar Press

Connect with NineStar Press

www.ninestarpress.com

www.facebook.com/ninestarpress

www.facebook.com/groups/NineStarNiche

www.twitter.com/ninestarpress

www.tumblr.com/blog/ninestarpress